YELLOWSTONE KELLY

YELLOWSTONE KELLY

A WESTERN STORY

CLAY FISHER

**BLACK
STONE**
PUBLISHING

This book is a work of fiction.

Printed in the United States of America

ISBN 978-1-4708-6192-6
Fiction / Westerns

1 3 5 7 9 10 8 6 4 2

CIP data for this book is available
from the Library of Congress

Blackstone Publishing
31 Mistletoe Rd.
Ashland, OR 97520

www.BlackstonePublishing.com

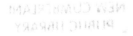

For my friend
John Martin Askey

YELLOWSTONE KELLY

This book is based upon the memoirs of a remarkable old man who died in 1928 in Butte County, California. His story as told herein is fictional romance, not factual biography, yet it becomes a practical impossibility to elaborate on his real-life adventures.

General Nelson A. Miles called him "a hero in war, a true American patriot in times of peace." The Sioux named him "the Little Man with the Strong Heart," and feared him above all the other scouts in George Crook's far-flung Department of the Platte. Of him, his fellow scouts cheerfully admitted, "he could smell an Indian in the pitch dark farther than most of us could see one in broad daylight." Still, today this strangely soft-spoken, politely educated eastern youth, whose name in his long-ago time and dangerous profession, like Abou Ben Adhem's, "led all the rest," is remembered only by a lonely mountaintop grave site above Billings, Montana.

Like the man, the marker is no longer important. Soon even the legend will be lost. The careless winds of time cover deep with history's cynical dust a hundred such obscure heroes and unsung stories of our western past. There can be no argument with this unhappy fact, even in fiction, nor does this account presume to advance any. It seeks, in the end, not to instruct the reader in the serious history of the Yellowstone Valley but merely to remind him, in honored passing, of the lighthearted, classics-quoting young Irishman who singlehandedly set the stage for most of that history.

His name, like his deeds, deserves better than to be forgotten.

It was Luther Sage Kelly.

C. F.
Bigtimber
Sweet Grass County

BOOK ONE
JUDITH BASIN

1

The four wolf hunters were neither young nor old, but of that indeterminate age which lies as surely beyond youth as it does safely short of senility. They were cautious, wary-featured men, not entirely at home in that eerily still Montana land yet not ill-matched to it either.

The day itself was far gone but holding brassy hot. For early September in a mile-high northern lonesomeness where killing frosts came any summer night, June through August, it was menacingly hot.

Down canyon, looking back toward the basin they had quitted in the four a.m. bone-chill of that morning's blackness, they could see the dust boils dancing beneath the contoured shimmerings of the heat mirage with which the low slant of the late afternoon sun was baking the outer valley floor. Jepson, the leader, slipped the straps of his backpack, stumbled toward an off-trail deadfall. Groaning, he sat down and waited in panting silence for his companions to come up.

"Best not turn the mule loose jest yet," he warned them. "We'll need to set a spell and think a bit, I allow."

The others nodded, saving talk.

Big Anse Harper, the man with the pack mule, obediently half-hitched the lead rope around a convenient snag of the deadfall, dropped gratefully alongside Jepson. "She's a powerful long uphill haul fer only one feed of cold fatback and no noon-halt coffee," he observed, not ill-naturedly. "Seems like we bin walkin' since last week. My feet ain't bin so sore since we used to make them thirty-mile night marches up the Shenandoah when 'Old Jack' got took with the notion to cut himse'f off a regiment of blue-bellies fer breakfast. Cripes Amighty—!"

"Well," grumped Jepson, "we dassn't to have lit no noon-fire out yonder on thet flatland. Likely you know thet well as I do." He bent his head toward the distant basin, the eyes of the others following his. The talk fell off.

Presently, Alec MacDonal, the third man, nodded his shaggy gray head, agreed in his pleasant Scots burr.

"Aye, Jepson lad, what ye say is true enough. 'Tis indeed a chancy land we're trespassin' on."

Caswell, the fourth man, said nothing.

They continued to sit, four thoughtful wool-shirted human limbs growing silently out of a dead-and-down Judith Mountain cedar spar seven thousand feet above sea level and twenty-seven miles from the nearest white settlement beyond Fort Buford, Montana, September 2, 1875.

Breaking the spell, Jepson dug out a big six-ounce cut of trade plug and passed it along.

"Shave it thin," he admonished needlessly.

"How many plugs we got?" asked Big Anse, paring with proper solicitude the one he held, before handing it along to MacDonal.

"Four dozen," answered the unimaginative Jepson. "It'll be aplenty, mixed in with a little red willow bark or larb leaves and allowin' fer a normal winter."

"Yeah," smirked Big Anse deliberately. "A normal winter and no unexpected company."

The tense swiftness with which the others jumped their eyes from the sun haze of the basin to the big man's calm face was the most eloquent reply they could have made. Yet Caswell, the least in years and last in experience among them, had to say it.

"You mean the Sioux, Anse?"

"Sure, why not, Yank? Them and the Cheyenne. Most likely the Sioux though, and then most likely the Hunkpapa."

"Well, we all knew that before we started out," challenged Jepson, not wanting the expedition to come down with a case of camp nerves the first day out. "Old Man Reed told us, and afore thet we was told at Fort Buford. No call to go to talkin' hostiles now. We ain't none of us come up here thinkin' we was on no church picnic." He paused, thinking it over.

Presently, he nodded.

"The game brings the wolves, and the wolves is what we're after." True to granite-headed habit Jepson picked up the dropped stitch of his own thoughts as though the others had said nothing and as though he and the cedar log were alone in the Montana world.

"To git prime wolf, you got to go where the game is. And when you git to where the game is, you wind up where the Injuns are at. It ain't really very complicated," he concluded with a humorless headshake for the unconvinced Caswell. "But at the same time, don't let Anse nor nobody else josh you none. We're passin' likely to see some trouble."

"Well, so long as we *see* it, we're all right," said Big Anse cryptically.

He stood up, reaching for the pack mule's rope. "I'm cooled out sufficient, how about the rest of you?" he announced tentatively. "I say let's git on over the ridge and set up camp fer the night."

Jepson did not move to follow him up off the cedar spar. Instead, he shook his head, looking around speculatively. "I'd say this looks purty good right here. We got water just down the gulch, plenty firewood waitin' to be picked up in sight of camp, reasonable decent browse fer the mule on close-in picket. I allow we'll throw down here."

"Aye," muttered MacDonal wearily. "Everybody's tired, Anse lad. We've done verra well today. No point in pushin' on anymore tonight."

"We'd ought to git deeper into the timber afore we build a blaze," grumbled the hulking southerner. "The heavy growth holds down the night-sky reflection. You know thet, Mr. MacDonal. You ain't no tenderfoot."

"Nope," demurred Jepson, before the latter could answer for himself. "I'd druther be out here on the flank of the ridge, in the fringe scrub. This way we kin see clean up and down the draw, and we're out where there cain't no sneakin' hostiles crawl up on us under cover, by Tophet. All we got to do is keep a sharp lookout."

"That makes sense to me," agreed Caswell quickly. "I vote with Jepson."

"And me," sighed MacDonal resignedly.

The wiry Scot was simply hot and tired and short on Plains Indian understanding. A Canadian woodsman, born and reared, he was a skillful hunter and trapper but relatively new, like the rest of them, to this Upper Missouri country. In no sense was he, anymore than the others, aware of the true and real depth of the hatred held by the Sioux and Cheyenne for the American invaders of their ancestral game pastures.

It would have been difficult to imagine a more dangerous combination of settlement innocents abroad in an alien and enemy country. Of them all, only Big Anse, the Georgia piney woodsman, had any instinctive feeling for the type of country they were in. And he was as tired as his companions.

"All right," he surrendered good-naturedly, "I'll not secede tonight." He put his huge knee into the bulging side of the mule's top-heavy load, called gruffly over his shoulder to the still disturbed Caswell.

"Come along, Yank. Give us a hand with this cussed pack. She's slewed around crooked as a bluetick hound's hind leg. I cain't seem to git a proper bite on the infernal hitch, to shake her loose …"

2

The fire burned low. It had been carefully laid, sent up no least telltale wisp of woodsmoke against the thinly moonlit autumn night. Replete with a heavy meal of cold mashed beans, broiled salt pork, yellow saleratus biscuit and tar-black coffee, Big Anse, Caswell, and MacDonal snored with their feet to the toasting coals.

Outside the fire's enfeebled light, crouched by a lone cedar which overhung the canyon and from whose rocky promontory there was an unobstructed 160-degree view of the campsite, John Jepson confidently kept the first watch.

It was now frosting cold and getting colder. In the four hours since sundown the temperature had dropped forty degrees.

Jepson pulled his blanket closer, shivered, and was not sleepy.

The night was so clear, it made a man's eyes ache with the shifting glitter of its frozen stars and the silvered glare of its sickle moon. But that was good. On such a still and starlit night, nothing, not so much as a friendly marmot, a curious deer mouse, or an inquisitive rock cricket, could have crept up on his carefully chosen campsite without being seen. As for anything the size of an interested Indian, why, he would have him spotted, sighted-in, and shot square center before he could have bellied to within anywhere near smoothbore trade gun range.

The shadow arose out of the seemingly bare ground not three feet behind him. It stood over him as silently as an ectoplasmic thing without substance of human flesh, no more real, no more tangible than an evil dream. Yet when it spoke to him, the deep easy voice destroyed any palpable illusion of nightmare or mental conjuration. And very nearly dropped John Jepson dead of a heart attack.

"Get up slowly, my friend, and turn around. Gently does it now. Leave the gun against the tree."

Jepson made a strangling noise in his throat but did as he was told. Swallowing hard to check the larynx-high hammer of his heart, he came about.

The figure which confronted him there in the coruscating light of the Montana stars was bizarre enough by itself. Yet it was not the sight but the sound of the apparition which string-halted Jepson's pulse and hobbled his struggling tongue.

The soft rich speech, beginning again now, was more than the illiterate New Englander's twenty-five years of self-education could surround, or his two decades of frontier settlement experience make sense of.

Still, to his credit, Jepson did not interrupt.

He simply stood there, letting his bearded jaw sag, while the vibrant baritone rolled with Orphic enchantment through the impromptu declamation—complete with a trained mummer's professional gesture!

> *"I could a tale unfold whose*
> *lightest word*
> *Would harrow up thy soul,*

freeze thy young blood,
Make thy two eyes, like stars,
start from their spheres,
Thy knotted and combined
locks to part
And each particular hair to
stand on end,
Like quills upon the fretful
porpentine!"

Jepson's jaw dropped another inch at the conclusion of this brief but appropriate borrowing from the Bard. Then his eyes began to smolder and his voice rasped harshly. "Jest what the infernal hell you talkin' about? You daft or somethin'?"

The newcomer laughed softly.

"I'm talking about the Sioux, my friend. And about the way you build your fire in thin timber, and how safe you thought you were, and how easy it was to show you otherwise."

Jepson shook his head like a surly dog with a contested bone between his teeth. "By Godfrey, I still don't git you! Nor what you're gittin' at neither!"

"No? Well, then, look at it this way. Suppose it had been the Sioux rather than myself who came up on you just now. That's where the 'harrowing tale' would have been unfolded and the 'freezing blood' spilled round about. Had I been a Hunkpapa brave, my friend, 'thy knotted and combined locks' would have been 'parted' to a final fare-thee-well by this time. Now do you see?"

John Jepson saw not.

"Dogged if I do!" he snapped. "Savin' thet you carry on like a crazy man!"

"Oh, that!" the other's second laugh was as quick and rich

as the first. "Shakespeare, my friend. Hamlet. The First Act, I believe. You see, I'm not alone an accomplished camp-sneak but a brilliant scholar as well!"

The graceful stranger's manner was so unique, the timbre of his voice so compelling, his moonlit smile so brightly swift, that Jepson wavered. But the disgruntled wolf hunter was thoroughly angry; angry as only a man can be who has been caught compounding an act of ignorance by a display of fear. And in front of a total outsider for more bitter measure.

"You tarnal fool," he gritted. "Sneakin' up on a man like thet. You tryin' to git yourself killed?"

"My friend," nodded the shadowed figure politely, "I might well ask as much of you. And I shall, but not here. Come along to the fire, and I'll ask it of all four of you at the same time." The smile was still there, but the suggestion was illustrated by an unceremonious shove from the speaker's gun muzzle. Given precious little choice, Jepson marched sullenly to the fire.

Here, on his mysterious guest's request, he stirred up the coals, threw on an armload of fresh-split cedar kindling, rudely aroused his sandy-eyed companions.

As the latter came muttering out of their blankets, the resinous cedar flared suddenly into new life, giving Jepson his first real look at the self-styled "brilliant scholar and accomplished camp-sneak." His three fellows, now thoroughly awake, joined him in the startled stare and in the gaping surprise which was its natural result.

Before them stood a slender fellow of no more than medium size, swarthy as a Gypsy, slit-eyed as a Sioux. He was a white man but such a white man as they had never seen nor secretly imagined.

Despite his lack of stature, his shoulders were grotesquely broad, his arms anthropoid in length and looking of latent power.

His hips were narrow as a Texan's, his legs as bowed and bent from clinging to the barreled ribcage of a prairie mustang as those of any pureblood Crow or Blackfoot. His entire body, encased in soft pearl-gray elk skin, seemed upon the slightest shift of movement to come alive with whipcord muscle. Despite the pleasant warmth of smile, the soothing depth of voice, and the apparent education, the impression he gave was distinctly primitive, disturbingly animal.

He wore Arapahoe moccasins, a Cheyenne bear claw choker, a low-crowned hat of the finest fifty-dollar light-cream beaver belly, a priceless belt of blazing Sioux beadwork. His armament was that of a high prairie war chieftain; a late model '73 Winchester rifle, a seven-inch Shoshone skinning knife, a Sheffield steel Hudson's Bay belt axe. His bearing, as well, was that of an Indian.

He stood with his trim feet set slightly apart, the toes turned just the least bit inward. His muscular back, square shoulders, and cavernous chest were frozen ramrod erect, as true and straight and unbending as the polished haft of a Hunkpapa buffalo lance. He held his dark head high, commanding notice of his hawk-bridged nose and defiant power of lean jawline. In truth, he composed a compelling yet puzzling picture of nature at cross purposes; a poised and dangerous young animal of great bodily strength and high male pride in feral manhood, yet these physical gifts compounded with gentle dignity, wry good humor, and a certain indefinable wild-creature shyness.

Returning the still resentful looks of the wolf hunters with a grin as plainly white-toothed as it was patently black Irish, the buck-skinned stranger nodded soberly.

"And now my friends we'll have a brief lecture on the wherefores and why-nots of white men building night fires along bare ridges of fringe timber in the upper intestine of Tashunka Witko's private hunting preserve."

"And who the hell," broke in Big Anse Harper pleasantly, warmed no little by the stranger's fey manners and always ready to admit his own ignorance in front of any man, "is Tashunka Witko?"

"Crazy Horse," replied the dark-eyed scout, straight-faced. "A somewhat prominent Oglala of whom I rather imagine you may have heard."

"Cripes Amighty!" gasped Big Anse.

"Good Lord!" breathed Caswell with great difficulty. "Isn't he about the biggest Sioux there is? Next to Sitting Bull, of course."

"Next to nobody," said the slender man unsmilingly.

"Sitting Bull's a politician, a medicine man. He doesn't fight. Crazy Horse is their real leader and a fanatic white-hater named Gall is their main war chief. That would make Sitting Bull about number three in my book."

Jepson looked at him without liking.

When he finally put the big question, he did so behind the lingering scowl left over from his earlier mortification.

"And jest who do you think you might be, mister, to be writin' any books on the subject?"

"Kelly," said the stranger evenly. "Luther S. Kelly." Then, after a searching look and a slow nod in receipt of their slack-jawed stares of disbelief:

"*Yellowstone Kelly . . .*"

3

"Cripes Amighty!" reiterated Big Anse. "I don't believe it. It's like seein' Jesse James or shakin' hands with Jed Smith!"

The others said nothing, just made sounds without words.

Each knew he was looking at a legend. The sort of ethereal human fabric most men die without ever seeing. Or ever coming near to seeing. Let alone standing close enough to, to reach out and touch for hand-feeling real. It was a vastly unsettling thing, and of them all only Big Anse Harper was able to answer for his amazement.

The huge Georgian was like a small boy who had hand-watered half a dozen circus elephants in happy exchange for five minutes of staring at *Colonel Wm. F. "Buffalo Bill" Cody & His Sixty Real-Life Sioux Indian War Chiefs in Their Death Defying Circle of the Flaming Wagon Train!* all performed, of course, within a thirty-five foot cartwheel of soggy tanbark to the wheezy brass pumping of *Mazeppa's Ride* or *Entrance of the Gladiators.*

He was, in a word, bug-eyed.

"I seen Custer once!" he blurted hopefully. "It was thet fust mornin' outside Appomattox Courthouse. My outfit was close up to the front ranks. We always was. General John Brown Gordon's boys, Mr. Kelly. The Raccoon Roughs from La Grange. Likely you heard of 'em. Most have, I reckon."

Kelly nodded, either out of agreement or the kindness of an easily reached Irish heart, and Big Anse plunged excitedly on.

"And it's blessed little wonder the Injuns calls him Yeller-hair, too! He was awearin' it thetaway even in them days. Clean down to his danged epaulets, it were! And yeller? Say, it was thet yeller it'd make a Fed'ral Gov' mint gold piece look new-grass green!"

Across from the aroused southerner, the intense darkness of the legend's face dissipated to another of the quicksilver smiles.

"You gentlemen would be the four wolf hunters out of Fort Buford by way of Reed & Bowles," said Kelly, somehow making it sound right and not like an interruption or an ignoring of Big Anse's friendly-dog harangue.

"We would," admitted Jepson, sensing the other's seriousness, smile or no. "And what business of yours might thet be?"

"That will keep," countered Kelly. "First you're going to sit still for that little lecture I promised you. Subject: 'The Cure and Prevention of Premature Baldness in Judith Basin,' or, 'A Fool and His Scalp are Soon Separated in Siouxland,' or—"

"Verra amusin', lad." MacDonal squinted narrowly. "Verra humorous indeed. But git on wi' it now, will ye? Ye're keepin' us up."

Kelly nodded and got on with it.

He did so in staccato bursts of five and six-letter words that had nothing at all in common with his previous flowery appropriation from Shakespeare or production of facetious titles for informal talks on Sioux haircutting techniques.

When he wished to, it was quickly clear, Luther Kelly could talk as plain and to the point as a Missouri muleskinner.

It was only the more remarkable that the blistering effect was achieved entirely without either the use or abuse of the Lord's good name, any reference whatever to the Devil's dwelling place, or any mention of the possible lack of legal wedlock surrounding the birth of a fellow man.

Profanity, dog-eared or highly decorated, was for less talented talkers than Luther S. Kelly.

When he had finished, the members of his hushed little captive audience understood several things inherent in their situation which had not been too clear to them previously.

One: they should never have left Fort Buford.

Two: before that, they should never have departed from Fort Berthold, and before that should never have waved farewell to St. Louis.

Three: they should now break camp and run for the Basin, bypassing Reed & Bowles, hitting straight for the River, and praying every jump of the way that the hostiles didn't spot their dust.

Four: once at the Big Muddy, they should lie up in the bank brush until *Far West*, *Prairie Queen*, or *Yellowstone Belle* came along, then halloo for help, go aboard, and stay aboard until the gangplank touched levee in St. Louis again.

His pertinent points made, Kelly stood back to await their acceptance or rejection.

Alec MacDonal, who in this moment of decision seemed to have taken over from the slower-witted Jepson, continued as spokesman for the wolf hunters.

"Aye," he averred thoughtfully, rolling the word as though it were a quid of high grade plug. "And what might ye say would be our alternative, Mr. Kelly?"

"Six months of Hunkpapa poker. With you boys betting your good hair against a problematical stack of wolfskins. And the odds ninety-nine to nothing in favor of the red brother taking the last pot and your precious pile of blue-chip peltries along with it."

"Verra, verra interestin'. And yer conclusion, lad?"

"Get out of the country and stay out of it."

The silver-haired Scot nodded, eying Kelly carefully. "It's fair drastic advice, mon. I imagine ye've some fair drastic reason fer offerin' it."

"I have."

"And ye might be induced to reveal thet reason?"

"For a reasonable consideration."

"Hmmmm." The craggy-faced Canadian hunter conceded Kelly the merest twinkle of a frosty blue eye. He was beginning to like this murderous-looking, gentle-talking, hard-bargaining, Indian-clad son of a black Irishman. He was clearly a man of parts and, moreover, of thrifty, unwasteful ways. "Now what might ye call a reasonable consideration, lad?"

Kelly shrugged.

"If I throw in with you, those Sioux odds drop to less than fifty-fifty, our way. You can stay up here with a better than even chance of going out next spring with your scalps still attached and with enough prime wolf to keep you in squaws and shag-cut for several summers."

"Aye, aye," MacDonal went along warily. "But the price, mon, the price!"

"My regular one-fifth of the total catch, plus ten percent of your four-fifths," said Luther Kelly.

It was not an unreasonable demand for the professional services of the most renowned Indian fighter and commercial meat hunter on the Upper Missouri. His uneasy listeners did not need MacDonal's conceding head-bob to understand that. But Jepson had had time to catch up with the conversation again. As nominal leader of the little company, he felt called upon to at least try to resume command thereof. He darkened his chronic scowl for the attempt.

"Fust things fust, mister. You said you had some fair drastic reason fer advisin' us to cut our sticks. Now you're offerin' to help us stay. I don't like a man that talks two ways at once. Now suppose you jest give us thet fust reason 'fore we go to talkin' peltry percentages. You hear me now?"

"I only hope you can hear me as well."

"Don't you worry about me. Git on with it."

Kelly smiled softly, shifted from his parade rest to lean lightly, palms crossed, on the muzzle of his Winchester.

"From a certain cedar ridge ten miles south of this campsite at dusk the present evening and through an excellent, thoroughly reliable pair of Union-issue field glasses," he recited flowingly, "I observed diligently engaged in following your clumsy track a war party of thirty-nine Hunkpapa Sioux Indians under a chief whose name is considered distressingly bad news from the Black Hills to the Big Horns."

Jepson shook his head growlingly. He had just been kicked in his stumpy teeth and did not like it.

But MacDonal was in no mood to await his companion's recovery. His Scots' spine was beginning to crawl a little, his old hunter's instinct commencing to close in on him.

"What chief?" he asked, head cocked sharply.

"Only the worst you could want." Kelly shrugged.

"His name! For God's sake, what's his name?" broke in the over-wrought Caswell, uttering his first words since the scout's arrival.

"His name?" Kelly delayed, savoring the situation with that curious detachment which is the particular narcotic of those long addicted to the drug habit of imminent danger. "His name is as bitter for the white brother as his heart is black for him. Even in Hunkpapa it leaves an evil taste on the tongue. *Pizi!* The Sioux say it as though they were spitting it out. In English it has the same effect—an acid, caustic, scalding word."

He paused dramatically, sweeping them with his fierce dark eyes.

Caswell was gray-faced, the beaded dank moisture of near nerve-break peppering his temples. Kelly, watching him, knew that he had finally gotten through to at least one of the four white fools confronting him. He knew something else as well. If his closing words did not convert the other three, none of them would live long enough to plant and poison his first wolf bait.

"His name," he repeated with deliberate monotone softness, "is Gall."

4

The Fort Buford men seemed to shrink unconsciously closer to one another. Noting this instinctive reaction, Kelly was satisfied. Clearly, none of his listeners was that new to the Upper Missouri he had not heard of Gall the Hunkpapa. Which was precisely what he had anticipated. And precisely what was fit and proper, considering the time and place and the nature of Gall's Montana reputation.

Sitting Bull's number one war chief was, in contemporary fact, far better known to the various white trespassers upon the Laramie Treaty Lands than was ever his more famous tribesman. He was to Sitting Bull and the Hunkpapa what Crazy Horse was to Red Cloud and the Oglala. Sitting Bull and Red Cloud made the headlines of the national news-press. Gall and Crazy Horse made the troop ambushes and emigrant wagon train burnouts behind those headlines. In the local way of looking at it, the former were very big Indians back east, the latter, very bad Indians out west. If some further comparisons might be made for the sake of character delineation, Crazy Horse, had he been born white, would have been of the stuff of Presidents—and of the very greatest Presidents. It would not have been too much, in Kelly's opinion, to have called him an Oglala Lincoln, so deep was his passion for freedom, so humble his love for his people.

By exactly the reverse token Gall was quite another Indian.

The Hunkpapa field marshal was pure, uncomplicated fighting man.

He was a red guerrilla raider in the murderous white tradition of Poole, Quantrill, Anderson, and Jesse Woodson James. His love for his people was savage, not humble. His passion for freedom was an instinct, not an ideal. He fought not for tribal liberty or to preserve a way of life, but only to defend his own personal right to take what he wanted, when and where he wanted it—including a settler woman's scalp or a Pony Soldier's hair.

Kelly had no personal experience upon which to base this vicious picture of the famed Hunkpapa. Neither had he any good reason to doubt its authenticity. A man heard what he heard in the river posts. If he didn't choose to believe all of it, or if he refused to testify vehemently and circumstantially to every last bit of its rumored fact, he could very quickly get himself considered an incipient squaw man and find himself cut off from the trust and confidence of his precious few white fellows in this alien red land. The far easier alternative to these natural doubts that any human being, even one of Sitting Bull's Sioux, could be as all-bad as Gall was painted by the settlement artists, was to simply accept the white version of his villainy uncensored by logical questions or common sense inquiries. Kelly had learned this very early. And he had not forgotten it. Weary and worn as the old saying was, a man in Kelly's moccasins had to buy it and believe it—*the only good Indian was still the dead Indian.*

And right now Gall was very much alive.

Waiting half-amusedly for his companions' plainly hesitant decision, Kelly was idly puzzled by the mixed bag of resentful scowls and suspicious side-glances being flung at him over the hunched shoulders of the conferees. Presently, Big Anse cleared the air. Seizing the corporate stumbling block, he brought it over and dumped it unceremoniously in Kelly's lap. "Them cussed hammerheads," growled the impatient giant, "are holdin' up over you bein' a bogtrotter. Kin you beat that?"

"Beat it?" laughed Kelly. "I can't even tie it."

"Well, all the same it's so. They're purely fretted over signin' on a flannelmouth."

"A what?" said Kelly, taken off guard.

"You know, a snake-chaser, a toe-kisser."

"Now, see here, Anse," grinned the unworldly scout, "are those supposed to be insults? If so, they're a waste of time. I've been worked over by experts. You should hear a Ree or Mandan or a Gros Ventre squaw cut loose and claw a man's hump for tracking dirt into the tepee or stumbling over the cradleboard in the dark and waking the baby. Mister, that's real Three Rivers insulting. White folks just can't shine with that kind of competition. You tell your friends to get on with the business meeting and never mind my politics."

"No, no," admonished Big Anse unhappily, "it ain't your politics, Mr. Kelly. It's your religion."

"My what!" burst out the other, losing half of his good-natured grin.

"Aw, you know." The big hillman was plainly upset. "Your bein' an Irisher and all that. Me, I don't care, though I will say I ain't no Pope-lover. But Jepson, him, and MacDonal, they're thirty-second-degree Masons, and Caswell, he's a hardshell shoutin' Baptist, and, well, damn it all, Mr. Kelly, you know how it is."

Of a sudden, albeit belatedly in view of his customary astuteness, Luther Kelly did indeed know how it was. It was, in fact, far from the first time his Irish name had run him up against the stubborn wall of settlement prejudice toward the legitimate sons of St. Patrick and toward their presumed first allegiance to the so-called "Pope of Rome." Kelly had never liked this experience in frontier intolerance, and he didn't like it now. Dropping the last half of his grin, he eased up off his haunches and moved over to the scowlers.

"My friends," he greeted them with warning softness, "it has been brought to my attention that you fear my religion more than you respect my professional ability. Or my Indian opinions."

He eyed them without amusement and until they dropped their defiant gazes in self-conscious confusion. Then he went on, scathingly.

"Allow me to amplify my pedigree. Also my social standing. Likewise my moral convictions.

"Firstly; I never knew of anyone in the American branch of the family who was bothered a great deal by prayer-rail knee calluses.

"Secondly; we are mainly North of Ireland stock, our line coming to this fair land in 1638 by way of one John Kelly, a merchant sea captain of strong character and more or less Episcopalian convictions. Old John came over not from the Emerald Isle but from Jolly Old England. He was a member of the original Roger Williams Colony in Rhode Island, and if he owed anything to the Pope, he never paid it. I myself do not believe in churches, nor do I attend the services of any church. I am a man of strong belief, nonetheless, and a devout disciple of the Christian faith. I hold there is a God and hope one day to meet him.

"Thirdly, however; I consider each man's religion his entire personal concern. I have as much respect for the Sioux's Great Spirit as I do for the Catholic's Holy Ghost or the Protestant's

Heavenly Father," Luther Kelly said. "To me one man's god is as good or as bad as another's, but it is *his* god. Hence, I don't cotton any small part to the drift of this talk, and I'll give you exactly five minutes to stop it, to come off worrying about the Pope, and to get on with taking or leaving my business proposition—amen!"

It then took less than Kelly's five minutes for the chastised company to declare him a full partner in the firm, plus his extra ten percent as required.

At first, with the empty-headed exception of Big Anse, who admittedly "didn't have good sense enough to be properly skeered," they all wanted to give up and to turn back at once. The discussion deteriorated along these frightened lines of total, immediate abandonment for perhaps the opening three minutes. Then Kelly, having allowed each of the three dissidents what he felt to be his full minute of floor time, stepped in and took over for his own sixty seconds.

Within that limited space, he somehow managed to convince the thickheaded Jepson, the wary MacDonal, and the shadow-jumping Caswell that if they would but follow his instructions, they could avoid any serious trouble with the Sioux. He made it honestly plain that there was no hope of avoiding the Sioux themselves, only of avoiding serious trouble with them.

"Doing business with these wild Indians," he told them, "is like riding a green-broke pony. You never know when he's going to pitch but you do know that he is going to, and so you are ready for him when he does.

"I myself," he announced simply, "have traveled many a lovely summer and long winter through these forbidden lands of theirs, and always alone, with no real protection whatever, save my reputation for sleeping lightly and shooting straight. In all that time, I have been attacked but once, and that when I first came onto the River as a youth of eighteen."

Big Anse, who had taken what he called a "Sunday suit shine" to the slender scout, broke in breathlessly as he paused, requesting an expanded detail.

"What abouten thet there fust time they jumped you? Thet brush you jest mentioned? The one where you was only a boy and new in the country and all, and them dirty red scuts—"

Kelly laughed, patting the towering piney woods giant on the bulging muscles of his shoulder.

"All right, my friend," he obliged, "there were two of them. Broken Back and Shuffling Bear, both Oglalas and both bad Indians. They ambushed me down near Red Mike Welch's place above Fort Stevenson. That was on a little trip I made to open up the army's mail route between there and Fort Buford, when the Sioux had had it shut off for something like six months and meant to keep it that way for a spell longer. Say maybe six years. Or eight or ten, like they bottled up the Bozeman Road after they shagged Colonel Carrington out of Fort Kearney.

"Anyway, one of them, I think it was Broken Back, had a fine double-barreled English shotgun. His partner had no gun but was one of the most interesting shots with a bow and arrow I ever met. In fact, he winged me through the knee with a broadhead buffalo arrow before I could fall off my horse and get my own artillery into action. I had a little brass-mounted Henry repeater—that was the first Model .44 short—for which I had given fifty-five dollars in prime sable but the day before. Now—"

"Cuss it all, Mr. Kelly!" exploded Anse with childish impatience for the main point and bother the minor details, "git on with it! What happened after the arrow hit you?"

"Oh," said Luther Kelly quietly, "excuse me, Anse. I didn't know you were in a hurry. They missed after that."

"And, and—?"

"I didn't."

"Oh," echoed Big Anse in a very small voice. And that was the end of the four and a half minute board meeting which officially formed the new Judith Basin wolf-hunting firm of Jepson, Harper, Caswell, MacDonal & Kelly, Ltd.

It was as well that no more time was wasted in its organization, for the new house was destined for a very brief career in the fur business; something less than forty-eight hours, as a matter of frontier record.

5

The following morning the party set out for the base of Judith Mountain, where Kelly's previous explorations had determined ideal conditions for wolves. They had but a few miles to go, and hence, about eleven o'clock, the weather being cooler and Kelly's memory of the ancient Sioux hunting trails having proved perfect, a halt was called to boil coffee and scout the immediate vicinity for their permanent campsite.

The scout's plan was to put up a green-log, rifle-slitted living quarters of heavy timbers, with an attached shed for cooking and a lean-to for fur storage made of lighter materials. The mule, Montana born and reared, would dig for his winter supper like any Sioux or Cheyenne pack animal and would find his own shelter from the fierce blizzards soon to come.

By noon Kelly had located the spot he sought, a thirty-foot naked rock cutbank crowned by dense scrub, down which no man and few animals could scramble.

A stout cabin built against the buttress of that living stone, surrounded as it was on both flanks and the front by a timber-free level of mountain meadow, would be impregnable to red attack.

To guarantee that impregnability, there was a fine spring, still alive in this driest month of the past year, bubbling happily from the base of the bluff. They had but to enclose this clean pebbled pool within the semi-heated confines of the cookshack to make sure of fresh, unfrozen water the winter through.

The spirits of the adventurers rose rapidly.

That built-in barometer of human blindness founded on the old adage of living in hope and dying in despair was functioning beautifully by the time Kelly had baked his companions a batch of the light, sweet frying-pan bread for which he was famous from Fort Berthold to the Three Forks, and had boiled them up a second pot of bitter pitchblende coffee.

They would have fresh meat that night, too, he promised them.

After a bit he would drift down south to make certain the Sioux had abandoned their trail, as it now appeared they had, to judge from the morning's uninterrupted peace and tranquillity. Once sure their Indian friends had veered off—Kelly hesitated to admit it but under the circumstances a man had to assume Gall's Hunkpapa had been influenced to healthier pursuits by Kelly's joining the Fort Buford wolf hunters—then they could fire a gun without fear of the report bringing a Sioux investigating committee down about their ears. And once they could do that, Kelly would have a spikehorn blacktail or yearling bighorn buck down and dressed before they could say Red Walker or Man-Who-Goes-in-the-Middle.

Eh? Who were they?

Nobody much.

Just two other names for their recent red-skinned shadow, Gall. He was Red Walker to the Cheyenne, Man-Who-Goes-in-the-Middle to the Agency Sioux, Gall to the wild Hunkpapa.

Small concern for that, though. The main thing now was that Kelly had to stake out the floor plan for their winter quarters before he went hunting. That way, while he was gone they could start felling and notching the timbers which would be needed. They were to remember, he admonished them, that for the main cabin walls they must select prime cedar spars with no less than twelve-inch butts three feet above the ground. For the cookshack and fur shed, they could use the six and eight-inch lodgepole pine which stood everywhere thick and bristled as the hair on an angry dog's back.

His companions accepted the orders in good part. There was no argument and everyone, even the morose Caswell, was encouraged, emboldened, eager to be at work.

Somehow it was difficult to feel any sense of depression or danger with Yellowstone Kelly in charge. The man's knowledge of the country and its animal contents—feathered, furred, finny, scaled, creeping, crouching, crawling, walking upright, or riding a spotted Sioux pony—was astounding. And the continual cinnabar shift of his talk from the apt quotation of Tennyson, Burns, Shakespeare, Poe, and Sir Walter Scott, apparently his boyhood favorites, to the picaresque colloquial idiom of the Missouri River frontiersman, was as bright and ebullient as it was bewildering.

Kelly was a man whose spirits picked yours up by the back of the neck and lifted them high, willy-nilly. Or, as occasion might demand (and had only the night before), he could grab your emotions by the throat and throw the fear of God into them. He was a true Celt, a contrast in sunny heights and plunging dark apprehensions. Yet he was not the typical Irisher of friendly fiction; that cocksure glandular son of the Auld Sod who loved nothing better than a good clean donnybrook among friends, or to sally forth with tilted bowler and itching fist to find a playful Protestant on Saint Paddy's Day. Kelly was that far rarer, more delightful product of Hibernian biology— the man of absolute brute strength who, fearing neither God nor the Devil, respected both. And who, being unafraid of any man who walked the earth in their images, would at once and graciously yield the path upon request, or even without asking. He was a humble and happy man, as lonely and free and clean in heart and mind as the restless wind which wandered the western plain. And he stirred men in the same way as that wind, making them sense his fierce yet tender love for this savage land and making them want to follow him wherever he might lead them across its mountained mysteries.

So his companions busied themselves almost excitedly with the routine chore of cleaning up the noon-halt camp, while less than ten minutes to the east, their new partner and self-appointed chaperon whistled softly to himself as he laid out the framing stakes for the winter quarters.

For his carefree part, Luther Kelly was well content with his new friends.

True, Jepson was a confirmed grouch, Caswell a congenital coward. But MacDonal was a delightful old pirate and Big Anse Harper promised to prove as friendly and useful as Daniel DeFoe's man Friday.

For a single-tracker like himself, a man who even in a society of insistently independent adventurers was noted as a "loner" and, in fact, actually called "Lone Wolf" by the Indians, it was not an unpleasant prospect to contemplate six months of snowed-in white companionship. Although he was then but twenty-six years old, Luther Kelly had already spent seven winters of solitary wandering along the frozen flanks of the Yellowstone and had little taste for adding a lonely eighth to the record.

Thinking back to the incident which had sent him loping off after the Fort Buford wolf hunters, the young Irishman slowed his work and frowned thoughtfully.

Dropping by Reed & Bowles on his way in to winter at one of the River posts, he had been told of the recent departure of the Judith Mountain trappers and had been suddenly seized with the compulsion to join them. Of course the fact that in glassing his back trail away from Reed's place as a matter of routine precaution, he had seen Gall's big party pull in and palaver with the old man, had had something to do with his decision. Especially when the Sioux had broken off their powwow to spur their shaggy ponies along the same track he himself was following—that of the four settlement incompetents from Fort Buford.

It had then become, after all, only an act of Christian charity to run up and warn the slow-witted sheep away from a certain shearing by the Sioux. Any frontiersman in his place would have done the same thing. It was a heap of bother, but what else was a man to do under the circumstances?

Kelly grinned suddenly as he considered this logical, self-justifying explanation. Bending lithely down, he drove in the last of the marker stakes and stood back to laugh.

Bushway! Why not admit the simple truth?

He was up here looking for the two things he had been living on since running away from home to join the Union army at fifteen. *Freedom and adventure.*

It was the opium of life to Luther Kelly, this wild free land of snowcapped mountains, dark timbered slopes, winding, clear-streamed valleys, and endless windswept leagues of golden buffalo grass. This virgin savage land and his unfettered freedom to roam in it. The freedom and the constant delicious sense of death and danger which came with it.

There can be no real life, thought Kelly, belting on his axe and turning for the noon camp, save that which is lived in the tingling shadow of death. How had Scott put it in *Lady of the Lake*?

> *Hope is brightest when it*
> *dawns from fears …*
> *And love is loveliest when*

embalmed with tears.

Something like that—anyway, the idea was the same. The old law of opposites. If a man wanted to see life he had first to get a good look at death. Kelly had been getting a good look at the Grim One for some nine years now.

He got another good look at him not nine years but nine minutes later.

6

The white scout froze, one moccasin poised unplaced above the ground. He was caught. As trapped and graven in mid-motion as a brush buck surprised in a fringe timber sneak around an open pothole meadow. Not sure he has been seen, not sure he has not. And wanting to make absolutely certain before so much as flicking an ear.

Presently, it was clear to Kelly that the Sioux had not seen him.

In the following moments of strained listening to their deep voices and intent watching of their impatient hand signs as they talked, first among themselves in Sioux, then to the fearful white hunters in English, something else became clear to him.

Where they had not *seen* him, they were *looking* for him.

Where had Lone Wolf gone? Gall was demanding of the Fort Buford men in his harsh English. Did they understand that he meant Lone Wolf Kelly? The one the white brother called Yellowstone Kelly?

With the question the Sioux chief paused, letting his nervous auditors think about their answer.

As they did, he added a pertinent directive.

They had better not try to talk to him with crooked tongues, for he knew very well that Kelly had come to their camp. Furthermore, he was in a hurry. He needed to locate the missing scout at once. It would be all to the advantage of his listeners to furnish their reply with a maximum of accuracy and a minimum of delay. *Hopo! Hopo!* was the exact way he put it in concluding Sioux, and even the ignorant Caswell understood this to be a Hunkpapa term dealing with speed in the utmost, immediate sense.

The four white men stood miserably beyond the blowing ashes of their fire. In the mind of each lay a clear path of loyalty to the absent scout. But the heart of none encompassed the courage to advance along the path. Of the four only Big Anse felt a genuine want to defend the whereabouts of his new friend, and he lacked the wit to implement the wish.

They had all picked up their guns at the unhidden approach of the Indian cavalcade, but had had no chance then, and less intention now, of using them. The Sioux understood that perfectly. The *Wasicun* fools were helpless. They were in a *wikmunke*, a trap. There was utterly nothing they could do, save comply with Gall's request for Kelly's whereabouts.

The watching scout was not surprised, nor did he blame Jepson when the scowling spokesman for the wolf hunters pointed eastward.

"He's over there a ways. By that rocky ledge. The one stickin' up out'n the trees yonder. You see the one I mean?"

Gall checked the rearing outcrop, then looked back at Jepson, nodding. "Me see. You lie Gall, *you* see!"

In his hiding place, Kelly stifled a swift chuckle. He loved the Sioux sense of humor. Gall's remark was entirely lost on his other white listeners, but it at once marked the famed war chief favorably for Luther Kelly. He had never met the murderous

Hunkpapa and would have circled forty miles out of his way to avoid doing so before now. Now, suddenly, he had a strange and entirely unwarranted feeling of kinship with the great white-hater.

"Sayapi, Red Paint!" barked Gall, deep-voiced.

A young subchief spurred his pony out of the warrior circle, slid him to his haunches in front of the Sioux leader.

"Take a dozen braves," Gall ordered in Hunkpapa. "Ride over and bring in Lone Wolf."

The youthful savage touched the fingertips of his left hand to his forehead in the Sioux gesture of deep respect, wheeled his pony to depart.

"Sayapi!" Gall stopped him. "There will be no shooting by my order, do you understand? Lone Wolf will make no trouble. We have his friends here, and he is an honorable man. Just tell him Gall wants to see him. For the sake of his friends, he will make no trouble. Do you hear me?"

"Hau, Uncle," nodded the youth, "my ears are uncovered. I hear you." He spun the pony again, flung up a lean arm, muscled and menacing as the twist of a copperhead's deadly length, swept it part way around the still-eyed circle. A dozen braves broke ranks and wheeled their mounts in behind his, returning his arm signal to indicate their understanding of the maneuver as they did so.

No oral order whatsoever was given, and for the hundredth time, Kelly marveled at the extrasensory Indian ability to communicate a complete thought without the use of a single spoken word.

But the white scout was not allowing his admiration for the red brother's gifts of perception to confuse his own sense of social protocol.

In coming up on the camp and from force of long, wary

habit, he had circled it completely. Accordingly, he now stood in the screening brush to the west, not to the east of the fire's wind-eddied ashes. The twelve braves in charge of the young man, who looked enough like the famous chief to have sprung direct from his leather-clad loins, were kicking their ponies around to start them eastward. In the small moment of their turning, a muffled stillness blanketed the suspended motion of the tableau grouped about the white man's dead fire spot. The sole noise to disturb that unnatural silence came from Kelly's direction. It was the metallic slotting of steel on steel, as he levered the cocking piece of his Winchester and stepped out of the timber behind the red visitors.

"*Hohahe!*" he called cuttingly in Sioux. "Welcome to my tepee!"

Gall did not move a body muscle.

He had heard the sound of a cocking rifle before now.

So had his companions. They sat like wooden gargoyle images, motionless upon their raunchy, hay-bellied little horses. Not so much as a slant eye shifted.

Beyond them, the dozen braves leaving to bring in Kelly were as wise. They checked their mounts without attempting to wheel them about. But their leader lacked equal seasoning.

Red Paint was furious.

He had been made to lose face, to look foolish in front of his fellows. This white *sunke*, this dark-faced Wasicun dog, had done this to him by stepping out behind him with his sardonic smile and sarcastic Sioux invitation. The intent was clearly deliberate, the insult immediately intolerable.

The angry young warrior whirled his pony hard around.

He did this with his knees because his hands were occupied with hipping, on the turn, his recent model US Cavalry carbine for a snapped shot at Lone Wolf Kelly.

But the latter was not to be caught napping at his own game.

The white scout had neither to turn his body nor to hip his weapon. He was already facing forward, lean body tensed, the Winchester held butt-low off his right flank. He had only to tip its octagonal muzzle and touch off its featherlight trigger.

It was a spectacular shot, as lucky perhaps as it was skillful, certainly.

Yet it was precisely the kind of life-staking, win-or-lose-the-works gamble upon which the slender Irish scout had built his enviable reputation among these savage dark-skinned people. Had the shot missed its tiny moving target and badly wounded or killed the Indian behind it, Kelly and his four companions would have been dead within the next thirty seconds. But the shot did not miss. The infuriated young subchief's prized Springfield went cartwheeling away out of his numbed hands like a thing suddenly seized with an independent, rebellious life of its own, its walnut stock shattered, its heavy steel trigger-guard bent irreparably askew by the smashing ricochet of Kelly's heavy .44-caliber Winchester slug.

The red watchers were not loathe to grant the beauty of the thing.

H'g'un! H'g'un! Growl the courage-word. Lone Wolf's medicine was still the strongest. His *hmunha*, his magic power to hurt, was still the most potent. His *wotahe*, his charm for personal protection, was still the best. Admit it, admit it! Nobody save Lone Wolf Kelly would have tried such a shot, none but he could have made it. It was no wonder Crazy Horse called him The-Little-Man-With-The-Big-Heart. It was a better name for him than Lone Wolf. Roll it on the tongue, it sounded good, "Little Big Heart."

Even Gall was impressed.

"*Hopa, hopa!* Pretty, pretty!" rumbled the Hunkpapa war chief in generous if expressionless tribute. "Lone Wolf has an eye like *Wanbli K'leska*, the Spotted Eagle."

"*Wowicake*, you say a true thing," agreed one of the two lieutenants flanking the Sioux leader, a man distinguished among the flat-torsoed company of his brothers by a remarkable paunch. "But then Lone Wolf had the advantage and also a better gun."

"*Ha-a-u*," acknowledged Kelly, before Gall could answer. "*Owotanla!* Frog Belly's tongue is straight as always!" He had met the squat Sioux many years before, or at least had seen him, and had never forgotten him. The memory was not mutual.

The fat brave glared at him, growling a sullen, indistinguishable answer. But Kelly was not deceived. Beyond rash courage, the average horseback Indian of the High Plains responded most emotionally to rank flattery. Frog Belly was average. Kelly knew Gall's big-barreled lieutenant was well enough pleased at having his name recalled by an enemy of Lone Wolf's caliber.

Gall's own continuing grimness, however, proved uncontaminated.

"Pick up your gun," he told the humiliated Red Paint. "You, Lone Wolf, go ahead of me. Take the mule to ride. We have work for you to do and it will not wait. Do you understand?"

"Work for *me?*" returned Kelly curiously. The conversation was now entirely in Sioux, a tongue in which the white scout was as fluent as his red host. "Then you were not trailing these poor *heyokas*, these simple clowns and fools from Fort Buford?"

"No. We were trailing you. Go now. Take the mule as I said. Take him, and we shall turn back south from whence we came. Our camp is but a little way down there. Hopo. *Hookahey*."

There was no chance to develop the debate. Not even for a speechmaker of Kelly's gifts. The dark-eyed scout knew that. He had two choices. Do what they asked and get shot later—argue about it and get shot now. To his recent business associates, he apologized hurriedly.

"I'm sorry, boys. This is one time I read a set of signs exactly backward. They were trailing me, not you. To that extent I brought them down on you. I'll do what I can to make it up to you by talking them off your track.

"Meantime, sit tight right where you are until things shape up. Don't try to run whatever you do.

"Also, meantime, goodbye.

"I've a hunch you won't see me again, or if you do, you won't want to look at me. Good luck—"

"*Take the mule*," repeated Gall, his face still, his voice monotone flat. "I won't say it again."

"You won't need to, my friend!" grinned Kelly in English. He took the lead rope from Big Anse, who had caught up the mule and led it in. Swinging aboard the bony beast with laudable alacrity, he completed the grin. "I learn very fast for a Wasicun! Hopo, let's get out of here."

"Hold on, cuss it all, Kelly—!"

Jepson had once again belatedly caught up with the rapid drift of current affairs. Or almost had.

He had not understood Kelly's allusion to the likelihood of their not wanting to look at him if they saw him again, but even his turtle-slow mind could translate what was going on in front of his small-pupiled eyes at the present moment. The unprincipled Irish rascal was throwing in with the Indians, leaving them, his helpless white companions, to the later and leisured mercy of the uncertain red men!

"You can't jest ride out on us like this! Mebbe you know where you're goin' and how you're goin' to make out. That's jest fine! But what in God's name is goin' to happen to *us*, man?"

Luther Kelly turned his head and laughed.

There was in the sound both an irrepressible outer humor and a certain plaintive undertone of Celt sadness.

"Mr. Jepson," he called back, kneeing the mule obediently in the direction indicated by the eloquent grace of Gall's rifle muzzle, "it's like Wee Robbie Burns told his frightened little friend, the Mouse—that 'wee, sleekit, cowrin' tim'rous beastie' for whom he had such great, gentle-souled compassion.

> *"Still thou art blessed compared*
> *wi' me!*
> *The present only toucheth thee:*
> *But, och! I backward cast my e'eon*
> *prospects drear!*
> *An' forward, though I canna see,*
> *I guess an' fear!"*

7

The Sioux caravan wound swiftly along the serrated spine of the ridge, where the trail led southward through airily spaced stands of hundred-year-old conifers. The occasional unexpected breaks of open grassland gave forth upon dizzying cliff drops and startling vistas out across Judith Basin to the apparent ends of the prairie earth. The motionless air of high noon hung redolent with the sun-released headiness of cedar, pine, and balsam, and with the even more pungent aroma of woodland humus arising from the deep-matted cone and needle floor of the forest.

Nothing stirred.

Even the birds were still.

"Of course," Gall nodded to Kelly, breaking the lazy sunlit silence matter-of-factly, "you understand that if you are not successful in the matter, we shall kill you."

"Of course," agreed the latter. "One does not expect to be rewarded for failure."

Actually, he did not know whether the Sioux chief was speaking literally or testing his nerves. That was the delightful thing about the Hunkpapa, or in fact about any of the wild Plains

Indians. You never knew what they were thinking or what they meant to do. Which was easily enough explained. Neither did they.

Yet in his eight perilous years along the Yellowstone, Kelly had learned the secret of staying alive among the unstable Sioux and their even more fractious first cousins, the Cheyenne. He had discovered the peculiar compound of emotions which separated them from their white brothers. The latter, at least by comparison, were mentally adults, conditioned in their behavior by consciousness, respect, or fear of settlement law. The Indians had the happy minds of completely undisciplined children, the killing reflexes of completely dangerous carnivores.

And like any other wild-born animal, the nomad hostile could smell fear. The smell of it set him crazy, made his heart bad, brought him to do things for which later, more often than not, he was abjectly sorry. But by that time it was far too late. The big trick was, Kelly knew, never to falter in front of them when they had you cornered. Never to let them get behind you for more than a minute. Never to allow them to maneuver downwind of you, where they could catch the smell of the fear in your sweat.

But knowing and doing were two different matters.

Gall had already explained what lay ahead.

His party had been on an Absaroka horse raid. They had made a good gather of the Crow ponies but not quite a clean escape. Half a dozen of the enemy had come up through the morning darkness at just the wrong time. There had been a little last-minute skirmish. Nothing much. Only five Crows killed and one shot in the leg.

It had been thought wise to bring the wounded one along. No use leaving a live witness behind to identify the raiders. Besides, a Crow captive was always a big coup. And this particular one bade fair to prove a *real* big coup.

But three days of hard riding to outdistance the Absaroka pursuit had been bad for the captive's wound. Very bad. Now that wound must have attention or the Crow would die. Gall did not want that. He wanted this enemy to live a long time. Aye, he had his personal reasons for desiring this thing, but they were none of Lone Wolf's affair, and Gall would not discuss them with him.

The Hunkpapa had stopped at Reed's to see if the old man had any white man's medicine that would heal the Crow's leg. It was there he had learned that Lone Wolf was but hours ahead of him on the foothill trail. He had set out at once to come up with him.

Why? Lone Wolf should know that. If anyone could draw out the poison from that wound, would it not be Lone Wolf himself? There was no time for false modesty. Gall had heard about his power to heal long ago. He had not forgotten it. He had seen it work with his own eyes, and he thought of it now, and he hoped that Lone Wolf remembered his big medicine well enough to do magic things with that Crow wound.

If he did not and the Crow died, it would be as Gall said. They would have to kill him. *Nohetto*, it was really quite simple.

As Kelly's searching mind struggled through this confusing welter of back-thought, the war party neared the Sioux camp.

Smelling the aromatic updraft of the woodsmoke down the ridge, the white scout made one last cautious try at clearing up the situation.

He put the proposition straightaway to Gall.

"There is but one thing which puzzles me in all this, my brother," he announced fraternally. "How did the Border People come to know of my skill with medicines?" He used the proper Sioux tribal division name for the fierce Hunkpapa to further the imposture of offhand comradery. "I had thought it a power which I had kept well hidden."

He knew better than to deny the gift with which the Sioux had endowed him. Right now it represented his only chance, or at least his best one, for saving his shoulder-long hair. But it was safe enough to question the source of Gall's information, indeed the very act and form of putting the query was a subtle flattery of the kind most dear to the Indian ego.

The Hunkpapa chief looked at him.

"You do not remember me?" he asked softly.

Kelly shook his head. In truth he did not, though there was a haunting familiarity about the renowned warrior's face and form which had bothered him from the first moment back at the wolf hunter's camp.

"Think back a long time," said Gall. "Many, many moons ago. In the camp of the English half-breeds. The pemmican-makers from the Land of the Grandmother."

Kelly's eyes widened. "You were with Sitting Bull!" he cried. "That time he came to visit the Red River Sioux half-breeds on their buffalo hunt." He shook his head again. "I can't believe that I would have forgotten you!"

"I was only a warrior then, a young man. I sat in the last rank of Tatanka's braves that day. You did not see me, but I saw you. You were no more than a boy. Very young. Very frightened. You thought we were going to kill you. Remember?"

Kelly remembered with a vengeance. And, too, with that sad twinge of ineffable poignancy which is reserved to a grown man's greatest love: that for the lost and long-ago beauty of his boyhood.

Seven years ago!

He had just gotten out of his three-year hitch in the Union infantry. Was journeying west with a band of mixed-blood buffalo hunters from Canada; commercial pemmican-makers from the Red River of the North country, as Gall had indicated.

The Red River breeds, Sioux by principal Indian derivation,

had advised him to buy a Hudson's Bay blanket coat such as they wore, and to adopt the blue broadcloth hood and red sash they affected as well, so that should they encounter any of the wild Sioux, the latter would not distinguish him for an American. He had gladly taken the advice, but the ferret-eyed Tatanka Yotanka was not to be misled by any such thin device.

When, far out in the buffalo country, Sitting Bull and his painted band had ridden suddenly into the peaceful camp of their half-breed brothers, the wily medicine man had singled out the young stranger at once. And had called him for a hated American on the spot.

Kelly's life had been saved by the quick thinking of the ancient half-breed whose wagon he was sharing on the trek. The old man had remembered his young American friend setting a broken arm for a little child earlier in the march—Corporal Luther S. Kelly had served ninety days of his three years in service as a medical orderly—and when Sitting Bull grew threatening, he called for the shy youngster to be brought forward.

Showing the neatly splinted limb to the curious wild Sioux, he had extolled the American boy's strange and wondrous powers as a healer of the sick, adding that he had been trained for this work among the Pony Soldiers. The Sioux, already familiar with the white man's doctors through both the Indian Bureau and the army posts, were impressed. When the half-breed patriarch concluded his oration with the explanation that the young American had been allowed to accompany the pemmican-makers so that he might minister to their ills or to the accidents of the chase, they accepted the fabrication without question.

Sitting Bull had even let the white-faced youth lance a bad abscess on the back of his neck and had been quite pleased with the relief afforded by the ex-corporal's crude surgery.

Since that time and thinking nothing of it, Kelly had always carried with him the lancet, forceps, set of probes, rusty surgical needle, bundle of catgut sutures, bottle of carbolic, and tin of camphorated tincture of opium with which he had absconded from the army; the whole conveniently contained in a buckskin bundle no bigger than his hand and transported with his other spare personal effects in his belt-slung war bag.

Inclining his head to Gall's last question now, he had good reason to be happy with the habit, and to remember with gratitude his ninety days of serving under army Surgeon John K. Blake at Fort Wadsworth in the desolate Dakota foothills these nearly eight years gone.

8

The ponies broke into a jingling trot.

Kelly tensed his hand on the mule's halter rope. He knew he was no more than seconds from getting the chance to demonstrate his surgical talents on a basis most bona fide doctors never enjoy— that of staking his own life on his ability to save the patient's. The grim thought occurred that this Indian arrangement might lead to a great improvement in the standards of modern settlement medicine, or at least in the careful practice thereof, and with the thought the white scout laughed aloud.

Gall glanced around, surprised.

"I don't remember anything funny about that visit to the camp of our English cousins," he said. "Unless it was sticking Old Tatanka in the neck with that little knife. That was pretty funny, all right."

Kelly did not remember the incident as being outstandingly hilarious but was quick with a second laugh all the same.

"Yes, that was it!" he exclaimed. "I was just recalling how frightened I was, even as you say. I thought my time had come when they told me that it was the great Sitting Bull who visited us. And then to think of me cutting his neck with the little knife! Do you remember him calling my attention to the warriors standing all around with their rifles pointing at me and telling me that they had been instructed to shoot if he cried out when the knife went in? That was pretty funny all right, just as you say!"

"I am glad you think so," said Gall.

"How is that, my brother?"

"Soon you will have a chance to try it again. Just the same way."

"I beg your pardon?"

The Sioux chief looked at him a full ten seconds. Then he said it very quietly.

"The guns will be around you again when you use the little knife. That's all."

Moments later, they reached the Sioux camp. Kelly committed it to memory with one sweeping glance.

There were no lodges or pack animals, as this was a war party, but the braves had erected a snug shelter cleverly woven of cedar fronds and pegged down, drumskin tight, with two expensive Four Point blankets of scarlet and black. This clearly had been built to house the wounded Crow. The unusual thoughtfulness shown in the construction of any kind of shelter for a fellow Indian, wounded or not, whetted Kelly's curiosity. At the same time, his proximity to the shelter's occupant was tightening the walls of his stomach with apprehension.

That Indian in there had better be in a treatable condition. He had better have a wound within the simple limits of Lone Wolf's peacetime army experience. If he did not—

But there was no point in such "ifs."

The devil take the red hellions. Win or lose, they were not going to be treated to any hesitation on Yellowstone Kelly's part.

He slid down from the mule, stepped quickly between Gall

and the cedar bough shelter. "I will go in alone," he said quietly, "or I will not go in at all."

Gall's face clouded.

"Now why do you say that?"

"My medicine will not work unless I first see the sick one alone."

"I don't believe you."

Kelly shrugged, feeling his stomach grow smaller still within him. "I don't care what you believe. My big medicine will not begin to work if I am being watched."

"It worked for Tatanka and there were a hundred and seventy of us watching you."

"That was different."

"How different?"

"That was a small thing. The air was clean. There was no evil spirit about." Kelly was stalling dangerously for time to be alone in the shelter. Time to think. To gather his mind. To figure out some desperate way to make a break for it if the injured brave were too far gone to help. He lied deliberately and skillfully, gambling on his knowledge of the Sioux fears and superstitions, as he played his trump bluff.

"*I smell death in this camp—!*" he said harshly.

Gall sprang back from the shelter as though the white scout had struck him in the face. The other braves, coming up in time to overhear the sibilant hiss of Kelly's remark, moved away as swiftly. Crouched and tense they hung behind their leader, slant eyes fastened on the dark-faced white scout.

"Go in," said Gall at last. "But remember that out here, the guns are watching you."

Kelly gave the hand sign of understanding, turned for the low entrance.

Ducking to pass within, his face paled. A moment before, he

had taken the name of the Dark One in vain. Now his fearful nose had just made an honest prophet of him. There was no mistaking that cloying, sweetish, fetid odor. Decaying human flesh. A man never forgot that smell once it had sickened his nostrils. Before he ever touched the suffering Crow's rumpled wolfskin coverlet, he knew what he would find beneath it. Gangrene. His patient was already rotten with proud flesh. Rotten enough to be smelled ten feet away on a wind-still day. Sight unseen, the captive Crow was as good as dead. And, likewise, Luther S. Kelly along with him.

Yet the white scout had received only his first shock of two that early autumn afternoon.

He got the second moments later, while his spreading pupils were still adjusting to the inner gloom of the noisome shelter and while he was still holding his hand on the burning forehead of the sufferer to gauge his fever.

The white-toothed flashing of the wan smile seemed to touch the hidden face with fading starlight for a fleeting instant, then was gone.

"Hohahe—" said a voice, as soft as the fall of a first snowflake. "I am glad that you have come. I have been waiting for you."

Kelly said nothing. He was literally unable to speak. It was all he could do to comprehend.

Gall's Crow captive was a woman. And, unless a man's straining eyes were playing tricks on him in the shaded darkness of that cedar shelter, a startlingly young and strangely beautiful woman.

BOOK TWO

CROW GIRL MEADOW

9

Kelly did not try to look at the girl's leg in the shelter. The dim light was far too uncertain for such a critical diagnosis. Further, the fouled air was unendurable. "*Owan-yeke waste*," he reassured his silent patient in Sioux, "everything here is good for the eye." It was a bald lie, but the girl, too, could smell the presence of death in the stench of her decomposing wound and was very frightened. It was, Kelly felt, no more and no less than any real doctor would have done for her—or *could* have, as a matter of apparent medical fact. On the frontier a man's instincts grew primitive. He could *feel* things. This girl was going to die.

He laid his hand lightly on her forehead again. She turned her flushed face gratefully into the coolness of his big palm as he did so, and he grimaced silently. "Do not struggle, and do not be afraid," he told her gently. "I am going to have them carry you outside now. That is so the clean sunlight can help me see what is the matter with your leg. I am here to make you well. Do you believe that?"

"I believe it, Wasicun," she murmured, pressing her cheek harder still against his comforting hand.

"And is your heart good for me, Crow Girl?" he asked her soberly.

"Yes," she said. "My heart is good for you, Lone Wolf." The husky accent was so low-voiced, he scarcely made it out, but he felt the slight movement of her head in agreement and, as he brought his hand away, felt also the swift course of the silent tears across her dark cheek.

He came stooping out of the shelter, his long jaw clamped, throat aching tight, black eyes smoldering.

Straightening, he flung his orders with peremptory abruptness at the waiting Sioux. When the latter did not move at once in response to the white man's commands, Gall whirled upon them, his face contorted.

"Do as Lone Wolf says!" he snarled. "Or account to me *hinmangas!*"

Since the literal translation of the concluding Hunkpapa term was "you and I tear each other with a knife," and since each of the sullen braves understood the peculiar tribal significance of the challenge, there was a rush of eager red hands to bear the suffering Crow girl out into the sunlight.

Observing the terse exchange, Kelly made a mental note of it. He had heard of the Hunkpapa hinmangas duels but had never witnessed one, nor talked with any white man who had. But even in the tension of his concern over his own immediate fate, he could not miss the reaction of Gall's hardened crew to the mention of the term. Quite certainly the combat must present some refinements of cruelty and courage-testing not included in the standard knife fighting of the plains tribes. He was given no more than time to file away the ominous fact for future reference before the braves were bringing the Crow girl toward him.

"Put her on this clean rock by the little stream, here," he ordered them, indicating a flat sheet of weathered stone which lay close to the source-pool of the welling mountain spring near which the Sioux had camped.

"Now you others cut four cedar stakes," he called to the remaining braves. "Cut them long and make them sharp and drive them deep into the ground at the four corners of the rock. Bring also four well-greased tether ropes, old ones that are soft and pliable, yet still strong. Hopo! Hopo!"

"What is it that you will do?" asked Gall, stern-faced, as the warriors went grudgingly about Kelly's orders. "Stake her out in the sun like a miserable dog of a *Tshaoh?*"

He referred to the Comanches, literally "the Enemy People," and to their frequent habit of torturing captives. Contrary to lurid popular belief, the North Plains tribes seldom mutilated their victims before death. Such barbarities were distinctly beneath the proud Sioux. Torture was the specialty of the southern Plains Indians and the haughty northerners held them but little better than brutes for the practice.

Kelly knew this, but had no time for tribal niceties.

"Exactly in the same way!" he rasped. "When you are cutting with the little knife, the least slip can mean the difference between living and dying. The one who is being cut must not be allowed to move. Especially," he added, eying Gall unblinkingly, "when the one who is doing the cutting is being watched by thirty-nine Hunkpapa rifles."

Gall broke his eyes from the white man's in time to see his braves lowering the Crow girl onto the bare surface of the sun-scrubbed rock.

His thin temper flared instantly.

"Bring a robe, you fools!" he roared. "Place it beneath her. And gently! What do you think you are handling there? A sack of Pony Soldier oats?!"

Before the startled braves could move, or Gall could further upbraid them, the chiefs angry orders were quietly countermanded. "*No robe*," said Luther Kelly softly. "The rock is clean. That is the way I want it."

Gall swung on him, eyes blazing.

Red Paint stepped in, shifting his knife belt.

The remaining braves moved forward, rifles coming up, wide lips tightening.

The warriors by the rock did nothing.

"What did you say?" growled Gall.

"There will be no robe," repeated Kelly. He did not raise the level of his voice, nor move so much as an eyelid muscle. The stillness grew as though it had life and form, swiftly and with a great heaviness. Red Paint was the first to find its weight intolerable.

With an animal snarl, he leaped at the motionless braves by the rock. "Here, you *sunkes!* Give her to me!" He seized the feverish girl from them, held her savagely yet tenderly as a child to his broad chest.

"Now bring the robe!" he barked. "*Hookahey—!*"

Again the white scout did not move, nor raise his vibrant voice. But there was, as always when he spoke with feeling, a strange compelling quality to the Irish adventurer's words. The departing Sioux halted in their moccasin tracks.

"There is going to be much blood, my brothers. And much need of cleansing waters to wash it away. There is to be no robe. No anything. Nothing beneath the girl but the stone, nothing above her but the sun. Hear me, my brothers. I will not touch her with the little knife unless I am obeyed at once."

He addressed the braves in form only. His words were for Gall and the sensitive Sioux leader knew as much instinctively.

There was a long silence while Red Paint pressed the girl to his breast, and Gall stared first at him, then across at Kelly. At last he bowed his dark head, made the submission sign with his left hand.

"Bind her on the rock as Lone Wolf says," he directed the defiant Sayapi. The latter hesitated as though he would not do it, then, without a word or look for Kelly, placed the now restlessly turning girl with exquisite care upon the sun-washed surface of the white scout's operating table. Stepping back slowly, his glittering eyes found Kelly's. Their glances locked across the slender body of the suffering captive with an almost audible click and fall as of steel tumblers going into irrevocable place.

"Do with her whatever Gall says," agreed the handsome Hunkpapa youth expressionlessly. "And while you are doing it, pray to your gods that what Gall says is not wrong."

The braves moved forward to tie down the Crow girl but Kelly held up his hand. "First bring a clean blanket," he instructed quickly. "And do you have any *hupistola?* Any Indian soap of the yucca root?"

The blanket was no problem, it appeared, but as to the hupistola, an ebb of negative headshakes washed around the waiting circle. In the midst of the little silence, Red Paint, who had stepped back to stand icily aloof after his surrender to Gall's will, called suddenly across the heads of his restless fellows. "Sayapi has better than that. Some *haipajaja*, some Wasicun soap!"

"No! Real soap?" asked Kelly hopefully.

"From the old man in the valley," interjected Gall. "He said it would be good medicine for the girl's leg. Better than nothing. We knew he lied, but we took it anyway, so that he would not think we were fools."

"He did not lie!" snapped Kelly, the prolonging tension of the exchange beginning to edge his ordinarily unshakable nerves. "Bring it at once."

"Bring it," echoed Gall to the fiercely proud Red Paint. This time the stony-faced youth touched his left fingertips to his brow without hesitation. He was back in a moment, after a quick search of the elk-skin parfleche slung across his pony's withers. He handed the grimy, lint-caked bar of soft-milled ash-and-lye settlement soap to the white scout and turned away without meeting his eyes. But Kelly had no time to worry about brooding Sioux subchiefs or countermanded Indian swains. Two lives were at stake, one of which happened to be his own. He flung up a long arm, waving it around the entire circle of his intent watchers.

"You will all go back by the fire now. Turn your eyes away from this spot. I must do a personal thing."

"How is that?" said Gall suspiciously.

Red Paint, in the same instant, saved words but joined in the sentiment by once again stepping forward and dropping his sinewed hand eloquently to his knife haft.

Kelly gave them both a scathing look.

"Would you then spy upon your own women bathing in a clear stream after a hot and dusty day upon the trail?"

The two Sioux flushed deeply, and Gall bowed his head in quick shame. "We will all turn away, of course," he murmured to Kelly. Then, gutturally, to his braves, "Go to the fire at once. As Lone Wolf says, this will be a personal thing. A warrior does not look at women bathing."

"I still need that clean blanket," the white scout called, as the group began to move away. "Who will bring it?"

It developed, again without a single exchanged word between them, that once more it was Red Paint who had the necessary article. He brought the blanket, a gorgeous new Hudson's Bay Four Point of black and scarlet, never used, gave it to Kelly and retreated after his fellows.

When he had turned away, Kelly got on at once with his risky and unwanted gamble.

He first cut away the girl's vermin-infested camp dress with his skinning knife, throwing the filthy serum-and pus-stained garment aside and trying not to look at the young body beneath it as he did. The girl said nothing and did not move to resist his probing hands. She was far too ill to think about a strange white man bathing her naked form with harsh Wasicun soap and soft mountain water.

Kelly sponged her methodically, all over, using the soap on a wadded handful of downy pine grass and cedar moss, rinsing away the residue of pore-deep trail dirt with copious hatfuls of running springwater dipped in his low-crowned beaver from the eddying rill beside him. His set face glistened with the pale sweat of nerve and thought control, yet despite his best efforts to detach himself from certain distracting male instincts, his breath was coming hard and fast before he got even to the girl's slender waist. He felt the guilt of his reactions but could not channel the latter regardless. Luther Kelly had never seen a woman's body before this one. And this one, fevered sick or not, was such a body as few men ever see. The young scout's hands were shaking like the leaves of an aspen grove before the first crash of thunder in a mountain shower as he finished cleansing the final soft contour of the dusky copper form upon the sunlit rock.

But he came at last, and shaking hands or nay, to the pitifully shattered knee itself. Giving it his first full look in good light, he nearly vomited.

The wound was fearsome.

Four days old and infected no doubt within the minute of its reception, there was no hope to treat it successfully. It was a raging, festering, gray-green, bulbous mass of sloughing proud flesh, protruding bone snags of sick white fracture splinters and yellow, crustingly granulated serous scab. The swollen angry area of the infection's spread, beyond the site of the wound itself, extended a good six inches above the knee. The entire right leg, below the knee, was a distended shapeless colon of flamingly discolored flesh.

Kelly knew perfectly well what was indicated—amputation. And high-up amputation. At least six inches beyond the head of the inflamed area into the healthy tissues of the upper thigh.

He also knew something else perfectly well.

The prairie Sioux did not practice amputation.

There was no use even suggesting it to Gall.

The Hunkpapa, in fact all the horseback tribes, were a body-proud race. To them, death was preferable to disfigurement. Knowing this, Kelly had no choice.

As was his perverse Irish way under pressure, he laughed. His hands were steady now, his black eyes unclouded. He threw the fresh blanket over her body above mid-thigh, signaled for Gall and Red Paint to return quickly.

"Now tie her fast to the stakes," he rapped out, when they had come up. "Tie her hard. Until the rawhide bites into the flesh to make it white."

Gall repeated the order to the first of his warriors to come up, and the latter fell swiftly to work spread-eagling the pale-lipped Crow girl as viciously as though they meant to put lighted pine splinters under her toenails, Apache-style, or to strip a roll of living skin from her firm young belly with a peeling-stick, after the fashion of the Kiowa and Comanche.

While they grunted unfeelingly about their ruthless trussing, Kelly was busy with the contents of his "big medicine" kit.

Squatting by the pebble-bottomed spring branch, he meticulously scrubbed needle, lancet, probes, and forceps with the fine white bank sand. Next, he repeated the process with soap lather, rinsed the instruments, and laid them to dry upon the surface of his granite surgery. He then opened the bottle of carbolic, placed it conveniently to hand, and was ready.

Making a thin roll of the soft leather instrument wrapping, he told the girl to take it between her teeth. "When you feel the knife," he said tersely, "this will keep you from biting off your tongue." To Gall and the brooding Red Paint, he muttered aside, "Stand close by her head, one on either side. See that she does not spit out the biting roll." The two Sioux nodded their understanding and stepped into position.

Kelly began his work.

He moved about it with the speed of brute mercy. There could be no help for what was to come, save to make it come quickly.

He carved away the curling layers of protuberant dead tissue in thick ugly gray slices. No sound issued from the rigidly braced girl, nor from the slant-eyed watchers surrounding her. The lancet sped on. Midway in the seventh cut, it rode searingly into living tissue.

The Crow girl screamed, spat the gag, convulsed, and went limp.

10

It went very quickly after that.

With the forceps Kelly picked out the eruptive bone splinters, arranging the damaged kneecap in as near its natural posture as his limited knowledge could suppose was correct. He then heavily irrigated the curetted wound site with more springwater drenches, augmenting the bleeding which was cleansing the incised area. When the loss of blood began to slow, he let the leg dry in the sun, meanwhile sprinkling the operative field with baking soda, a tin of which he always carried in his war bag for the manufacture of frying-pan light bread. The bleeding stopped entirely within three or four minutes.

The moment it had, Kelly took the needle and bundle of suturing gut, grasped them in the forceps, plunged the whole into the water he had ordered the Sioux to boil meanwhile for the purpose of sterilizing some undyed trade cotton which one of the braves had bought at Reed's Ranch.

He grimaced wryly at the crude contrast in civilized aim and savage method; the Sioux were boiling the bandaging cotton in a green buffalo paunch!

Kelly pulled his hand quickly away from the steaming Sioux cook pot. Moving back to the girl, he made his simple sutures, laterally, across the gaping openness of the knee, pulling the edges to within an inch of each other and thus holding the kneecap, under pressure, in place for the bandaging.

He wrapped the hot, wrung-out cotton stripping as he had been taught in the service, leaving it just free enough to accept a pushing fingertip beneath its edges. This done, he splinted the knee with pliant green willow withes, set the splints by wrapping them firmly in the remaining cotton, covered the whole, ankle to mid-thigh, with a piece of clean manta, or canvas pack covering, bound in place with plaiting rawhide.

When he had made his last tie and trimmed its ends, he stood back, making the simple hand sign of completion to the red audience.

The Sioux were entirely fascinated.

Gall was openly impressed.

He stepped impulsively toward Kelly, his left hand raised palm out in the lingua franca arm signal of Indian peace with respect and friendship the prairie over. At the same time, he growled, "*Waste! Waste!*" in his grizzly-deep Sioux bass.

It was a rare tribute coming from the Hunkpapa who stood second only to the great Sitting Bull in the tribal councils of his, the fiercest of all the Throat Slitter people. Kelly recognized the goldenness of the moment, struck while the Indian mood was malleable.

"*Haho*, thank you." He bowed soberly. Then, straightening to look at Gall as one chief to another, "I have done what you asked me, my brother. The girl lives and is greatly relieved. It is time for you to keep your part of the bargain."

Gall nodded thoughtfully. But before he could speak, a tall shadow fell between him and the white scout. "What bargain?"

said Red Paint flatly. "We only promised to shoot you if you failed."

"The unspoken part of such a promise," replied Kelly quietly, "is that you shall free me if I succeed." Then, with deliberate acidity. "Are you a Mandan dog-eater or a Hunkpapa warrior? Will you sneak around your word like a Pawnee pony stealer or stand beside it like a Sioux chief?"

Kelly, of a sudden, was no longer blarneying his red hosts in protection of his hair. His Irish was up at last, and he had had enough and more than enough of Red Paint and of Hunkpapa tongue-splitting in general.

"You, Sayapi!" he barked at Red Paint. "Answer me, I am talking to *you!*"

The young chief's face writhed. His eyes narrowed to Mongol slits. For the third time in ten minutes, his hand went to his knife. This time it did not stop. The ugly weapon came away from its sheath in a gleaming arc of upraised naked steel as Sayapi leaped and struck at the unarmed white scout in one eye-blinding movement of animal speed.

Swift as was the youth's attack and lightning fast as was Kelly's sidewise dive to avoid it, the third member of the brief dialogue moved quicker still.

Gall struck with the speed of a hurled buffalo lance.

Coming from the side and slightly behind his berserk subchief, he was beyond Red Paint's field of vision. The young chief did not know for some seconds what had happened. He sat in the soft dirt and churned up pine needles where he had landed, shaking his head to clear his blurred sight of the lingering shock of the fall Gall had given him.

Kelly was shaking his head a little, too.

Seizing the leaping youth from the rear, Gall had raised him bodily over his head, whirled him once full around, slammed him back-flat to the ground in less time than it had taken Kelly to simply leap aside and regain his balance in avoiding Red Paint's initial lunge. And the latter was no stripling. He stood three inches over six feet and must have weighed at least one hundred and ninety-five pounds.

The white scout had never seen an equal combination of speed and brute strength applied with such exact science. As was his careful habit, he made a mental note of the fact against future possible need: Gall, second-in-war-command to Crazy Horse among the combined Sioux bands, was everything that frightened settlement talk had said he was in savagery and fighting skill; and he was, beyond that, physically the strongest man Luther Kelly had ever seen. Small wonder, Kelly recalled grimly, that his Hunkpapa friends had shown such little stomach for his offer to oblige them in a hinmangas duel. To fight a man like Gall with a knife, regardless of the rules, would be like tackling a Bengal tiger with a toothpick.

Again, there was time only to file the thought.

Gall was lifting the young warrior to his feet, and the latter was twisting away from him, livid with shame and repeated loss of face. Gall let him go.

"Pick up your knife," he told him, kicking the weapon toward him. "Go quietly, and give thanks to Wakan Tanka that you did not kill Lone Wolf, who had no weapon, and thus bring dishonor on my lodge."

To Kelly he added with head-shaking regret, "*Wonunicun*, Lone Wolf, it was a mistake. I apologize for my nephew."

Kelly nodded, surprised to learn that Red Paint was actually Gall's blood nephew. But he said nothing, and the Hunkpapa chief went on.

"Sayapi is young, and he hates the white man, yet he is not a coward. It is the girl that made him do that just now, do you understand? He has looked at her and is a little crazy because she has not looked back at him. *Nohetto*, that is all. Do you not see?"

Kelly felt like saying, "Yes, he did not see," but instead he nodded gravely that he understood.

It was clear enough to him that Red Paint was jealous of the girl, but he, Kelly, being himself completely without personal experience in the field of romance, was certainly no expert on love signs. He had made little from the Hunkpapa youth's behavior toward the Crow girl other than to assume, from his proprietory action in seizing her from the warriors before the operation, that she was his personal captive, and he was naturally concerned with her arriving home in good condition so that he might strut to his haughty young heart's content in front of the envious eyes of lesser youths. After all, to take a beautiful Crow girl in a pony raid conducted by the great Gall himself, in which no other Sioux had brought home so much as a scalp—let alone an enemy horse— was a little more than just something for a young man only now turned twenty.

Kelly conceded his density on the way of a red man with a red maid and was careful to keep his thoughts on Gall and his own immediate escape from the Sioux camp.

"Hau, my brother," he waved politely, "these things will happen. A man understands." Then, as indifferently as he could. "With Gall's permission I will go now ..."

The famed Hunkpapa looked at him a long while. This time there was no nod, thoughtful or otherwise. There was no sign of any kind at all from Gall.

Just the slant-eyed, emotionless, unfathomable Sioux stare.

11

"Go in peace," said the Sioux chief, after a time which seemed to Kelly like eternity compounded.

"Thank you," answered the latter, touching the fingertips of his left hand to his forehead before signing them gracefully toward Gall. "Do my friends and I also have your permission to hunt up here this winter?"

"What do you hunt?"

"We are out after wolf pelts. It is my thought that it will be a good thing for the game up here to thin out the wolves a little. What do you think?"

"It will be a good thing. You may stay."

"Thank you."

"Stop thanking me. Just go."

"There is still one thing more. About the girl. A way to carry her on the trail," said Kelly.

Gall queried the white scout carefully on the subject. As carefully, Kelly described to him the method of making a travois stretcher, used by the army where pack animals or riding mounts but no ambulances or field wagons were available. Long poles were cut and a regulation litter made up. Then, the forward, longer end of the poles were fastened low to the pack or riding saddle fenders, while two men on foot bore the rear ends. In this way the occupant of the litter could be transported quite swiftly and with little or no discomfort.

Gall thanked Kelly and promised that such a litter would be at once constructed.

"Then there is just the matter of giving the girl this medicine to ease her pain." The scout held up the container of camphorated tincture of opium, the army's standard anodyne. "It will take but a moment." He did not wait for Gall's approval but turned at once back to the rock and the silent Crow girl.

She had regained consciousness. He smiled at her and gave her the medicine, bringing some water for her to swallow with it. She obeyed quietly, letting him raise her in his arms to drink and then to lower her gently back, as trustingly as a child.

"I heard what you said to them about the travois," she whispered, staring up at him with a directness that went through him like a fever chill. "I am grateful for that. The leg hurts very much."

For the first time, he noticed that her eyes were gray; as gray and clear as springwater in a limestone pool. He had seen it in the Crows and knew that among them it was not uncommon, but had never seen the color peculiarity so strikingly demonstrated in any of her Absarokan tribesmen as in this young girl.

"It will hurt much less in a little while," he told her, made uneasy by her unfaltering gaze and dropping his own dark eyes before it. "The medicine will make you forget it for many hours."

She smiled as she surprised him in his overt study of her pagan beauty, and he blushed like a schoolboy caught looking at teacher's shapely ankle.

"I must go now," he mumbled clumsily. "Is there any last thing I may do for you?"

"Yes!" she replied quickly, and to his certain surprise. "You may take a message for me!"

There was an urgency in it that would not be denied, and he bent slightly over her. "To whom? Be quick with it, girl! We do not have all fall. The Sioux will be coming over in a minute."

"I have a brother," she murmured. "He is a scout for the Pony Soldiers. I do not know where he is now, but you can find him. He is not unknown," she put in proudly.

"His name!" gritted Kelly, stealing a nervous look toward the Sioux. "Hopo—!"

"You could not pronounce his name in my tongue," smiled the girl. "But the Wasicun call him Curly."

It hit Kelly like the bounce of a four-pound war club off good solid skull bone.

Curly! Of course! Why hadn't he remembered?

For the past few seconds, he had been studying the Crow girl's flawless features openly, haunted by a growing conviction that he had seen her somewhere else before this—yet knowing he could never actually have done so and forgotten her. Now it was all clear.

Curly, the best full-blood scout the army had according to reports along the river posts. Curly, the friendly Crow, the intelligent, easy-smiling, soft-voiced *Kangi Wicasi*, the loyal Absaroka guide who had cast his lot with the Wasicun Walk-A-Heaps and Pony Soldiers from boyhood. And Curly, the handsomest one male human being Luther Kelly had ever seen, red or white or black or any shade in between. That was where he had seen the girl's perfect face before; striking feature for striking feature mirrored in her brother's classic profile.

"I know him," he told her, recovering from the side thought with another covert glance at the waiting Sioux. "Not as a brother or a friend but by reputation. I will be able to find him and give him your message."

Now, out of the tail of his darting eye, he saw Gall start toward them. "Hurry now!" he warned her. "Is it that you want me to tell your brother that Gall, the Hunkpapa, has captured you?"

"Not Gall. Sayapi. Gall is good. Red Paint is the devil who shot me. He knew I was a woman, too. He told me that later, laughing about it. Saying he could see my body in the dark and wanted it. So he shot me low down as I ran away. I wish he had killed me, or I did wish it until—"

"*Nohetto!*" interrupted Kelly harshly. "That's enough of that! Did Red Paint tell the others he had shot you deliberately?"

"No, he told them it was an accident. And he talked Gall into thinking it would be a big coup to bring me back here. They hate the Kangi Wicasi, but Gall would have left me when he found I was a woman. He has a brave heart, but he dotes on that Sayapi—!"

"He also rides herd on him pretty roughly!" Kelly couldn't help saying in English, before dropping rapidly back into Sioux. "But the message!" he rapped. "It *is* that you want me to tell Curly Gall's band has you captive?"

"Yes, that is it. Curly will come. He will bring the Pony Soldiers to punish these Sioux dogs!"

"I will tell him." He shot another glance at the nearing Gall. "It is goodbye now." Gall was almost up to them. "May Wakan Tanka walk beside you."

"Lone Wolf—!"

Her soft cry caught him turning to check the scowling Sioux chief's approach with a disarming grin and careless hand sign to say that he was coming now.

"Yes—" He threw it back, side-mouthed, over his shoulder.

"You heard Gall say that Sayapi had looked at me?"

"Yes, yes." He kept his smile on Gall.

"And that I had not looked back at him?"

"Yes, what of it, girl? Hopo!"

"Only this," she said, the whisper so fiercely soft, it spun him back around to face her, the gray eyes stabbing so deeply into his that he felt the look clear to the toes of his Arapahoe moccasins, "I *have* looked back at you!"

Kelly had no answer. He wheeled away from her.

It was not a matter of time. He could not have made her a logical reply given the remainder of the winter in which to phrase it. The girl's strange avowal had caught him squarely in the center of the meadow. There was no chance to reach the trees.

He was still standing there, completely routed, when Gall's deep voice touched him on the shoulder.

"Hopo, hurry it up now. Look yonder at Sayapi's pony."

Kelly did as he was told, grateful for the rescue from the clear-eyed Crow girl's growing spell.

His gratitude was short-lived. He felt his scalp tighten, the individual nape hairs on his neck come erect.

"I do not see Sayapi's pony," he said in a small voice.

"Of course," replied Gall, his savage features a study in Sioux inscrutability. "That is because he is gone. And Sayapi with him."

"I see your point," admitted the white scout hurriedly, "and a little more beside." He legged it unashamedly for the pack mule, swung aboard him, kicked the bony brute around. "Sayapi has taken ten braves with him!" he said to Gall.

"Twelve," corrected Gall. "The same twelve who lost face with him when you smashed his gun up there by the Wasicun's fire."

> *"Thirteen Sioux on a dead*
> *man's trail,*
> *Yo! ho! ho! and a bottle of*
> *wolf-bait—!"*

Kelly shouted grinningly as he put his heels into the mule. The latter broke into a lumbering run up the ridge track, headed for the wolf hunters' camp.

"What did you say?" called Gall, cupping his ear for the galloping scout's answer.

"Lay on, Macduff—!"

Kelly yelled back over his shoulder.

> *"And damn'd be him that first cries,*
> *'hold, enough!'"*

12

Kelly had an unexpected, not altogether pleasant surprise awaiting him when he slid the lathered mule up to the ashes of the wolf hunters' campfire. His companions were gone.

He had only begun to clench his long jaw in anger at this desertion and more, at this disregard for his parting admonition to sit tight no matter what, when his wide mouth relaxed and the bad light went out of his black eyes.

Clear and ringing, off to the east, came the chonking of a double-bitted axe swung by a man who cut his notches deep and clean. Moments later he heard the clear tenor carry of Big Anse Harper's "*Timber—!*" followed by the breaking crash of an eighty-foot cedar septuagenarian careening earthward through the slender arms of its lesser fellows.

By thunder! That was more like it.

The boys were over at his cabin-site stakes, felling trees. Evidently, they had made up their minds, independently of what happened to him, to stick it out. Good for them! They were showing more spunk than a man would have thought.

Not two hours before, when quick thinking had been the

order of the moment, MacDonal, the shrewd Scot, had taken over from Jepson, the stubborn State of Maine man whose bulldog grit and Yankee acquisitiveness had envisioned the venture in the first place. Now, facing a probable Indian fight for their isolated lives, both MacDonal and Jepson had willingly subordinated themselves to a towering hillbilly oaf whom they had twenty-four hours previously been treating on a par with the pack mule.

It reminded Kelly of the war.

A man in the ranks learned very fast when the bullets were flying. And the first thing he learned was that under fire, sergeants frequently became captains and colonels, while captains and colonels as often turned into blundering privates of the line, with suddenly no more sense of how to direct an attack or order a retreat than the newest recruit in the regiment.

It more than simply pleased the watching white scout to see the two older wolf hunters jumping to the big southerner's commands. There was a reason for Kelly's gratification. What Big Anse's commands had accomplished in the two hours Kelly had been away could well mean the difference between standing the Sioux off or going under for keeps. The Georgian had already cut and notched enough timbers for the others to have up a good three feet of wall entirely around Kelly's ground plan for their winter quarters. And, in addition to the wall already in place, there was enough other timber down and trimmed to get on with the raising at the rate of a foot an hour.

The scout stepped silently from the screening pines, calling clearly across the meadow to avoid drawing a shot from the nervous Caswell, on rifle guard while his companions worked in the timber.

Caswell ran toward him, exhibiting a relief and gladness that would, Kelly thought, have been a grand fine flattering feeling in a stronger man. In Caswell, it only made a fellow's skin crawl with embarrassment. Nevertheless, Kelly accepted the weakling's gratitude for what it was and did not let him suspect that he was any less glad to see Caswell than Caswell was to see him.

The others were only seconds behind Caswell in crowding around him, Big Anse being the first to put his welcome into words.

"I'm tolerable glad to see thet mule, Mr. Kelly." He grinned awkwardly. "I was just gittin' set to snake them big butt-cut cedar sticks fer the roof stringers out'n the timber by myse'f."

"Aye!" Dour Alec MacDonal actually laughed. "Now we can hitch the two of ye together and have a team of donkeys. That is, if the mule has no objections, lad."

"Little man," observed Big Anse without anger and picking the small Scot up by the collar of his sweat-soaked shirt, "one day you're goin' to git me riled. If you do, I'd be beholden to you if you'd pick a bright sunny day. Buryin's alius give me the fantods when there's a gray drizzle drippin' or a scud of cloud bank clabbered up and puckerin' to rain over the family plot." With the half-meant warning, he put MacDonal back down and yielded the floor to Jepson.

The down-easter came right to the point.

"What happened and where do we stand now?" he demanded of Kelly, as the latter handed the mule's halter rope to Big Anse. Kelly put him straight in less time than it took Big Anse to get a good grip on the exchanged rope. When he had finished, it was still the perverse Jepson who wanted a precise clarification. "Well," he demanded bluntly, "where does that leave us? Do we stay or don't we?"

Before anyone else more qualified could deliver an opinion, Big Anse stood surprisingly forward.

"We'll jest make another vote of it, by Gawd," he announced quietly. "Jepson?"

The glum-tempered easterner was no stranger to Indians, but the Hunkpapa Sioux were a far cry from the community-dwelling Mandans, Iowas, and Sacs of his experience along the lower river. "Turn back," he said flatly.

"MacDonal?"

The Scot took a little longer to think about it, yet in the end he too decided Gall's brethren were much more risky a cut of the red deck than the peaceful Crees of his Canadian boyhood. "Aye, clear out," he said.

"Yank?"

Caswell was an honest coward. "Run for it!" he blurted.

"Mr. Kelly?"

"I'm for seeing it through, Anse."

"And me," nodded the giant Georgian in quick agreement.

"Phineas—?"

"Now wait a minute!" snapped the humorless Jepson, but he was too late. Anse already had his huge paw wrapped tighter around the mule's halter rope.

"Phineas," he said, "you vote to go or stay?" And with the question, he gave a tremendous jerk on the rope. Willy-nilly, the startled pack animal's dozing head snapped an automatic yes. At the same time, his offended bray echoed angrily enough to have been heard back in Judith Basin.

"What did he say?" asked Kelly, cupping an ear.

"He's fer stickin' it out!" cried Anse delightedly.

"I rather imagined he would be," admitted the black-haired scout, meanwhile watching the others anxiously to see if they were going to go along with the big southerners crude charade.

The sampling showed little promise.

Apparently, the opposition was not amused at being disenfranchised by a talking jackass.

13

There was a goodly silence then while the five men stared stubbornly at one another, and the mule eyed Big Anse resentfully. Not knowing he had been granted the glorious right of suffrage, Phineas was wanting only to maneuver his backside around to where he could plant a set of ironshod heels in the ex-Confederate's burly hams. Before he could accomplish this, Kelly's irrepressible Irish came to the top, easing the pressure for man and beast.

"We'll toss a coin, boys," he suggested lightly. "Heads we stay, tails we shag on out of here."

"Toss it," agreed MacDonal. "I've half a mind to stay regardless. The more I look at this country, the more fur I see in it. I canna help but be thinkin' we'll make a tidy stake if we put out our strychnine just so."

"You will that," Kelly assured him. "Have you got a silver dollar on you, Scotty? None of your Canadian tin, now. I want United States metal."

"And ye shall have it, Mick," the pawky little Scotsman arrowed him back. "I'm prepared to advance ye the sum requested and 'tis fer loan at a reasonable ten percent, the same as yer services, lad."

Kelly laughed, reached into his war bag, and brought out a bent and verdigrised ten-cent piece. He threw it to MacDonal. The latter picked it out of the air, dug a mint-fresh US dollar out of his own buckskin moneybag, flipped the shining coin to Kelly with an eye twinkle of Celt understanding. The scout caught it expertly. "Heads we stay, tails we go," he repeated, balancing the heavy coin on forefinger and thumb knuckle.

"Ah, no you don't!" inserted Jepson quickly. "I don't trust your deceivin' Irish ways. We'll call it in the air," he concluded, jaw thrust.

"In the air it is!" Kelly laughed again and threw the coin high.

"Heads!" yelled Jepson defiantly.

"Tails!" cried Kelly happily.

And in the moment of their contrasting upward looks, the faces of both men changed color and contour.

The single shot came crashing from the meadow's edge to the west. It caught the coin still turning lazily at the apex of its arc. It hit it, sent it whining away at a weird glancing angle. It struck the rock wall above the cabin site, ricocheted crazily off a quartz outcrop, spun to a stop in the dust at Big Anse Harper's feet.

The hillman leaned over, picked it up.

It was drilled nearly dead center.

"Purty good shot," he said laconically, suspending it with the promise of completing thought to come as the others eyed him, not wanting to look behind them toward the meadow's west fringe. Big Anse turned slowly to face the site of the shot's origin, finished his doubtful compliment as his suspicions were confirmed, "fer an Injun," he conceded unhurriedly.

On his calm words, the rest of them came unwillingly around to take in the view westward.

It was a mountain vista, well designed to widen white eyes and shorten Wasicun breaths.

Sitting their tail-switching little prairie mustangs at the edge of the meadow's backing timber, the low sun behind them flashing ocher red off their lance blades and rifle barrels, were twelve war-painted Hunkpapa braves. Fronting them, the smoke from his great shot still wisping thinly from the muzzle of Luther Kelly's spoils-of-war Winchester, his handsome face as blank as an unlettered limestone head-marker, sat the thirteenth.

"*Onhey!*" shouted Red Paint, levering the empty brass casing spinningly out of the white scout's priceless rifle and throwing the weapon to arm's length above his head in the signal for the charge. "I will count the first coup!"

On the excited boast, he slammed his moccasined heels into the flanks of his spotted stud and sent him careening wildly toward the startled white men. Behind him his twelve braves echoed his hoarse challenge as they beat their scrubby mounts unmercifully with rifle barrel and lance shaft to race Sayapi for the honor of taking the first scalp.

"What did he say?" yelled Big Anse to Kelly as the five white men dove for the cover of the low cabin walls.

"He was betting his friends," yelled back Kelly, leaping the cedar log barricade, "that he'd be the first to get his knife under white hair this afternoon."

Then, grabbing Caswell's old Springfield away from him and shoving the paralyzed army teamster to the safety of his knees behind the log wall, he added grimly, "Hold low and get their horses down."

But Sayapi's Sioux veered off too far out in the meadow to have any of their ponies downed by the white fire. There was a good reason for that. One with which "Lone Wolf" Kelly and his friends had nothing whatever to do.

From the south rim of the open grassland fronting the scout's cabin site, the third member of the argument made his position known with true Hunkpapa simplicity—charging Red Paint as straightaway as the latter was bearing down on the beleaguered white men.

In an Indian, as in any other fight, two's company, three's a crowd. When Red Paint saw his uncle coming hellbent across the meadow for him, backed by twenty-four of the twenty-six older warriors remaining loyal to the war chief, he lost faith in his new independent medicine. He did this because Gall was making it very clear by the way he was slicing in between Sayapi and his white targets that he intended to rescue Lone Wolf and his four friends even if he had to ride down his favorite nephew to do it.

Red Paint's temper was as thin as his famous uncle's. But he was no more a fool than was the latter. He had been trained in war by Gall himself. He knew when to stay and when to go.

Swinging his pony northward, he turned the charge with a precision no white cavalry could have approximated. His twelve braves streamed after him, not a pony faltering or missing a stride in the fluid shift. "Beautiful! Beautiful!" cried Kelly excitedly, as the young Sioux, seeing that Gall had halted his forces in mid-meadow and did not mean to pursue the issue, again flanked his troop in full gallop and brought its wiry mounts to a nostril-flaring stop, facing his uncle across the winnowing mountain grass.

"Hear me, Sayapi!" called the latter. "After you had led your braves out of my camp in anger, I gave these Wasicun permission to hunt our lands through this winter. I gave Lone Wolf to understand that we Sioux would not bother him and his friends. I now give you to understand the same thing. I won't say it again." He paused, then added sharply. "And one more thing; I am keeping the girl now. I will keep her until she is well and can say rightly with whom she chooses to ride."

"*He-hau*," waved young Sayapi, greatly subdued in Kelly's opinion. "I hear you, Uncle. Now you hear me." As he went on, Kelly quickly lost the impression that he had just formed. "This Lone Wolf has insulted me twice. I have sworn to kill him for that. You cannot stop me, I take your orders no longer." He paused exactly as Gall had, then yelled angrily, "And here is one more thing for you! I want that Kangi Wicasi girl. She is mine. I counted the first coup on her, and I want her back right now, do you hear?"

"Come over and get her," suggested Gall flatly.

With the proposal, he pointed over his shoulder to the timber behind him. Following the gesture, Kelly saw the two missing Sioux of Gall's group standing just within the fringe pines, holding up the rear poles of the wounded Crow girl's pack-pony travois.

Sayapi looked across the meadow a long time, moving his dark glance repeatedly from his uncle to the girl. He wound up looking at the empty-faced Hunkpapa chief. His only reply to Gall's unblinking invitation was to throw up his lean rifle arm once more, in silent signal to his followers, then wheel his paint stud and gallop away to the north. Without a sound his braves followed him. In ten seconds the stillness of the late mountain afternoon had refallen across the shadowed meadow.

"You were lucky," said Gall, reining his blue roan war-pony to a nervous halt in front of the unfinished cabin fortress. "I think Sayapi would have gotten you."

"He might have done so," admitted Kelly ruefully, "since you gave him my sixteen-shooter and I had only this old Pony Soldier one-shot."

The "sixteen-shooter" reference was a misnomer in actual ballistic fact, but Gall understood it. The scout was using the Sioux name for all the later lever-action repeaters, taken from the early Henrys which had, indeed, held sixteen of their short .44-caliber shells. The same went for calling the older Springfields "one-shots," though with more accuracy.

"I gave it to him because you had broken his," apologized Gall seriously. "I thought it might take a little of the bitterness out of his heart. But he is too much like me. Anyway, you were lucky. I think there are only two things that will make Sayapi break a charge once he has started in."

"Gall is one of them," grinned Kelly. "What is the other?"

"Death."

The Irish scout nodded. As far as he was concerned, the two reasons were synonymous, the terms interchangeable. Gall was a very dangerous Indian. The kind you could never risk extended familiarity with; that you had to keep the steel in front of. His whole relationship with the Hunkpapa was getting on shaky ground. It was time to show a little steel.

"Well," he said boldly, "I am glad to know that your word is better than your sign." He touched his forehead properly. "I salute you for keeping your promise to me."

Gall stared at him stonily.

"What do you mean about my word and my sign?"

Kelly had made the statement deliberately, of course. It was his conviction that without keeping the hostiles under the continued spell of what might be called a northern frontier version of the south's white supremacy, they could not be controlled. As with the ex-captive black hordes of the late Confederacy, the numerical odds in their favor were simply too great to accept any lasting case of social equality. Hence, he had taken this moment to cut Gall back down to Indian size. He did not want to do it, nor did he like to do it. It was simply a case of necessity.

"You sat on the blanket at Laramie?" he said quietly.

"You mean that time Makhpiya Luta lied to us?"

"I mean that time. But Red Cloud did not lie to his brothers. He wanted peace, and he signed the white man's paper for the Sioux. So did some others that I remember."

Gall's face clouded. His eyes looked far away.

"It is true I touched the pen," he said, with a strange softness new to Kelly. "But I did not understand what I was doing, I did not know what the paper took away from the Sioux." He made a helpless sign. "I was there only as Sitting Bull's delegate. It was his fault. He should not have sent me. I am a warrior, I cannot read."

"But you understood that the paper meant peace, that you were to kill no more white men?"

"Yes."

"Yet you have continued to kill more? Is that not a true thing?"

"Yes."

"It is what I meant by your word being better than your sign."

"I knew all along it was what you meant, my brother," admitted the head-bowed Sioux chief, almost inaudibly.

Kelly nodded and let the silence grow.

This side-thrust mention of the Laramie Treaty of 1868, Kelly's first full year on the River, had left an acid taste in the Hunkpapa's mouth. The Irish scout had meant that it should. A white man must never leave an Indian without impressing him that he, the white man, is always at least one full step ahead of him. It may have seemed a poor way to return Gall's recent good treatment of him, but Kelly was satisfied he had made just the right stroke.

"No matter," he concluded graciously, purposely attempting to sweeten the aftertaste of his bitter reminder of Sioux perfidy, "I am glad that I have your word now, and I know that you will keep it."

Gall's reaction completely confused him.

The great Sioux leader's craggy face took on an expression of ineffable sadness. His oblique black eyes were even farther off on the distant horizon. The peculiar humble softness the scout had noted before in his deep voice burred even lower.

"In all the time that I have been a grown man," he said to Luther Kelly, "in all the time that my father was a grown man, and before him his father, back to the earliest time in my people's memory of touching the pen with the white man, even unto the time when all the Sioux lived east of the Big Muddy and had no horses, no Indian has ever been the first to break a treaty." He turned his pony to go, adding without bitterness but with the weight of a lifetime of useless, losing war. "You may well be glad that you have my word, my brother. It has never been dishonored."

Gall was gone then. He did not look back, nor did any of his braves.

Kelly, watching them go, failed to feel the relief such departures usually inspired. For the first time in his long years on the northwest frontier, he had met an Indian to whom he did not feel superior. More than that. In the brief moment of Gall's soft goodbye, Luther S. Kelly had felt very clearly that the Hunkpapa was second-best man to *nobody* in that hushed mountain meadow.

14

When the last of Gall's warriors had cleared the meadow and were lost in the forested slopes to the east, Kelly roused himself from his strange depression. It was no time to be weighing white wrongs against red rights. Leave that to the bumble-heads in the Indian Bureau. Kelly had a problem of immediate survival on his hands.

There was a practical guarantee that Red Paint would be back in the morning. As certain was the supposition that Gall would not be around to chaperon his white friends the second time. The chief had clearly wanted to get on with his journey; to get the girl to the main Hunkpapa camp which, Kelly understood from conversation overheard among Gall's braves, was over near the mouth of the Musselshell, a good three days eastward.

What the Sioux chiefs sudden interest in Sayapi's pretty captive might amount to, Kelly did not care. Moreover, he did not even try to guess. It was a dangerous omission of imagination. As with the nephew before the uncle, the white scout's innocence of heart signs was to prove a costly ignorance indeed.

At the moment, however, his only concern was for his own and the four other white scalps in his charge.

"Whether we stay the winter or not," he told his companions tersely, "we've got to fort-up for right now. Best way to do that is finish the cabin as planned. We've got a melon-slice moon and plenty of Montana lanterns to light the job." He threw an explanatory arm upward toward the blazingly starred night sky. "I suggest we get on with it right now. Any better offers?"

There were none.

Big Anse seized his axe and passed the mule's halter rope to Kelly.

"I'll cut and notch all thet the four of you and Phineas kin haul and set in place. Like them Hunkpapa boys say, 'hopo! Let's go.' Let's build a fire under our backsides. It's a sight better than havin' the Sioux set one under the bottoms of our bare feet, by Gawd!"

Kelly only agreed with a curt nod, not bothering to disabuse the others as to the Georgian's popular misconception of the Sioux as torturers. Right now the impression would serve as a good spur, and right now a good spur was what Luther Kelly needed.

By the scout's educated guess, the brief September dusk was only minutes away. Its fall would leave them twelve hours of darkness in which to get up and roof over the cabin walls before daylight brought back Sayapi and his now thrice-humbled braves. It would be a herculean effort, even for five frontier-hardened men and a Montana-bred mule. Kelly set his big jaw, brought out his best grin to cloak its grimness.

"After you, Harper." He bowed to the delighted hillman, sweeping the pine needles with the brim of his beautiful beaver hat. Then, starting off behind Big Anse's proud lead, he clucked to the eye-walling Phineas, flung a long arm dramatically toward the sun's last thin rim, even then slipping beyond the cloud-banked shoulder of Judith Mountain, and rolled the startling quote thunderously forth:

"Move eastward, happy earth,
*   and leave*
Yon orange sunset waning
*   slow:*
From fringes of the faded eve,
O, happy planet, eastward
*   go—!"*

As Big Anse and Kelly moved into the darkness, the three remaining wolf hunters stood staring after them, the Irishman's elfin bit of Tennyson still ringing in their uncomprehending ears.

"The mon's entirely daft," said Alec MacDonal to the bewildered Jepson and Caswell. "Dippy as a Slave Lake loon, or I will buy the drinks all winter."

"Drunk, more likely!" snapped Jepson, whose busy blue-veined nose and sharp simian eye had previously noted that Kelly carried an unannounced and unoffered bottle of Kentucky bourbon in his war bag. "He totes a pint along. I seen it in his sack."

"If so," countered the Scot, "I'm put in mind of what Abraham Lincoln told them that was wantin' him to get rid of General Grant because of his boozin'."

"You mean," said Jepson irritably, "thet old wheeze where Abe says, 'What brand does he drink? I'd like to send a barrel of it to my other generals?'"

"Aye, mon, that's the one."

"Well, so what? Where's the point in it fer us and Kelly? Drunk or sober, he's still crazy!"

"Aye, lad, and there's jest the point," said Alec MacDonal, picking up the hand axe and starting off after Big Anse and the Irish scout. "I canna help but wish we were all as crazy as he is."

In the next nine hours, five men and a mule—by sweat and

starlight—built a notched and mortised cedar log cabin twenty by fourteen feet square, complete to unchinked fieldstone fireplace and raftered over, heavily sodded roof.

Kelly, standing back with Big Anse to survey the finished fortress, felt proudly that as much had not likely been done before, by so few in so short a time. He was proud of his work and proud of his workers. He had reason to be. Hidden talents had come to light under his cheerful, driving example.

Jepson had been a shipbuilder in his east coast youth; what he could do with an ordinary camp axe by way of fitting and interlocking contrary timbers was pure witchcraft. MacDonal had for years bossed a Canadian logging crew in really big timber; he knew a dozen ways to move a down and trimmed "big stick" sawlog with a little pack rope, and the one available draft animal, that most men would have been at a loss to budge with sixty feet of log chain and a steam winch. Even Caswell had come through; remembering that in his Nebraska boyhood he had cut prairie sods for roofing a cowshed, and fashioning now a sod-cutting rig of their sturdy camp shovel set behind Phineas with a pair of pack rope tugs and a spare axe helve singletree, he had peeled away the clean furrows of meadow turf like bow waves from a keelboat cordelling up an eight-mile current. Lastly, of course, Big Anse was a lifelong artist with the double-bitted steel, having worked in timber from the time he could toddle and tote a splitting wedge.

But the best thing about this new-found esprit was that Kelly did not enjoy it alone.

The joint effort had drawn the little company together and now, as they leaned pantingly on their axes or shovels staring at their handiwork in the frosty light of the Montana morning stars, the community feeling was far different than it had been only short hours before, when Jepson had refused to trust Kelly to so much as toss a coin without trickery.

"She's about four a.m., boys," said the scout, breaking the proud silence as he eyed the changing sky professionally. "There's a full two hours for you to catch up on your sleep before we get the kind of shooting daylight the Sioux like. I'd suggest you all bed down inside, right off."

"Yeah? How about you?" demanded Jepson quickly.

Kelly smiled. Though he could not see the gloomy New Englander's face, the change in the latter's attitude was unmistakable. This question was mothered by honest concern, not fathered by specious doubts.

"Mr. Jepson," he reached through the darkness, putting his hand on the older man's bowed shoulder, "you don't need to worry about me. I'm used to going three days without sleep if need be; presently I've been but two."

"Nobody's worried about you!" denied Jepson, as quickly. "I jest don't want you sneakin' off on us agin!"

"Aye," MacDonal backed him. "We're payin' ye a handsome ten percent fer yer services, mon, remember that. We've a right to know what ye do with yer time."

Again Kelly could not see the speaker except as a blurred silhouette in the morning blackness. But he could sense the gruff out-countryman's change of heart as certainly in the tart little Scot as in the grumbling Jepson.

"That you have, gentlemen," said the scout, seating himself on a convenient stack of cut timbers with an obvious sigh of resignation to his humble status as an employee of the company. "And you shall have an accounting in detail the moment I return."

"The moment you 'return?'" exclaimed Jepson.

"By Gawd, now wait jest a minute here!" It was Big Anse, beside himself with childlike excitement. "If you're agoin' summers, I'm agoin' with you! I got a hankerin' to learn me some of yer Injun tricks."

Kelly shook his head.

"No, nobody's going with me. You all get some sleep. You won't need a guard, the Sioux don't move around at night, but come daylight and I'm not back, post a sharp lookout."

"Now see here—" MacDonal began, then broke off, sensing something wrong. "Kelly, lad? You hear me?"

There was no answer.

The four men rushed as one to the pile of cut and stacked lodgepole pines upon which Kelly had been perched the moment before. Big Anse blundered over and around and behind the tumbling heap of dislodged poles like a green bird dog breaking on the point to put a big covey to flush from dense cover. His yelp of disappointment was equally canine and keen.

"Cripes Amighty, he's gone! Mr. Kelly! Mr. Kelly! Where the hell are you—?"

Once more the only answer was the stir of the freshening dawn wind through the crested heads of the summer's rustling crop of stem-cured meadow hay.

Luther Kelly had disappeared into the same element from which he had originally arisen to join the Fort Buford wolf hunters twenty-four hours before—the solid mountain ground.

15

Kelly had both a purpose and a plan. Sayapi's camp should not be hard to find. He would have trailed his uncle a short ways to ascertain his intention and direction—to make sure Gall was truly bound for home—then would have doubled back to wait for daylight. He would almost surely have lain up not far east of the white cabin site. The prevailing wind in this part of the high country, east to west, would only make the searching out of his bedding grounds so much the easier, providing Kelly was right.

He was, and it did.

He had not drifted three miles through the night when he caught the acrid faintness of banked woodsmoke. Another two miles of quartering this vagrant scent to its pungent source brought him to the edge of the Sioux camp.

It was set in the open on a small stream bank, after the nomad Indian custom. The ponies were on picket—an uncommon situation which gave the white watcher an unwarranted sense of security—about a hundred yards downstream in a swale of rich September hay. There was no horse herd guard that Kelly could see, and he did not look too hard. With the ponies on picket, a man did not have to worry about a guard being out. The braves were all spread out around the fire, moccasin bottoms inward, rolled tightly in their stolen US army or honestly traded-for Hudson's Bay blankets. Kelly had come out on an elevation twenty feet or more above the campsite. There was thick timber immediately behind him and an open boulder-dotted slope directly below him. It was perhaps eighty yards to the little stream and the Sioux fire.

He gauged the wind both with wetted finger and by studying the drift of the wisping woodsmoke from the banked embers. It lay almost due into him, quartering a bit to the south, toward the horse herd. That was not good. A stray shift of air current, possible at any minute in a high mountain draw, could carry his alien scent to the shaggy ponies. Still, it was a standard risk. The enemy getting winded by the home-camp horse herd had saved more Indian bands from extermination than any amount of warrior-manned outposts or picket lines had ever accomplished. There was no watchdog, human or canine, to compare with the raw-nerved, hypersensitive little mountain mustangs. Knowing this, a man took a tight hold on his luck and prayed that the breeze would lie steady for the ten minutes he would need. And while he was still praying, he slid on over the edge of his elevation and went gliding soundlessly toward the sleeping camp.

In less than three minutes, Kelly was crouched behind a buffalo-sized boulder not thirty feet from the Indian fire and set in the damp sand at the edge of the noisy little creek.

Reaching inside his elk-skin shirt, he brought out a small buckskin bag of the type in which the horseback brave habitually carries his war paint and personal medicine. It took him perhaps another thirty seconds to load and pack the little bag with the damp creek sand. Thus weighted, it hefted just so when grasped by the draw-stringed neck and swung tentatively into the tensed muscles of his thigh. He was ready.

Now came the part that shrunk a man's stomach. That put a tingle in him from his neck hairs to the beaded tips of his moccasined toes.

Which one of those shapeless sleeping Sioux lumps was the one he wanted?

The devil take it! If a man knew that, it would cut his gamble in half. And where would his fun be?

Kelly grimaced acridly and went on in.

He started the way he had to start, by picking an Indian and working around the circle from him. He had gone over four braves, using up five precious minutes, before he came to the one he sought. Even so, he was lucky to hit red pay dirt that quick. He acknowledged his gratitude with a quick-flung grin to the starry vault above and got on with the real business of the evening.

Sayapi was curled peacefully on his right side, the purloined Winchester wrapped in his loving arms like a favorite squaw on a February night. There was no chance, nor was it any merciful part of Kelly's plan, to pry the young Sioux painlessly loose from his unearned prize.

Luther Kelly appreciated his red brothers more than did the run of his fellow white frontiersmen only because he knew more about them. He looked at the Indian with the common eye of the times. The red man was like any dangerous big game; you had to admit his bravery and sometimes even the beauty of his wild abilities, but you never let that blind you. He was still an Indian and not worth wasting a drink of good whiskey on.

Kelly studied the angle of Red Paint's head dispassionately. It was set just right, turned nicely away from the white scout to expose the bony processes behind the left ear. The sand-packed buckskin pouch went home almost soundlessly. Above the brawl and chuckle of the creek, the small noise it made could not possibly have been heard. It was just the least sort of pleasant little "tunk"; and Sayapi relaxed to it as satisfactorily as though he had been permanently anesthetized by a hickory pick handle or a ten-pound rock.

Kelly deftly lifted the Winchester from his cradled grasp and lay beside him without another move for a full minute.

Nothing stirred.

The thought cynically crossed Kelly's mind that Cooper would never have made things work out so well for the deer-slayer. Truly, if he, Kelly, got away with this bald invasion and lived long enough to later write it up in his memoirs, he would have to remember to add a bit of what Mark Twain called "the stretcher" to it, to liven it up for the readers. It just wouldn't wash, the easy way it was going.

At the moment, no matter, he was still lying in the middle of a circle of twelve healthy young Sioux who had *not* been sandbagged. Any man in such a spot was scarcely in a position to settle back and start dictating the exciting story of his life and times along the Yellowstone.

Kelly came soundlessly to his feet. Lean body bent nearly double, he started away from the slumbering Sioux circle. His trained eye automatically swept around it with a last glance. Something registered belatedly. He stopped, frozen in mid-crouch. He had gone over four Sioux before coming to Sayapi. With the latter, that made five. Now he had just seen that, beyond the unconscious young chief, there were not eight but only seven blanketed forms.

Of such oversights are scalp belts inspired. He had made a very bad medicine miscount. *There had been a horse guard out.*

He wheeled instinctively, coming upright and shifting his grip on the Winchester's barrel as he spun about. "H'g'un!" snarled the Hunkpapa horse guard, and struck for his bowels with his buffalo lance.

Kelly got far and fast enough aside to avoid the blade's finding his vitals, but took its searing rip through the meat and muscle of his left side between hip point and ribcage. The Sioux came with the thrust, lunging off balance, and the white scout shattered his face bones with the steel-shod, in-driven stock of the rifle. The next instant the camp was alive with blundering, stumbling, cursing braves. And Luther S. Kelly was running for his life straightaway up the boulder-strewn slope to the west of Sayapi's swarming campfire.

In the coal-pit darkness of the timberland, Kelly easily lost his pursuers.

There was much running around and shouting and blind firing, after the Indian manner of making a great show. But there was precious little sincerity of chase once the trees began in earnest, and a man could not see a knife-swing past his nose, nor tell a friend's from a white man's shadow in the small time such a one as Lone Wolf Kelly would give him to make up his mind in the matter.

Within seconds Kelly was able to drop his speed to the tireless, high-shouldered lupine gait that was his peculiar style of covering long ground.

Forty-five minutes later and without incident, he reached the cabin-site meadow.

As he moved across the open ground, the backing pine and cedar timber was beginning to sharpen its murky silhouette against the ghostly half-light which grows just ahead of the coming day. He was pleased to note, by the orange-bellied smoke issuing from the stone chimney of the little log fortress, that his friends had followed orders this time and were up and on the alert. A few seconds after that, he was stepping through the door behind them with a softly laughed "Surprise, boys! Guess who?" and moving cheerily in to join them where they sat crouched around the fire waiting for the charred coffeepot to bubble over.

That was as far as the good spirits went that morning.

One glance at the resentfully worried faces turned to him over the hunched shoulders was enough to let Kelly know that once again the wind had shifted against him in his absence.

"Surprise, is it now, lad?" said Alec MacDonal, coating it with an inch-thick frost rime of Scotch sarcasm. "Aye, and likely we've got one fer ye, as well. Only ye'll not be needin' to do any 'guessin' who' about ours. Jest turn yer smilin' Irish eyes to yon far corner, mon"—the diminutive Scot hunched his head and shoulder unhappily in the direction, grimacing wryly—"that's it, right to your own wee cozy bedroll, there."

Kelly came around, peering through the firelight into the darkened corner. He saw the shapely form beneath his bedding move to come up on a coppery elbow and greet him with the white-toothed flashing smile he remembered as though it were not five minutes since he had last been warmed by its shy glow.

There was a painful silence then while Kelly was not able to speak and the Crow girl apparently saw no reason for doing so.

Alec MacDonal felt otherwise.

Behind him, the furiously blushing Kelly heard the Scot's reedy voice begin.

"She speaks a bit of English, ye know, lad. And I've picked up a wee smatherin' of Sioux in my Canadian travels." Kelly winced, waiting for the rest of it, knowing it was coming and knowing, too, there was no honorable way in God's great dark green Montana timberland that he could duck out from under it.

"She tells us," concluded MacDonal witheringly, "that she has *come back to share Lone Wolf's fire and to sleep beneath his blankets forever!*"

16

Kelly did not say a word to the girl. Turning his back on her deliberately, he stood stroking his jaw and staring at the ground, as was his habit when taken with a problem of plainly serious proportions.

He knew the uselessness of challenging the Indian mind, once its purpose has been publicly announced. There was no point whatever, at this late hour, in quizzing the Crow girl as to her motives and meanings. Besides, it made no real difference why, or by what heroic labor of pain, she had made the journey back to the white camp. The only and whole point now was that, regardless of her feelings, she could not be allowed to stay there. Not unless he and his friends meant to make an awfully short winter of their sojourn in Gall's game preserve—say, such as being prepared to leave for Fort Buford within the next five minutes.

Kelly had no intention of leaving.

He had always wanted to winter in the Judith Basin foothills. Moreover, he was beginning to enjoy the company of his newfound friends and was looking forward to a long, snowbound time of cabin-snug good fellowship and intellectual comradery.

In his pack he had his beloved thin rice-paper editions of Scott, Poe, Burns, Tennyson, Shakespeare, and the Bible. Caswell spoke as though he had had some formal education, MacDonal clearly had a superior if untutored mind. Both men could be developed and drawn into worthwhile fireside literary debate. This would be a fine winter, perhaps the very best he had spent since coming on the frontier.

No, confound it! He was not going to let himself be euchred out of this anticipated pleasure by any immoral snip of a grateful Indian girl!

He brought his black eyes up from the floor, and they were snapping. Bobbing his dark head to the worried waiters-by-the-fire, not one of whom had uttered a sound through his frowning silence, he put himself on company record with a great deal of righteous conviction.

"I will take her back to Gall as soon as there's light, boys. The red rascals won't miss her much before then, and I'll be able to meet them about midway on the trail back here. That way it will make it right with them, saving face and all that nonsense, you see, and we will then be able to go on with our hunting plans.

"On the other hand," he warned them, following a little pause, "it would be very bad if they trailed her back here before I got started back with her. They're always ready to believe the worst of a white man, especially where their women are concerned, and there would likely be a lively time convincing them we ever had any intention of returning this rather attractive one at all. Do I make my point?"

They nodded that he did.

"There are no objections then?"

There were none.

"Good! Then I propose to make up a batch of bread and have breakfast. Any takers?"

There was a chorus of good-natured assents as Kelly grinned and went to work. Everyone was vastly relieved, and within a few minutes the coffee was brought to just the right rolling boil and removed to settle out. By the time it had, the scout's irresistible light bread was ready. The heady twin odors of freshly baked frying-pan rolls and richly simmering mocha erased even Jepson's habitual gloom. With pleased grunts and chewings, he cautiously allowed that "fer what started out to be a sinful mean one, this here day looks better by the minute."

When Kelly had finished his own food, he took a cup of coffee and a piece of bread over to the Crow girl.

"Eat this," he told her gruffly in Sioux. "It will return your strength. When it is daylight," he went on quickly, "I am going to take you back to the Hunkpapa. You understand," he qualified defensively, as she remained silent, "that I must do this. You are Indian, you know that they will come for you. We have no choice, nohetto, there is no more to it."

Still the girl said nothing. Neither did she reach to take the coffee or the bread. Kelly's eyes narrowed.

"Did you hear me? Take this food. Drink the *pejuta sapa*, anyway. It is good black medicine. I made it myself. And I have sweetened it heavily for you with the real *can hanpi*, the real white man's sugar."

He held out the cup once more, adding caustically in English and referring to the known Indian weakness for sweets, "That ought to please your red soul. You'd probably stab a man in his sleep for half a pound of real white sugar."

When there was still no answer from the girl, he knelt quickly by her side. She only turned as quickly away from him, putting her face to the log wall and clutching the blanket more tightly about her dusky shoulders.

He put the coffee and the bread aside, took her none too gently by a tensed arm, forced her back around.

"When a white man speaks to you, Crow Girl—" He began in formal frontier rebuke, then broke off helplessly, struck speechless in mid-superiority by the oldest weapon in the female world: Crow Girl was crying.

Kelly did not know why, but the sight of that lovely young face stained wet with the salt tears of shame and worn gray by the pain of her shattered leg, plus the pathetically small look of her huddled, no bigger than a child, under the worn blanket, nearly unnerved him.

His rough hand went impulsively to her cheek, brushing back the disheveled auburn-black hair and patting the small head mechanically, while his thick tongue tried in vain to form words his humbled mind refused to supply.

This young girl had him going. If not already gone. He was completely baffled by her strange effect on him. In his entire experience, Kelly had never before seen a grown or nearly grown Plains Indian crying; in hard fact he had never even seen one of their blank-faced, shoe-button-eyed children weep. Now this young Kangi Wicasi woman had shed open tears twice within the past twenty-four hours. And both times in his behalf!

The white scout winced.

At a time like this, a man had to be honest with himself.

Even a great simpleton like Luther S. Kelly caught on eventually.

Toughen up, Kelly.

And smarten up.

Horseback Indians did not weep from bodily hurt. This girl had cried when he first saw her in the Hunkpapa camp shelter, because her heart had been touched by his gentle words to her. She was crying now by the reverse, cruel token of his necessarily heartless decision to take her back to Gall, and by the harsh, unkind way he had told her of that decision.

But admitting the impact she had had upon you, and then

being guided by the admission, were two vastly varying situations. It would very probably cost him his life, as well as the lives of his four friends, to give this Sioux captive the sanctuary she sought. He knew the Hunkpapa mind in such matters. There could be no possible compromise with Gall. The moment the war chief discovered Crow Girl had gone, he would come after her. When he did that, there remained no doubt he would find her.

Over their coffee and bread, his comrades had told him the girl had shown up outside the cabin on one of the Sioux ponies. This borrowed beast she had painfully dismounted from, whacked across the rump with her heavy willow crutch-stick and sent galloping back up the trail to the Sioux campsite from which she had fled upon him. For Gall to track the familiar bare-hoof prints of one of his own mounts in the damp humus of the forest trail would be an elementary exercise. Something the Hunkpapa chief could do at a long-going lope. And unless Kelly intercepted the Sioux party somewhere along that telltale track with an obvious bid to return the escaped girl—

He dispelled the unpleasant end–certainty of the thought with a decisive headshake, spoke gently to the girl, still using Sioux.

"Do not weep anymore, now," he smiled. "Eat the food, and sleep a little. I will do the same. We will talk more when the sun has warmed the mountainside," he lied deliberately, turning away.

Back at the fireplace, he dropped his voice carefully.

"Watch her," he instructed Big Anse. "I've got time for an hour's nap before I start back with her. Luckily, there's no rush. Gall won't travel until daybreak. Still, there's no way of knowing how far or fast he will come. Better wake me up when the first sun hits the tips of that high ridge." He motioned toward a broken line of peaks to the west, concluding, "Do I make myself clear?"

"As gravel-bottom branch water," Big Anse grinned. "Any

chance of taggin' along with you, Mr. Kelly?" he went on. "Jest in case them red guts turns off balky on you."

Kelly looked the huge hillman over, decided there was a very good chance. He could use the outsized southerner's tough company and he would need an extra hand with Phineas and the crippled girl.

"All right," he agreed quickly. "Now don't let me sleep over an hour, you understand?"

Anse and the others nodded that they did. Satisfied, Kelly turned in. He was in deep sleep within sixty seconds. Beyond him, in her darkened corner, the Indian girl relaxed in relieved turn. Presently, her peaceful breathing was added to the exhausted scout's. The fire cricked and popped with drowsy, permeating warmth. Lulled by its resinous reassurance and drugged by the flavor and fragrance of their first deep-puffed pipes of the day, the Fort Buford wolf hunters let down. Good coffee, hot bread, strong tobacco, and pure inner contentment had their seductive ways. When Kelly's hour had passed and Big Anse moved obediently to awaken him, MacDonal put out a restraining hand.

"There now, lad. No need to be hasty. Let the poor devil rest. He's not had a decent sleep in three nights."

"But he said to be sure and git him up," insisted Anse. "I dunno, now."

"Aye, and he also said there was no great rush," grunted MacDonal. "Now ye do as I say, lad. Let him snooze another wee bit while. The same fer the little Injun lassie yonder. The poor thing's all run out, like a frightened fawn."

"Sure," said the taciturn Jepson. "There cain't no harm come of it. Let 'em sleep."

"Well," muttered Big Anse, unconvinced. "I dunno. But most likely you're right. It ain't even full light so far and the sun's not yet quite tippin' them yonder hawgbacks of his'n. I allow it won't hurt to give 'em another few minutes."

Perhaps there was a potential of truth in the easygoing Georgian's allowance.

The ill-fated wolf hunters never found out.

It was not a few minutes but a full hour later when Luther Kelly awoke of his own accord and sat up, wide-eyed.

He narrowed his dark glance to the bright glare of the glass-clear Montana morning shimmering beyond the unhung frame of the cabin's doorway. From there his startled squint jumped to the distant crags of the western ridge. The clean pink wash of the climbing sun lay far down its timbered flanks. His misguided friends had let him sleep past his allotted hour. There was no question of that. The only question was whether or not they had let him sleep too far past it.

"You poor fools!" was all he flung at them, before leaping for the doorframe and a full view of the cabin-site meadow beyond it.

"Good morning," said Gall, easing his blue roan to a halt not twenty feet from the cabin door and expressionlessly signaling his followers to spread out behind him in a trapping semicircle. "We are grateful that you gave the girl shelter. Now bring her out."

17

Kelly eyed the Hunkpapa chief with what he trusted was a passingly fair impression of white scout supremacy.

"I was just leaving to bring her back to you," he bluffed boldly. "My companions let me oversleep, or I would have met you on the trial."

"You lie," said Frog Belly, the fat subchief who was Gall's right hand in battle.

"Your tongue is crooked as a sick snake's track," barked Tokeya Sapa, the Black Fox, who was as lean as was Knaska, the Fat Frog, rotund. And who was, moreover, Gall's left hand in war, as Frog Belly was his right. "I can see beyond your shoulder into the little log house. The girl is still sleeping there in the far corner."

Gall kneed his roan pony toward Black Fox, peering in through the cabin door along the line of his lieutenant's scowl. Kelly saw his eyes contract.

"I did not think you would lie to me, Lone Wolf," he said slowly. "I thought you and I had looked at one another and spoken like brothers."

Shaking his head, he turned his gaze on Kelly, and the scout was amazed to see that he was not angry but strangely hurt. Once more his previous Indian opinions were given a sharp shake, his professional sangfroid faltering under the Sioux leader's steady glance.

"I have not lied to Gall," he defended uncertainly. "I have told you what I meant to do. But I was very tired. I had not slept for three suns."

"Bring the girl out," repeated Gall flatly, and Kelly saw that the palaver had gone against him and was over.

He did not say anything at once, because he did not know what it was he wanted to say. Nor did he move, by virtue of the same indecision. But in the pause, another spoke and acted for him.

"It will not be necessary to bring her out," said a strained voice at his elbow. "I am ready. I bring myself out."

Kelly came around to see Crow Girl, leaning gray-faced on her willow crutch, just behind him. Her slight body was twisted grotesquely in the painful effort to balance its full weight on the left leg alone. Her clear gray eyes, dark now with suffering and shame, looked past him as though he were no more than a piece of the lintel or the jamb or the threshold of the door opening.

"Because Lone Wolf lied to us," announced Gall, dismissing the girl after a close hard glance to make sure she was all right, and turning back to Kelly still somewhat sadly, "we will take his mule for the Kangi Wicasi woman." He returned his hurt frown to Crow Girl. "If this one can ride a Sioux war pony through the blind night with that bad knee, she can sit astride a Wasicun pack mule in the bright sunlight."

Behind him in the cabin, Kelly heard Big Anse growl, "You and what Union army, you slit-mouth red son! You lay a hand on Phineas, I'll dot your damn eyes for you square in the middle!" But he had no time to spare Anse so much as a grin. He was too concerned with Gall.

Watching the latter narrowly as he spoke about Crow Girl and the mule, Kelly was again puzzled at the savage chieftain's soft attitude. It left a man with a mighty uneasy feeling. And but one possible conclusion. Gall, second only to Crazy Horse in Sioux Nation military command, had given a personal trust to both the captive girl and himself—a trust which both had unknowingly held and, hence, unknowingly dishonored.

He set his blunt jaw unhappily.

For a man who had been on the frontier as long as he had and who held such a fancy settlement reputation for his surpassing store of wild Indian savvy, Yellowstone Kelly was a pretty sorry specimen. He had to admit now that in the past few hours, he had learned more about the "insides" of those same wild Indians than he had in the past several years. Still, he must not let this ounce of new insight overbalance the far greater weight of his older knowledge. Indians were still Indians. In the present very touchy situation, the least aggressive word or overt motion might mean five white scalps drying in the Judith Mountain breeze on their belt-dangling ways to the Hunkpapa winter camp on the Musselshell.

He opened his mouth to cede the mule to Gall, along with the pretty little Kangi Wicasi captive, hoping to advance the talk from this firm base to a reconfirmation of the war chief's permission to winter-hunt the Sioux-held foothills.

The arrangement was never reached. Nor even broached.

Crow Girl moved proudly past him, chin held high. He stood aside, surprised, and as he did, haughtily tilted chin or not, he caught the sun sparkle of the farewell tear glinting down the pale, dirt-streaked cheek.

That did it for Luther Sage Kelly.

His long arm, thick and hard as a sun-dried cedar post, shot out. His hand, big enough to wrap and lap itself half again around her small arm, closed like a No. 6 bait-pan trap above her elbow. "Stand right where you are," he told her quietly, "I have changed my mind."

The sick girl looked at him, and it was reward enough to last a man his whole life. Which was well. His whole life might be over within the next ten seconds.

He heard the rash of cocking rifle hammers ripple through the Sioux ranks, and the low mutter of animal growlings which muffled the hammer clicks. But Kelly was suddenly Kelly again. His overweening hunger for excitement was singing in him like the feathered whisper of a war arrow or the mean whine of a ricocheting rifle slug.

The dark flash of his grin struck the tension from his face. His black eyes danced. He took his hand away from the girl, turned his flicking smile expectantly on Gall—and waited.

Behind him he could hear the groans of despair from Caswell, MacDonal, and Jepson. But he could also hear Big Anse Harper's happy curse, "Keep the red sons uh bitches busy, Mr. Kelly, I'll need a minute to git the boys to the front-wall rifle slits!" and his heatless smile only grew the wider.

Gall looked at Frog Belly, then at Black Fox.

"I don't like it," said Frog Belly.

"It's a trick," muttered Black Fox.

Gall receipted their opinions with a nod, turned to the crouching Kelly. "I want the girl now. Give her to me."

"That is just the trouble, brother."

"What is the trouble?" frowned Gall.

The white scout bobbed his head with unthinking speed, the reflex answer surprising him as much as it did the Hunkpapa chief. "I want her too—!"

Gall returned his excited stare with one of enforced calculation. Black Fox was right. There was a trick hidden somewhere.

"And what makes Lone Wolf think he can take her?" he

probed slowly.

"This!" said Kelly, and snaked his Winchester from its leaning place just inside the doorframe.

Gall's glittering eyes widened at the sight of the recovered rifle. Now there was even a little excitement in his heavy voice. "Did you kill Sayapi?"

"Only a little. I hit him behind the ear while he slept. I left him *telanunwela,* dead yet alive," shrugged the white scout, using the Sioux phrase for unconsciousness.

"Why did you not kill him?" Gall could not comprehend such charity. "He would have killed you. In fact," he added thoughtfully, "he *will* kill you."

"Would you kill a sleeping enemy?" Kelly asked, stalling to give Anse and the others time to get set.

"I have done it."

"Would you kill me thus?"

"Of course."

"Well, you see, my brother, that is the difference between a Wasicun and a *Shacun.*"

"It's a bad difference, Lone Wolf. It will get you killed one day."

"I don't sleep very often," grinned Kelly.

"I have heard that," nodded the other. "And very lightly too, I understand."

"Yes, very lightly, too."

Gall shifted his pony two steps away from Black Fox's mount. Kelly did not take his eyes from him, but he could sense and hear the other Sioux behind their chief moving their horses to insure shooting room.

"Well, Lone Wolf," said Gall, "here is an end to talk. Let us now see what we are going to do."

"Yes," replied Luther Kelly, low-voiced, "let us see." And as he said it, he hipped the Winchester, letting its octagonal muzzle study the region of Gall's quill-worked war shirt just beyond the cartilage of the prosternum and slightly below the left breast.

It was a long, nerve-tight standoff. But Gall was a real war chief. He saw the rifle slits in the cabin's front wall, and he saw protruding from them the four barrels of the Wasicun wolf hunters' guns. He added to that unwavering number the beautiful new sixteen-shooter of Lone Wolf, which was wandering his shirtfront in little lazy circles around his heart. When he had done that, he had his total. And his answer.

Five white rifles cocked and aimed meant five Sioux saddles emptied as the minimum price of an immediate conclusion. The final figure could easily be far more. Gall had not risen to his high place in the war councils of the wild Sioux because he was a hothead or a fool. True, his flaring temper had made him a famous and feared hand-to-hand fighter. But it was his ability to control that murderous trait under pressure which had made him the tactical terror he was to his white enemies.

He demonstrated that dangerous control now.

A later time would do much better than the present, he cautioned himself, for taking the measure of Lone Wolf Kelly. Besides, revenge, like a piece of prime buffalo meat, only grew the sweeter with proper aging.

But Gall was also intensely honest. His way was never the devious, nor the split-tongued way of Sitting Bull among the wild, nor Red Cloud among the tame Sioux. He always said what he had to say.

"I owe you a life," he pointed out to Kelly, "so I will not fight you now." The scout knew he referred to his sparing of young Red Paint, but said nothing, and the war chief went on.

"But you must know that you are no longer welcome here. That I will fight you the next time we meet. That I will try to kill you if I can. Nohetto. I go now to make my peace with Sayapi.

Look well to your watch fires, Wasicun."

"What about the girl?" asked Kelly curiously, as the Hunkpapa turned his pony away.

Gall stopped.

"What *about* the girl?" he emphasized, stony-eyed.

"Do you still want her?"

Gall looked at the tiny Crow girl, not at Kelly. He looked at her a long time and until she dropped her eyes. "I will always want her," he rumbled, fierce gaze softening. "As long as I shall live and look up to the sun, that long will she stay in my heart." His eyes swept the little cedar-rimmed mountain clearing as though they would fix it forever in the future accounts book of his memory. "I will never forget this place," he finished softly. "Nor will you," he charged his impassive followers. "From this time forward, it will be called 'Crow Girl Meadow' among our people."

He spun the roan viciously around, dark arm flashing skyward. "Hopo! *Hookahey!*"

"Hopo," echoed Frog Belly without enthusiasm.

"*Hookahey,*" grumbled Black Fox in agreeing disenchantment.

The twenty-six outmaneuvered Sioux swung their shaggy little ponies and were gone across the meadow and into the trees. The time of their passing counted fewer seconds than the number of gaudily dyed horsehair tassels bobbing from their buffalo lances. And, when they had disappeared, the only sound to break the returned lovely quiet of the mountain morning was the compressed company of long-held breaths exhaling from their white watchers.

18

Once again there was a vote of war in the little white camp. There was no doubt now but what the question of stay or go had assumed the proportions of life or death. Gall had so announced himself. Furthermore, he had stated his intention of forgiving Sayapi. This could only mean the Sioux band would be back at full strength, the odds against the wolf hunters again raised to their former eight-to-one. It had been gamble enough when they had only to guess at the solvency of Gall's guarantee not to harm them. Now that he had promised to kill them, the company barometer dropped like hot lead from a shot tower.

Even Big Anse was depressed. And Phineas, disenfranchised. The vote went four-to-one in favor of getting out at once, Kelly being the lone dissenter.

The mercuric-tempered scout, not smiling now and sober as a Sioux, was no longer humoring any Quixotic ideas of danger and adventure. The happy Irish inspiration which had made him grab Crow Girl's arm at the last minute had had time to take a bad chill. Hence there were no frontier heroics, real or imagined, involved in his decision. He saw it as a simple case of humane consideration; the selfsame impersonal pity the soldier shows when, on the field of battle, he raises the head of his enemy whom he has just mortally wounded and gives him to drink from his canteen: to move the Indian girl now would be to kill her.

Gall's departure had given him his first chance to reexamine her closely. When he had replaced the blankets about her shaking form, he knew what he had to do.

Her fever was raging again, the rotten stench of the gangrene returning. It gave a man no choice. He had to open up that leg again. At the same time, he could not ask his comrades to wait, nor could he join them with the girl. To subject her to the rigors of the forced night march now necessary to get the others safely out of the foothills and back to Reed's Ranch in the outer basin would be to finish her as surely as putting a gun to her temple and pulling the trigger.

She was going to die anyway. The least a man could do was to help her do it with dignity and with all possible peace of mind. That much was no more than God expected of any of his little sparrows. How was it the line in the Scriptures went? *Inasmuch as ye have done it unto the least of these, ye have done it unto me?* Something not far from that. In any event a man of Kelly's simple faith had no option, nor did he ask one.

The anxious wolf hunters, glum Jepson and cowardly Caswell included, urged him with a heat which warmed him wonderfully to take the Indian girl and get out with them. They could and would gladly rig a litter like the one the Sioux had made for her, slinging it from the aprons of Phineas' aparejo and trotting by turns at the rear poles. But the scout would not see it. Big Anse then pleaded clumsily to be allowed to stay on with him and the "little redskin lady." Kelly remained quietly adamant. His reasoning was equally immovable.

It was his fault, he repeated calmly, that the Hunkpapa had

come down on their camp in the first place. It was his fault that the girl had led the Sioux raiders back onto them in the second place. It would be his fault if they did not reach Reed's alive in the third place. And their best chance of reaching Reed's, he stressed, lay in Big Anse Harper.

Anse was the only one among them who could track, trail, read sign, or smell an ambush well enough to guide them out. He was, in effect, the only one of them who had what Kelly called "a natural built-in feel for Indians," and despite his lack of experience, these superior native instincts made it imperative for him to accompany his friends. If Big Anse would listen to him and the rest of them would listen to Big Anse, Kelly could guarantee them they would all be shaking hands with Old Man Reed before daybreak.

At first the hulking Georgian was obdurate, but a compromise was reached by late afternoon. He would take the others into Reed's, then return with Phineas and an emergency load of ammunition, salt, sugar, and tobacco. All of the present supplies, including the deadly little black bottles with their neat St. Louis pharmaceutical labels, *Alkaloid of Strychnia*, were to be left with Kelly.

They were not to imagine, the scout chided them good-naturedly, that his actions were heroic or his position hopeless. He was doing what he was doing because he wanted to do it and because he saw a very good chance of getting away with it.

Gall was certain to go to the main winter camp on the Musselshell for reinforcements before attempting his promised assault. Indians simply fancied far better odds than eight-to-one when trying to take an alerted, forted-up bunch of white hunters. That meant at least a week of pony travel time, going and coming back. By then Big Anse would have returned with the mule and the girl's leg most likely improved enough for them to put her aboard Phineas and pack her out to Reed's well ahead of Gall's curtain-call return to the cabin-site meadow.

This specious argument was uneasily accepted, as twilight closed in over the Judith Basin foothills.

Now, as the little group waited anxiously inside the cabin for full darkness to follow the short autumn dusk, the scout had a final warning for them.

Within the past hour, a new need for urgency and dispatch of movement had appeared; this, in addition to the Sioux's Musselshell timetable.

There was a change in weather coming.

Kelly could smell snow.

"Now wait!" he ordered Big Anse, who immediately wanted to stay again. "Let me qualify that before you start bellowing like a fly-bitten bull in a dry wallow!" The big man quieted down with a trusting grin, and Kelly got on with it. It was a deliberate lie but as white as the snow it was twisted about.

They were to remember, he reminded them, that they were at nearly eight-thousand feet and far north. An early fall storm could mean trouble. He could remember winters when the high country had been closed in as early as late August. But the way the wind smelled to him right now, the storm was perhaps three days off. Beyond that, he compounded the falsehood (the wind smelled of big snow not hours away), it would most probably be a normal light autumn fall. Something like three or four inches. Six at the most. Anyway, Anse would have ample time to get back from Reed's and the others to get started from there on out to Fort Buford before any really rough weather came on.

Big Anse, new to Montana and the merciless abruptness of the meanest winter weather in North America, accepted the fabrication and the discussion ended in an awkward silence.

The five men shook hands, all around, with considerable feeling.

Their terse, spoken goodbyes were by no means the full measure of the Fort Buford wolf hunters' feelings for the fey-humored Irish scout. Kelly was a man who talked very well to other men but to whom other men invariably experienced difficulty in talking. The most obvious explanation for the apparent perversity was his truly deep shyness, a peculiar reticence to trust his feelings to his fellows which was almost Indian in its intensity. It was his nature to befriend others while not allowing them to befriend him. It was possibly this very Siouan fear of being rejected which made him understandable and acceptable to the implacably wild Hunkpapa and Oglala. But in the present case, it only sped and made awkward the last words between him and his white companions.

The darkness was down now all around them.

They filed swiftly out of the little cabin, Anse bringing the mule from the unfinished fur shed lean-to where he had been stabled since Gall's departure.

"Good luck," said Kelly softly as they moved away into the gloom. "You'll make it all right."

"Sure we will!" Big Anse's reply echoed confidently. "We got the world by the tail on a downhill pull, goin' back. From here to Reed's, the trail drops forty feet a minute!"

They all heard Kelly's quick answering laugh, then the last words any white man would hear from him that raging winter of 1875-76. "Remember what Sir Walter Scott had to say on the subject of advancing down the mountainside, boys!" he called cheerfully.

"Huh—?" Big Anse questioned wonderingly. "How's thet?"

"*Even the haggis, God bless her, can charge downhill—!*"

The Georgian thought it over a moment, gave Phineas a hard jerk with the halter rope. "What the hell's a haggis?" he asked his three companions. Fortunately, Alec MacDonal was following next behind him. "A haggis," recited the wiry Canadian

BOOK THREE
SOUTH PASS

19

Five hours after the Fort Buford wolf hunters left the little cabin in Crow Girl Meadow, the wind began an uneasy restless moaning through the pine and cedar tops.

It was a northwest wind coming down out of the Aleutians and coursing along the frozen spine of the Canadian Rockies. Yet it was strangely warm and gentle in the beginning. It held that way for exactly one hour, then dropped away to a dead, ticking-watch stillness.

Kelly, only a few minutes returned from the weirdest game hunt of his life, glanced up from his work over the girl's knee.

The silence became a tangible thing. The cold creeping in the uncovered cabin door had texture, body, and literal feel. Like a bad mist along the Big Muddy's bottomlands. Or the raw blind sea fog Kelly could remember shrouding up the Potomac when he had been a green, underage recruit in Company G, Tenth Infantry, stationed in the capital ten long years before in the spring of '65.

He waited, poised on one knee, listening.

That peculiar earlier warmth in the air? The beginning gentleness of that wind? Now this dropped-pin stillness? *Aii-eee*, as the Sioux would say, no *waste*, no *waste:* not a good thing at all.

The girl, eyes closed to endure the pain of his uncasing her splinted leg and his pulling away of the serum-glued cotton bandage from the reopened knee, now looked up at him, eyes wide. She was in time to catch his apprehensive glance out the door, to share his tense attitude of strained listening.

"*Wanitu*," she whispered quickly.

Kelly shook his head. "*Wasiya*," he corrected.

Crow Girl's face grew frightened. Wanitu was only the normal wintertime, Wasiya was the Blizzard King, the particular god of the wild Montana snowstorms which were things fearfully apart from the peaceful happiness of Wanitu's otherwise snug and sleepy shelter.

"He comes so soon?" she asked plaintively. "The Winter Giant comes now?" She tried a wan smile, wandered off aimlessly. "So soon, so soon—"

"The sooner the better," Kelly assured her grimly, setting his teeth at the sight of the knee as the last of the matter-caked bandage came away. "You had better make a big prayer to whatever the Crow People call Wakan Tanka that the old devil comes tonight. And that he decides to stay a long time when he gets here."

"Why is that, Lone Wolf?"

She was still managing the smile, and Kelly grimaced. The pain in that hideous green and purple lump which had once been a knee had to be enormous. Yet as long as Indian flesh and nerves could endure, she would not "make his heart sad" by showing it.

"If the Winter Giant strikes tonight and strikes heavily," he told her, "we are spared, you and I. We are given a little longer to live."

"But," she protested, "if he fills the south pass with snow, your friend who is as big as a bull buffalo will not be able to return with the mule, as I heard you planning it. We will not be able to escape then."

Kelly forced a grin, reaching for her forehead to check the fever. "If the snow fills the south pass, will it not also fill the north?" he asked her quietly.

Crow Girl brightened. "*Hau, tahunsa!*" She actually laughed it, her gray eyes lighting up for the fleeting moment of her little pleasure. "I see! I see!"

What she had seen, before the pain darkness dulled her eyes again, was that if the snow was too deep for Big Anse and Phineas, it would be too deep, as well, for Gall and his blue roan gelding. What she meant by "*hau, tahunsa*" was "Yes, cousin," and the unthinking use of the generic term for anyone the Sioux have accepted into the tribal group pleased Kelly greatly.

But what he was looking at pleased him not at all.

The knee was very bad again. Worse than he had expected. Still there was nothing to do but go ahead with the girl's own heathen suggestion. His Pony Soldier medicine had fallen flatter than the wind-muffled report of a mile-distant rifle shot. Perhaps her pagan Kangi Wicasi witchcraft would do better.

But that was impossible. More than that, it was preposterous. The treatment Crow Girl had remembered from her wild childhood, and for the main ingredient of which he had just spent the past five hours hunting, was the product of a disordered red imagination.

The hot paunch of a young bull elk killed at midnight in the first quarter of the new moon?

God forgive a man for lending his heart to such heresy and for surrendering his good Christian mind to such heathen mumbo jumbo. Still, he could not forget what testy old surgeon John K. Blake had repeatedly roared at his orderlies when one of the post hospital's ignorant country-boy patients would request some unorthodox medical therapy for the relief of urgent pain. "I don't give a continental damn what it is!" the irate doctor would explode. "If it helps the poor son of a bitch to rub the back of his ear with a corncob, order him a load of cobs!"

Kelly grinned twistingly at the army memory, took his hand from Crow Girl's brow, shed his wry smile. The poor little thing was burning up. God help her. If her Kangi Wicasi medicine did not work, she would be dead before another sundown.

"If I do anything wrong, you will tell me." He forced the reassuring calmness, arose quickly, went to the doorframe where he had hung the young wapiti bull, his mind turning desperately.

Maybe—just maybe—the whole crazy luck of the last twenty-four hours would hold. It had been fantastic. Getting his gun back from Sayapi after bungling on the horse guard. Bluffing Gall right down to his breechcloth with nothing but a fancy Winchester. Getting his four friends safely away before the snow set in. Gambling that Gall would find Sayapi and that both would go to the Musselshell before returning to the cabin clearing, and apparently winning the gamble hands down. Lastly, getting this weanling bull out of a stray herd which had accidentally yarded up not a mile from the meadow at the first smell of snow. And getting him at night, quartering away, with one shot which had gone clear through him, flag to fore-chest, without so much as nicking the precious stomach! He-hau! Incredible would be a better word than fantastic.

Or maybe even preposterous!

His Shoshone knife slipped into the yielding belly just under the prosternum, slid downward with no sound to the genitals. The smoking viscera spilled outward, and he caught and severed the stomach from its esophageal and intestinal ties. As skillfully, he trimmed it of its clinging pieces of interorgan fat and heavier adherences of muscle, slit it down its ventral surface, and emptied its vegetable content on the floor.

Moving quickly with it toward Crow Girl, he asked, "Have I done with it as you said?" She smiled that he had, and he went on. "And it is now to be placed around the knee so that the inside of the uncleaned paunch comes to bear directly upon the wound itself?" Again she smiled, adding, "Aye, and fastened firmly there so that the natural juices may feel their way into the wound, drawing out the poisons that Sayapi's bullet left within."

Kelly knelt beside her, capping the purulent knee with the still-steaming paunch of the young elk, binding its greasy casing securely in place with salvagings from the old cotton strips.

"No," remonstrated Crow Girl, as he finished tying off his dressing wraps and reached for the splints, "do not replace the willow sticks. I will not move the leg, awake or asleep. In three days the bad smell and the yellow sickness will be gone. It is but one of the secrets of my people. You will see."

Kelly returned her sober look, nodding thoughtfully.

"Perhaps I shall. I have already seen quite a few of the 'secrets' of your people in but two days. What might I not see in three?"

The blizzard came first.

It blew crazily from every quarter of the mountain compass for forty-eight unbroken hours, then crashed to a wind-still halt as suddenly as it had begun.

The sun shone brilliantly that third morning. From earliest light, it poured down on a new mountain world of snow white, timber green, and startling, winter-sky blue. By ten o'clock it was warm enough to unpin and throw aside the thawing green elk hide Kelly had improvised into an emergency storm door. The fragrant pine– and cedar-distilled wine of the mountainside air flowed into the windowless cabin, washing out the staleness of two days and three nights of cooking and living odors and carrying away the decomposing offense of the elk paunch still bound to Crow Girl's knee As it did, Kelly came once more to stand over her and to look down at what he did not want to see.

But the clean morning light fell revealingly about his small patient, narrowing Kelly's dark eyes sharply.

She was still asleep, but her breathing was deep and easy now, no longer shallow and labored as it had been. Her face was neither flushed brick red nor paled fish-belly gray, the way it had been alternating since her return. Dropping beside her, he touched her forehead. Cool. Almost cold. As heatless, indeed, as April runoff water. He took her wrist. The pulse was slow, steady, strong.

My God! Could that miserable elk gut possibly have passed her through the crisis? Broken the fever? Beaten the gangrene? Actually drawn the pus and poison from that terrible wound? Literally have saved her slender leg and savage life?

No, impossible.

This was coma; that last merciful unconsciousness from which the traveler to that distant bourn of no return never recovers. His nose told him that, even as his heart leapt with unaccountable hope over the prior prospect. The stench from that cursed knee was worse than ever. Here, so close to her, its moribund nausea was unmistakable. The fever was gone too late, the pulse not slowed in time. Those strangely beautiful and disturbing gray eyes would never open again. Crow Girl was dying.

Then, even as the dread diagnosis formed in Kelly's tired mind, the blankets beneath his big hand stirred suddenly.

Crow Girl moved her dusky black-lashed lids, sighed happily, opened those same strangely beautiful and disturbing gray eyes that were never going to open again, and sat up, yawning luxuriously.

20

It was Kelly's nose, really, which had betrayed him.

What he had smelled was the elk paunch, turned very high from its sixty hours in the heated air of the snow-sealed cabin. But Luther S. Kelly was a hardhead.

When Crow Girl had fully enjoyed her awakening yawn and told him as much, he would not believe her. It was not until he had removed the paunch at her order and subsequently thrown it as far out across the meadow as he could, then sponged off its adhering residue from about the wound site, that he was made an open-mouthed convert.

Call it heathen witchcraft or no, that wound was as clean as the cross grain of a fresh-cut buffalo steak. The angry purulence was drawn entirely from it, it was already beginning to close and heal, the slim leg above and below it had returned to its normal size and perfect shape.

From that hour, Crow Girl's recovery was as swift as that of any vital young animal. Her inherent Indian urge to live healed her with a speed which bewildered Kelly and which had her limping about the cabin without her crutch-stick in the first week. By the second week, when he gingerly removed the boiled cotton bandage which was all she had permitted him to use, the wound was closed. By the third week, the girl was actually hinging the knee and, save for a slight limp which she would in all likelihood carry for life, might never have been struck by Sayapi's cruel bullet.

Now began the happiest time of Luther Kelly's life: the hidden winter months which frontier legend insistently whispers he spent with the young Absaroka woman, H'tayetu Hopa, Beautiful Evening, in the tiny cabin at Crow Girl Meadow high on the sheltered south flank of Judith Mountain.

The first of the countless many wonderful days was the one beginning the third week of his small patient's remarkable convalescence.

By this time it was abundantly clear to Kelly that his guess as to both Gall and Sayapi having returned to the Musselshell for reinforcements had been correct. Not a Sioux moccasin print nor a Throat Slitter pony track had appeared to mar the virgin snows of the cedar ridges above Judith Basin. Furthermore, the first blizzard had been succeeded by two others, lesser in force but heavy with new snow and guaranteeing the closure of the only two trails into the Cedar Ridge foothills buttressing the white scout's skillfully chosen campsite. Barring a January or February warm-wind chinook, always an uneasy possibility in high Montana, he and his gray-eyed Indian miss were snowed in until the late spring breakup took the ice out of the lower rivers, to begin draining the mountain snowpack above.

The prospect of the chinook did not worry him unduly.

These "silver thaws," thought to be occasioned by freakish west winds blowing across the Washington Cascades from the heated offshore Pacific Ocean current coming down past the Alaskan Peninsula, were far from every-winter occurrences. And, even if one *should* hit them, he and the girl could run ahead of it faster than Gall and Sayapi could come in behind it. Ponies or no ponies, their snug meadow was only a long one-night foot trek to Reed's Ranch, where it was a three-day forcing horseback lope from the Hunkpapa main camp on the Musselshell.

So it was that Kelly's iron conscience was at rest, his immature adventurer's heart soaring high that remembered Monday morning of the third week.

And why not?

Ahead of him he could see nothing but the engrossing snowbound prospect of refuting Dr. Johnson's dismal observation that "life offers more to be endured than to be enjoyed." And he had meanwhile undertaken preparations to meet the pleasant emergency.

He had made himself a trim set of Sioux snowshoes against the time when the last of the young bull elk would have been eaten, necessitating a fresh kill. He had also made, against the first moment she would be well enough to ride upon it, an exquisite little cedar and willow-bark toboggan for Crow Girl. The present crystal bright morning was the conjunctive time for both events. The smell of snow and pine and pure mountain ozone was overpowering. Before he had gone a hundred yards, Kelly was whistling and grinning and picking up to a frisky trot, as happy as though he had good sense.

Behind him his tiny passenger, bundled to her dimpled chin in Sayapi's gorgeous red Four Point blanket, laughed joyously and chattered as incessantly as a small child.

Finally, Kelly had to chide her into silence.

They really did need meat, he told her, and if she was going to carry on like a magpie the entire morning long, they would have nothing for their supper save the few marrowbones and scraps of hock gristle left of the elk. She subsided looking a little hurt but clearly understanding the requisite niceties of the stalk. A short time later, he cut fresh mountain sheep sign and, after but a ten-minute follow, dropped a fat yearling ewe out of a band which was just moving down from the higher peaks and had, accordingly, not been shot over since the past fall, if then.

He hung and gutted the young sheep quickly, wanting to get her hocks slit and her carcass slung for handy backpacking before it froze. He had just completed the latter task—forcing the front feet through the twin slits made between bone and tendon of the hocks to lock the front and rear legs together like those of a range calf roped and thrown for burning—when Crow Girl's soft voice startled him from the top of the twelve-foot cutbank overhanging the gully in which he had dropped the ewe.

"I think you had better tie me up like that too, Lone Wolf!" laughed the panting Indian girl. "I don't think I can walk back to the little sled now. I am so weak from following you—"

As she said it, and before he could think to warn her back, she had started down the treacherous bank. On her second step, the weakened knee gave way, and she fell headlong toward the broken-edged boulders littering the gully's bed.

Somehow Kelly got over the sprawling carcass of the sheep and under the cutbank before Crow Girl's plummeting body struck among the waiting boulders. It was thus her slender frame met not the jarring shock of thinly snow-clad granite but the muscular cushion of elk skin–covered arms.

She had not cried out at either the onset or termination of her fall, as would have a white girl. Now she lay quietly, both slim arms encircling her rescuer's neck, her soft form passive in his cradled grasp. Kelly stood there, not able to open either his mouth or his arms. A most peculiar feeling of weakness began to take him behind the knees. At the moment of its inception, Crow Girl chose to peek upward at his stern face from beneath a properly shy downcasting of sooty black eyelashes. She blushed daintily, sighed inaudibly, snuggled her dark head the least bit closer against his broad chest. His arms tightened instinctively, his pulse leapt, his heart hammered against his ribs as though it would beat its way out of their trapping cage by main wild force. Crow Girl laughed aloud, squirmed her young body deliberately against his. She slid her silky cheek along his cording jaw, found and brushed his ear with open lips, bit him suddenly and savagely on the neck.

He straightened up as though someone had slapped him in the haunch with a hot marking iron. He did not put Crow Girl down reprovingly, nor set her upon her feet primly. He dropped her. Right squarely on her shapely rear. And he did it not as a directed act of conscious moral volition but as a matter of involuntary muscle flection.

Kelly was not shocked, he was stampeded.

To begin with he had never in his life held a young girl in his arms. Much less had one teasingly move her body against his. Or bite him libidinously below the ear. Not to mention laughing wickedly about the whole thing while she was maliciously about it.

Furthermore, he had been all his active masculine life too interested in the adventures of the male animal to even think about the machinations of the enemy sex.

Right from the age most boys are starting to notice the nubbining-up of Sister Sue or the bottom-rounding of Cousin Clara Mae, or devoting their extra classroom hours to boring strategic knotholes in the schoolhouse privy's unpainted partition, young Luther Kelly had been a man's boy concerned only with the world of men.

In another day and time, he would have been a Knight Templar or Crusader of the Malta Cross, a captain under Cromwell, a cutlassed leader of a John Paul Jones boarding crew, one of Lafitte's volunteers at New Orleans, a voyageur for Jacob Astor or Pierre

Chouteau, a disciple-at-buckskin-knee of Bit Throat Bridger or Broken Hand Fitzpatrick, or an unpaid Ranger under history-tall Sam Houston in his dream of Texas Empire.

But when his own minute struck, the hour was too late. Even the War Between the States, that wholesale maker of heroes, was nearly over. He had had to lie three years onto his age (using the common dodge of the time to mark a number "eighteen" on the bottoms of his shoes so that he could tell the recruiting corporal that he was "over eighteen") just so he would not miss the opportunity entirely. And then for his trouble had drawn six miserable months of barracks tour north of the Potomac! The only fighting he saw was among his drunken or quarters-fevered messmates of Company G on payday.

When his three-year hitch was at last up, only one frontier to explore, only one final land to conquer, lay open to the dreamer of crusaders, kingmakers, robber barons, buccaneers, fur traders, mountain men, and builders of Lone Star Empires in the clouds—*the West!*

A frontiersman, a real frontiersman, the *puritan* high plainsman, the one cast in the mystery of silent space, endless sky, and shining mountain-mold of a Jedediah Smith or a Father De Smet, was never a squaw man. That was for the Bridgers and the Bents and all the rest of the *commercial* buckskin brigade. The true believer was a loner like Luther Kelly. He might be a doer of incredible deeds but he was above all a dreamer of impossible dreams: a spellbound sitter on the sides of magnificent mountains; an awed looker-out over limitless rolling buffalo pastures, never-ending sunlit stands of pine and cedar, rushing falls and long-still pools of boulder-broken glass-green water; and a drinker-in of all the wild restless wine, borne hauntingly upon the western wind, of what might lie beyond the last far shining range, cloud-capped and softly calling across the lonely miles.

Kelly, in his years along the Yellowstone, had become such a mountain sitter and such a seer of far ranges.

Accordingly, he had become the legend that he already was in 1875. With his matchless knowledge of a land long closed to all white men but himself, he had become a sort of "all things to all men" who might stand in need of his wilderness advice or services. By the same lonely token, his life had been without feminine contact. To women, even to the dusky Mandan, Sioux, Cheyenne, and Gros Ventres maidens who had tested his moral immunity in the course of unavoidable trading post or Indian village social contacts, he had been as nothing, as they and all other women had been as nothing to him.

It had been a comfortable and vastly safe arrangement of woman-shy male security.

Now, suddenly, it was in the gravest danger.

Kelly, for all his innocence, sensed that instinctively as his hand now went unthinkingly to the whitening marks of Crow Girl's clean teeth upon his bronzed neck.

Scowling defensively, he stepped back from where she still sat gazing up at him in wide-eyed astonishment at having been so rudely deposited upon her pretty backside. On the point of returning his angry look, the Indian girl found herself bubblingly unable to oblige. Instead, she laughed again, the childish, ringing bell clarity of the happy sound only serving to darken Kelly's black Irish scowl. He turned away from her, went quickly to the side of his kill, tested one of the quarters already beginning to "set up" in the sunless chill of the gully bottom, wheeled growlingly on the innocent-eyed Crow Girl.

"Get up!" he snapped at her. "We must go back now. It is too cold here. The ewe's body is beginning to stiffen up. Hopo!"

"Give me your hand," she requested demurely, holding up her own slender red fingers for him to take

He obliged ungallantly, pulling her to her feet, still angry with her and with himself.

"Lone Wolf," she said softly.

He had already turned away to pick up the trussed ewe. "What is it now?" he grumped testily, trying the "hold" of the sheep's inserted forefeet in the rear-quarter hock slits to be sure of his "packing lock" before slinging the game across his shoulder. "Be quick with it," he repeated. "This cursed cold will have this ewe's body stiff as a Sioux cradleboard in another minute."

Crow Girl nodded obediently, but caught his eyes with a look that put his nape hairs on end.

"A small moment ago," she murmured, with an inflection of throaty meaning no man could miss, "when you held me so strong and so close and when I twisted myself against you, I felt *your* body stiffen. Was that also the cold, Lone Wolf—?"

21

The cedar fire snapped amiably and talked garrulously back at Kelly as he fed it up preparatory to laying it over with some seasoned gnarls of deadfall pine to make a bed of broiling coals for the sheep's ribs he planned for their supper. The long day since their return from the hunt had gone well. Crow Girl had put in the entire afternoon working down and fleshing out the green hide of the bighorn ewe for later tanning. Now she had just gone out to carry away the meat and fat scraps of her labor, and Kelly, waiting for the resinous cedar to slow its crackling discourse and die back a bit, looked around the little cabin and found life good again.

Perhaps he had misinterpreted the girl's disturbing little antic back there in the sheep gully. Perhaps there was some Indian connotation to the neck-bite which he did not understand. Perhaps he had only imagined she had wantonly thrust her body against his. Perhaps the whole thing had been simply a thoughtless child's spontaneous impulse of meaningless gratitude.

Yes, surely, that last explanation was the right one and he, Luther Kelly, was a man who had been too long alone.

This little Indian miss could not be over eighteen, the same credulous age he had been when first he topped the Missouri's bluffs behind Fort Berthold and stood like stout Cortez, "silent upon a peak in Darien," stricken senseless with the wonder of a land that was like another planet to him. That must be the way it was with this poor little thing; she was just overcome with being the lodge guest of the great Lone Wolf, awed at having been so devotedly cared for by a feared and famed Wasicun scout, wrongly taken with the honor, even though entirely without connubial reward, of serving as the woman of the legendary Yellowstone Kelly.

Assuredly, without putting any great strain on one's own modesty, this reaction was understandable.

And add to the Indian girl's certain knowledge of his frontier reputation the fact that, one way or another, the army's stolen surgical kit or the green elk paunch, she owed him her leg and her life, why then you had your reasonable answer.

By thunder, the more a man thought of it, the more sense it made and the clearer it became to him that the girl was not going to follow in the body-fawning footsteps of her red sisters in his past. The average young Indian woman, when it came to winning blanket privileges in a decent white man's bedroll, had no more moral compunction than a Mandan camp dog trying to tail-wag her way into her red master's roundhouse in mid-January. But this gray-eyed Absaroka child was different. He had said so from the beginning, and it was still true.

Outside, now, he heard the quick, light tread of her returning footsteps. His thoughts interrupted, he turned his expectant glance toward the doorway.

She came in without a sound to stand just within the elk hide, waiting for her eyes to adjust from the outer splendor of the dying sun to the warm inner gloom of the cabin. As she posed there in the gaudy wrappings of Sayapi's scarlet Four Point, Kelly thought she looked exactly like one of the beautiful little *hanpospu hoksicala*, the miniature gaily blanketed buffalo hide ceremonial dolls carried by the Sioux *Wiyan Wakan*, or Holy Women. Either that, or like the elfin, delicate women of Old Nippon in their butterflied kimonos, which he recalled seeing pictured in his geography book the last year he had attended school at Lima Academy back in New York. Yes, that last was it, and he could even remember the heading on the page above—*Captain Matthew Calbraith Perry Voyages to the Land of the Rising Sun.*

Well, regardless, she was something out of a picture book.

Her auburn-black hair, that peculiar coppery red over blue-black sheen which was encountered occasionally among the Plains tribes, particularly the Crow and the Oglala Sioux, was piled atop her head in Empress Eugénie fashion, secured there with a bit of polished elk horn she had apparently had with her when captured by the Hunkpapa. That effect, alone, when a man was eight years accustomed to seeing all Indian women (and most whites!) with their hair either in down-hanging plaits or not groomed at all, was stunning. It gave Crow Girl, standing with the blanket swept moldingly about her, revealing only her slim hands and dainty bare feet, the appearance of having just stepped from the most modern and elegant of baths.

Which, as the complacent Kelly was shortly to find, was an illusion only in detail.

Crow Girl swayed toward him and toward Phineas' canvas pack cover which he had spread before the fire in lieu of a buffalo robe or some better floor cover for them to dine upon. As she came, and instinctively, Kelly found his feet, backing away from her in sudden nameless alarm.

But he had not far to back. He was against the log wall in one step, and she was between him and the cabin's sole exit in two. For the first time in nearly a decade of skillfully dodging red warriors, Lone Wolf Kelly found himself Indian-cornered by a slip of a girl who did not come up to his shoulder and weighed no more than a weanling antelope fawn!

Trapped, he tried to bluster. But no sound came from his frantically moving lips.

Several did, however, from the freely curving lips of Crow Girl.

"Do not be afraid, Lone Wolf," she laughed softly. "It is only that I have been snow bathing. It is an old custom among my people when one has been long ill and confined to the lodge in wintertime. It cleans the body and sends the fire racing through the blood. It returns one to usefulness among her tepee mates or to her loved one."

With supreme effort, Kelly broke his eyes from hers, managed a step toward the slab of sheep ribs he had hung across the room. "That is good," he mumbled thickly. "*Waste, waste.* Now we will broil the ribs and then—"

He got no farther, either with the evasive maneuver to reach the ribs or the stated intent to rack them for cooking.

Crow Girl did not move a muscle, save to let Sayapi's blanket slip a calculated six inches. It was enough to bring into eye-corner view a rounded copper shoulder and, below that, the ripely curving lusciousness of a farther sight designed by a bountiful nature to stop any normal man squarely in his tracks. Luther Kelly was normal. He stopped. And swung his head around and stood and stared, trembling like a leaf, at the first uncovered breast he had ever seen.

Crow Girl smiled at him.

It was not a wicked or a wanton smile but a sweet and womanly and almost shy smile, an ages-old unspoken promise of warm surrender which in three seconds put more crazy hammer and wild flutter into a man's heart than all the abandoned smiles of sheer lusting could have done in a hundred years.

"I have made myself ready for you, Lone Wolf," was all she said, and dropped Sayapi's blanket away.

Beneath it she stood as God had made her.

They lay before the fire, burned very low now, the garnet glow of its hard-pine coals exaggerating their shadows and projecting them across the packed earth floor to dance with fitful grace upon the rough log walls beyond. It was very warm and still in the far corners of the little cabin, out past the fireplace. And very calm and peaceful and languorous beneath the lamb's-wool nap of Sayapi's fine blanket, there in front of it. It was a time and place for that halting smalltalk with which lovers—who have never mentioned love—are wont to cautiously explore or painfully explain the awkward (yet wondrous!) fact of a physical fait accompli. And to get around, better late than never, to asking one another those few little overlooked personal statistics so convenient to a friendly understanding; such as true names, birth dates, honorableness of intentions, and the inconsequential like.

"Are you happy, Lone Wolf?"

"Ummmmmm."

"You are not angry with me?"

"Nnnnnnn."

"You are not ashamed?"

Kelly checked his drowsy mumble. He would have to consider that. He actually did not know whether he was ashamed or not. It had not come to that yet in his mind. He looked into the fire, thinking it over.

"*Niye osni tona led?*" he finally asked her in Sioux, meaning, "How many colds—how many winters—had she been there? How old was she?"

"*Wance zaptan,*" she smiled, watching him out of the corner of her eye, knowing he would be shocked.

He was, and rightly.

Good Lord! Crow Girl was not the eighteen he had guessed, after all. She was not even seventeen. Nor, God forgive him, sixteen. She had just told him she was only *fifteen!*

"Then I am ashamed," he answered humbly, breaking his unhappy pause and not having the courage to look at her as he did.

"You need not be, Lone Wolf. I was to have had my *tanke yanke isnati* in another moon."

"Yes," he insisted glumly, "but you did not have it. That is the point." She had referred to the tribal ceremony in which a young girl lives completely alone outside of the family lodge for a given period upon reaching sexual maturity, and prior to which no young man may look upon her seriously. Had he but known, he started to tell himself, then shook his head angrily. Had he known it would have made no difference at all. When Crow Girl let that blanket fall, no man in Montana could have … He abandoned the apology abruptly but kept his eyes on the fire. "I am still ashamed, yet I am happy too," he admitted hesitantly. "It is a hard thing for me to say it. I am not a good talker with women."

"You don't have to say it," shrugged his slender companion encouragingly. "A woman can tell without talk."

"A woman, perhaps," muttered Kelly, overcome by his pseudo moroseness.

"But I *am* a woman!" she cried. "A *full* woman!"

She came up on one slim elbow, startling him into a stolen side-glance as she slipped the blanket from her shoulders to support her indignant claim of nubility with the thrusting evidence of her proud breasts. "Will you look at me and say I am not!" she demanded of him, her anger as specious as his regret.

Kelly decided he would do neither. At such a time, a man would do well to keep his eyes on the fire, his thoughts on the future, his opinions of female maturity to himself.

She laughed, reading his mind aloud for him.

"You are afraid to look! The great Lone Wolf is frightened by a woman's body. And the Sioux call you 'The-Little-Man-With-A-Strong-Heart.' They should call you 'The-Little-Boy-With-A-Weak-Heart!'"

"Cover yourself," said Kelly sternly. "To be bold and brazen with her body is no test of a real woman."

He hoped she would agree, was vastly relieved when she did.

"I am sorry, Lone Wolf." Her blush of contrition was as genuine as had been her flash of indignation, but before Kelly could take advantage of it, she was away again. "It was only that you made me feel like a full woman. Ha-a-u! *Pte h'caka!*"

It was one too many for Luther Kelly.

The social mores of New York were still too far from those of the Yellowstone. East was east and west was west. Even eight years on the River had not prepared a man to accept gracefully from an unclad fifteen-year-old Indian girl the glowing compliment that she considered him "the real bull buffalo."

There had to be an end to this fireside tête-à-tête at once. Because a man had been crazy for five minutes did not mean he had to make a career of it. The time to start getting that idea across to the reckless talking Absaroka girl was right now. It must be made plain to her that this had been a single accident of surprised passion, not a habit pattern for their enforced future together. Still, at the same time, a man could be kind about it.

"I have been calling you Crow Girl," he announced with studied soberness, deliberately ignoring her eager, waiting smile and addressing the fire as though he had far more important things on his mind than those which had just now been recovered by Sayapi's blanket. "But what is your true name? The one by which your people call you."

She looked at him quickly, then shrugged. It was all right with her if Lone Wolf wanted to change the subject. One could still hope this did not mean he *really* wanted to change it.

"H'tayetu Hopa," she replied demurely. "It came about because my father said my eyes had the color and coolness of a clear summer twilight. Do you like it? Do you think it is pretty?"

"'Beautiful Evening!'" he exclaimed, genuinely moved as he always was by the Indian art in painting names. "It is lovely, very lovely."

"I like 'Crow Girl' better," she said flatly. "It is the most beautiful name I ever heard."

"Now how in the world can you say that?" laughed Kelly, beginning to feel and be grateful for the margin of smalltalk safety growing between them. "It is a very clumsy name for one so slight and graceful."

"Of course," she said. "It is only because you gave it to me, Lone Wolf."

"I?" he echoed, surprised, thinking he had gotten the name from Gall.

"Yes." She dropped her eyes, suddenly and confusingly shy now. "In the little shelter the Hunkpapa made for me. Where you first came to see my leg. Do you remember? You asked if my heart was good for you, and you called me Crow Girl. Since that moment my name was changed."

"Do you really want me to call you that—Crow Girl?"

"Yes."

"Then will you do me a favor in return?"

"When I do not do as you wish, I will be dead."

He turned away when she looked up at him and said it, but not quickly enough. The fire's light was not so low, but he caught the warning glimmer of the tears again brimming those great black-lashed eyes.

"Then call me Kelly," he requested hurriedly. "I do not like

Lone Wolf, nor Little Big Heart, nor Man-Who-Never-Lays-Down-His-Gun, nor Little-Man-With-A-Strong-Heart, nor any of those other foolish Indian names I have been given by your people. Do you understand?"

"Yes."

"Can you say Kelly?"

"Yes."

"Let me hear you."

"No."

"Why is that?"

"I would rather say it my way."

"And what is your way, you stubborn minx?" He smiled condescendingly, led into the trap so beautifully he never saw nor suspected it.

"This way—!" she whispered fiercely.

And brought her lean body meltingly into his, sealing his surprised lips with the clinging hunger of her kiss and receiving the answering wildness of his embrace as deeply and easily as the warm sands receive the angry sea.

22

From that hour, the relationship between the white scout and the Indian girl deepened with the high-country snows. Beyond the understandable enjoyments of being young and strong and alone and in love, the first-time physical fun of "keeping house," as it were, nearly every day brought some new surprise of subtler, more lasting appreciation.

For his part Kelly, who would have wagered a factory-fresh Winchester against a seven-dollar Hudson's Bay smoothbore that he knew what there was worth knowing about the wild Plains Indians and his way of life, discovered that his knowledge was superficial. It was all concerned with trailing and tracking, hiding and seeking, hunting and being hunted, ambushing and avoiding ambushes, shooting and getting shot at, bluffing and calling, stalking and being stalked, and, in continuing kind, limited strictly to the mastery of the main article of Indian war—the holding down of your own or the lifting of the enemy's hair. And to Kelly, quite naturally, as the owner of one of the most sought-after scalp locks in Siouxland, the Indian had always been "the enemy."

Oh, he had learned much of the community life of the

tame Mandans, Arikaras, and Gros Ventres who made of their windowless roundhouses virtual mud-wattled cottonwood parasites to the palisaded hosts of the white man's trading forts up and down the east bank of the Big Muddy. And he had many a fine red acquaintance among the humbled people of the peaceful tribes. Men like Bloody Knife of the Arikara, for instance, a hunter and warrior as famed and fearless as any Oglala or Hunkpapa. But these civilized Indians, driven into the protecting arms of the white brother by the merciless persecution of their own wild cousins, did not count in the frontiersman's coldblooded scale of values. They were simply "friendlies," well tried, if not to be trusted.

Quite another matter were the Indians who still ranged west of the Missouri. These unhaltered "mustang" bands of Sioux, Cheyenne, Arapahoe, Crow, and Blackfeet were proven and predictable "hostiles." They were "the enemy," not only to Kelly but to every white man and every white man's Indian north of Fort Laramie or west of Fort Lincoln.

For eight years Kelly had accepted this standard Montana version of the rebellious horseback tribes, applying it in particular to the Sioux with whom he was most familiar. Still, he did not let lack of familiarity breed carelessness. While he had had very little contact with the Crows and Blackfeet, whose home camps in general lay westerly and northerly of his beloved lower Yellowstone Valley, he regarded them as no better risks than their Sioux, Cheyenne, or Arapahoe cousins. It was true that the Blackfeet had never come back from their almost total decimation by the great smallpox epidemic earlier in the century, and could at this late date be practically discounted as a power on the plains. But the Crow, called Absaroka by themselves and Kangi Wicasi by the Sioux, were numerous and great travelers. Kelly many times heard but never listened to the story that they had taken the white man's path. Only one tribe ever had done that and stuck with it. That had been old Jim Bridger's adopted people, the Shoshones, or Snakes, and they made a careful point of staying out of Sioux territory. As for the Crow, if he met a party of them on the trail, he was just what he would have been with a band of Oglala Dirt Throwers or Hunkpapa Border People—The-Man-Who-Never-Lays-His-Gun-Down.

Now all that past prejudice was being badly shaken.

During the silent, swift winter months of 1875-76 in the little cabin at Crow Girl Meadow, H'tayetu Hopa, the gray-eyed Absaroka child-squaw, gave him a new sight of Indian life, setting to grow in him a seed of sympathy and understanding for her nomad people which was to bear a strange bright fruit in the destiny of her Sioux cousins where history lay tragically in wait for them along the icebound banks of Tongue River.

From Crow Girl he learned the silently total obedience to the male, to the hunter, to the provider, which is the whole instructed purpose, from the time she is old enough to walk and to bear wood and water, of the Indian woman's life. This discovery, alone, was enough to make a renegade of any man. His own society, based upon the diametrically opposed philosophy of the sacred cow or the queen bee—"all hail the fertile female"—had not prepared a fellow for any such service as Crow Girl had been trained to provide.

Yet beyond her unbelievable anticipation and eager submission to his least lordly whim or lowest male passion, the Indian girl amazed him with her practical abilities.

Did he need a new pair of calf-high, flesh-out, wolfskin winter boots, he had them within the week; and of the most beautiful workmanship in design, beading, and delicate quilling he had ever seen. Did he, on the other hand, make an exceedingly heavy killing at one of his strychnined baits and need an extra hand at skinning out, the tiny Crow girl could strip and flesh out the pelt of a hundred-pound buffalo lobo as swiftly as any man he had ever hunted with. Or she could gut a buck, pack eighty pounds of meat up or down the mountain, build a fire in any weather, with or without flint and steel. Make a pine bough bed or a willow thatch wind shelter. Or a wolf set, or a rabbit snare, or a grouse net. Or do any other of the thousand-and-one things a skilled scout or hunter could do to live and be happy in the wilderness.

As for herself, Crow Girl simply thanked her Absaroka gods for letting her be Lone Wolf's woman. Past serving him, she delighted mostly in listening to the many strange and wondrous stories of the white man's world beyond the Minnisoso, the big muddy river, which her Wasicun mate had to tell her. If, from Crow Girl, Kelly learned much about the Indians he had not known before, Crow Girl learned from him everything she was ever to know about the white man. Yet, unlike the Irish scout, the Indian girl did not change. She loved this one paleface with a devotion and a blindness and a loyalty of passion which was beyond measure. But as for any other white man, or all other white men, Crow Girl did not yield a single one of her red prejudices.

Though she listened to Kelly read his books before the fireplace and even learned to recite for him in her halting new English the entire soliloquy from Hamlet, as well as scattered bits and pieces of Poe's "The Raven" and sundry of his favorite isolated lines from Burns, *sic* those from "To a Louse on a Lady's Bonnet"—"Oh wad some power the giftie gie us to see oursels as others see us!"—she never understood what she was saying except that it made her man and master cry out with delight or give her a quick kiss or squeeze, for any one of which small favors she would gladly have died or have done anything else within her Indian comprehension.

Yet it was precisely the limitations of that same comprehension which, in the end, very nearly defeated Kelly. As the winter wore on and Crow Girl began to show her child, he became increasingly aware of her growing discontent. Still, he was helpless either to stem or understand it.

The wolfing had gone beautifully. There had been no trouble making good bait kills, sheep, elk, blacktail deer, and even stray wintering buffalo being plentiful, and he had taken up to twenty-two grown wolves from one strychnined carcass in a single night. As February and March wore away into April, he had a great load of prime pelts cached in the fur shed against the coming spring runoff and the opening of South Pass down into the Basin. He quit baiting, then, to give his full time to Crow Girl, now six months heavy with child and badly needing attention.

But nothing he could do or say seemed to penetrate her deepening melancholy. Shortly, he knew that he must do so, must somehow reach her retreating primitive mind or stand to lose her. And there was that in the increasingly far-eyed quality of her depressed restlessness which warned him that the latter possibility was no idle chance.

As May burgeoned and the spring melt began in earnest, Luther Kelly realized that any next morning might open the pass. *That* morning, when it came, would be the one when he would awaken to find the pine bough bed by his side empty, its soft blankets long cooled of the fragrant warmth of H'tayetu Hopa's dear form. He must not let that happen. He must find out what was troubling her and find it out before it was forever too late.

As is usual with young men in love, the obvious did not occur to Kelly until well past the eleventh hour.

Then it struck him as the greatest inspiration ever received by mistreated man.

He would *ask* her what was the matter!

Kelly got his answer in almost as little time as it took him to ask for it.

Crow Girl burst into tears and told him she was homesick. That she wanted to go back to the lodges of her people. That she could not face going into the white man's settlements with Lone Wolf and living there in the shameful way of a Mandan or a Big Belly. That she wanted, above all, to have her baby among her own free kind. It would be an Indian and should be born and reared as an Indian. Could not Lone Wolf see that?

Kelly nodded that he could and put his arm comfortingly around her.

Actually, her odd statement that her baby would be an Indian did not catch at his conscious thoughts. He let it pass as a figure of red speech, not a literal announcement of heredity. She would naturally think of her child as an Indian. The fact that it was as much his as hers would not have entered her wild mind. Well, he had no argument with that. Let her see it that way and be happy.

He had no argument, either, with her wish to go home.

He understood that and, moreover, it fitted into the thought which had been growing of late in his own mind—he could not and would not, in the final hour, take this unspoiled child of nature into the filth and degradation awaiting any of her dark blood in the settlements.

At the same time, he realized, she could no longer follow him upon the hazards of the hunting and scouting trail. Not with the little one to come so soon now.

What more natural, then, than letting her return to her people? And what more reasonable than his returning with her to live out his life as an adopted member of the tribe?

This last was not as melodramatic as it sounded.

Other white men had done it and successfully. There was

Cetan Mani, Walking Hawk, of the Oglala Sioux, for example. He was rumored to have been a full colonel in the Confederate army come to the frontier in '66, but two years before Kelly, and living now with his Indian mate, North Star, as a full war chief with Crazy Horse's band. It was a thought which, once faced, actually fired the imagination. And he, Kelly, had seldom been caught short on that commodity.

Eagerly, he told the sobbing Crow Girl of his decision, pledging her that he would never depart from it and that they would live out their lives as Indians. He further promised that they would leave for her Kangi Wicasi homeland the moment the trails were clear, tarrying at Reed's Ranch only long enough to leave a message for Big Anse to go up and bring out the furs.

The way the Absaroka girl looked at him, the way she kissed him through her tears, the way she crawled into and curled up in his arms and went to sleep like a trusting, happily tired puppy there in front of the fieldstone fireplace, was all the reward any man could have asked for his small sacrifice of white superiority.

The following morning, May 27, Kelly glassed the south pass from the granite outcrop above the cabin and decided it was open enough. After all, they were in no position to be taking their sweet time about getting out. The first day they could travel would be the best day for them to do so. From what he could see through the field glasses, this was that day.

He aroused Crow Girl, telling her to make ready for the trail. He, meanwhile, would go out while it was still early and drop a fat buck for fresh meat on the march. He would be gone no longer than half an hour. Not sighting game in that time, he would return, and they would go out on black coffee and cold bread.

Crow Girl's delight was candescent enough for a man to warm his hands by. Kelly left the cabin with his heart as high as the turreted snows of the distant Big Horns. He had cut his sign and downed his buck within ten minutes. Had skinned and quartered out the saddle he wanted within ten more. Was topping out on the landmark rock behind the cabin within the third ten.

And was throwing himself flat on his belly in the slushed snowpack within the following five never-to-be-forgotten seconds.

Below him lay a sight he would remember to the grave.

Thirteen winter-ragged Sioux ponies standing hipshot in the morning sun just outside the open elk-hide door of the little cedar log cabin in Crow Girl Meadow.

23

Kelly thought fast, faster than at any time in the previous eight years of necessarily quick Indian thinking. Yet each new trail along which his racing mind leaped hopefully led only to some new dead end of despair. There it wound up trapped by a swiftly growing circle of inescapable facts.

Inescapable and frightening.

Sayapi had badly outguessed him on the vagaries of Montana weather. The youthful subchief had anticipated the melt-off by at least seventy-two hours, giving himself the exact time to come from the lower elevations along the Musselshell to the mouth of South Pass just as the trail to Crow Girl Meadow opened. He must also have defied the Sioux taboo against night traveling to have gotten up the pass into the meadow so early in the morning. Furthermore, his presence here without his brooding uncle almost guaranteed there had been another break between the two and that young Sayapi was once more running unhaltered, on his own.

These were very dangerous conditions.

They let you know you had seriously underestimated Gall's

nephew both as a man and as an enemy. Now, too late, you realized the headstrong Hunkpapa youth did not carry his uncle's fighting blood in vain. He had more of Gall in him than a quirky temper, an inbred distrust of wandering white scouts, and a constitutional hatred of home-building Wasicun breakers-of-the-buffalo-grass. He had that rarest of Indian inheritances—a quality shared to Kelly's knowledge among the major Sioux only by Crazy Horse, Gall, and Sitting Bull—the ability to put together a plan of campaign and to follow it out in painstaking military detail.

Now the young devil had Crow Girl and twelve hard-memoried friends along to make sure that he kept her.

The next move was Kelly's. The moody Sioux youth would know that. Would be waiting down there right now for him to make it.

Well, at any rate, Kelly thought grimly, it was nice of him to wait. He might just as well have set out to run him, Kelly, down on his way back to the cabin.

Might have? The thought put the flattened scout's scalp to tingling eerily. Might have, bushway! He almost certainly had! There was no one down there in that cabin right now but a bound and gagged Absaroka girl with a minimum bodyguard of at most three or four warriors. Sayapi and the rest of his boys would be out doing the same thing Kelly had just been doing. Hunting. Only they would not be hunting a fat young blacktail buck. They would be hunting a fatheaded young black-haired bull. A white one about twenty-six years old and mortal apt not to get a great deal older.

Kelly lay still for another two or three seconds, long enough to flash his eyes right and left in that flicking ninety-degree head-motionless viewing arc, the trick of which white scouts who survived their first season in Sioux country had quickly acquired from their friendly settlement-Indian instructors. He saw nothing.

The next move was academic and made faster than the twist in midair of a falling cat to put its feet beneath itself.

He had five shots. There was one shell in the Winchester's chamber, four more in its magazine. He had used a round on the blacktail buck, had loaded but six to begin with, a happy carelessness which he was regretting even as he whirled, got his knee propped under his sling-arm, and began dropping running Indians.

They had been in a soundless crawl-up behind him, working their ways out from the backing timber forest's edge across the boulder-strewn surface of the granite outcrop. The moment Kelly came up off his flat-muscled middle and slewed around to face them with the Winchester shouldered, they sprang into full charge, Sayapi fearlessly leading the wild yelling rush.

This Indian, Kelly remembered thinking as his trigger finger tightened for the squeeze-off, is a very brave and a very foolish and a very dead Indian. A man almost hated to center him, but this was no time for moral regrets. Sayapi had a gun too. And was very clearly bent on using it. Kelly crooked his finger on in, setting his cheek for the jump and slap of the .44-.40 recoil.

The heavy charge boomed, belching forth its characteristic mouthful of greasy smoke and fat orange flame, and the white scout's eyes widened in disbelief.

Somehow, in some fantastic way no truly just God would ever have sanctioned, the best offhand shot in the Upper Missouri drainage basin had missed an Indian on foot with a knee-braced, deliberately aimed shot from less than sixty feet!

Fortunately, for at least one famous general officer and several hundred unsung troopers of the US Army who had not yet had the anticipated pleasure of meeting him, Yellowstone Kelly's next four snaps were all meat-in-the-pot shots.

A different kind of outcry at once overlay the triumphant

closing yells of but a moment before; the agonizing, stricken-animal sounds men make when a big-caliber bullet slams into them at pointblank range. For some it is a high crazy whimper, for some a low angry growl, for some only an explosion of released air from smashed chest cavities, for some no sound at all beyond that of the leaden slug's own soapy smack of going home in deep-hit flesh.

But your Indian, Kelly knew, would cry out if possible when seriously hurt. A stoic in most other realms of suffering, sneering at wounds which would make the strongest white man weep with fear, the red warrior wanted his companions *and* his enemies to know when he took a real coup in open battle. There were two reasons for this. First, his inordinate pride in having taken a dangerous wound, second, his desire to signal his brothers that while still alive, he was out of action. Hence, Kelly was sure, as he saw his subsequent four targets grab their bellies and go down, that Sayapi's original twelve were now eight.

But the young Sioux himself, an impossible target with his weaving pantherine speed, was on top of him while the last of the four braves was still falling.

The finger-sized bore of the subchief's brand-new .50-caliber Springfield trap-loader gaped yawningly as the mouth of a twelve-pound howitzer not eight feet from Kelly's face.

The white scout did what he could; threw his empty rifle slashingly at the other's head.

Sayapi had to duck and shoot or not shoot at all. His off-balance discharge went four feet over Kelly's hunched shoulder, whined harmlessly out and away across the empty meadow air: Sayapi saw the white man's powerful body hurtle toward him. Saw the long, thick-boned arm snake back for the leaping blow. Tensed, too late, his own great strength. His foe's clenched fist, gnarled and knotted as a black oak burl, exploded alongside his heavy Sioux jaw with a crack like a breaking ridgepole, and Gall's magnificently muscled six-foot nephew dropped forward into the ground-slush to feel his way about on hands and knees, helpless as a cradleboard infant, until his ringing ears could clear and his sightless eyes uncloud.

Kelly did not wait for the adjustment.

Leaping over the stunned Hunkpapa youth, he scooped up his rifle on the run and turned to speed southward down the treacherous decline of the granite outcrop. He had not taken three steps when the solitary bowman among Sayapi's band of modern gun-bearers rose up from back of a rock-based snowbank six pony lengths off his left flank.

The Sioux had his arrow nocked and drawn to eye on the noiseless rise. There was nothing Kelly could do, save throw himself twistingly aside on the run. He heard the familiar venomous hum of the shaft behind him as he did. Then, for the second time in his frontier life, felt the numbing shock of an arrow wound. He staggered, regained his balance, drove on. The arrow, pinioned slantingly through six inches of meat and muscle just above his hip, tore at him with gasping pain at every straining leap.

Behind the cursing bowman the other four of Sayapi's trailing crew burst from their boulders, loading on the run and yelling down to their three companions, left to guard Crow Girl, to race down the meadow and cut the trapped scout off when he sought to come off the rock. The guards, who had dashed out of the cabin at the first sound of firing, shouted back their understanding, headed for the lower edge of the open grassland belling for all the world like three lean red hounds on a hot track.

Kelly, however, had no intention of going near the meadow, the cabin, or the cabin's captive occupant.

Sayapi had clearly won this round. Crow Girl was his—for the time. Kelly's only chance of getting her back alive and unharmed lay in saving his own life. His only chance of saving his own life lay in precipitous flight.

With a little longheaded Irish wit mixed in.

Toward both ends he knew of a hidden declivity in the outcrop just ahead. This blind gully had a good bottom of packed detritus and led not down toward the meadow but back up into the timber. In another moment he had plunged over its eight-foot lip and was running for his life along its smooth floor. He was out of it, into the shadowed line of the first trees, as the pursuing Hunkpapa drew up on its edge and fell into an excited palaver over the clear line of his moccasin prints in the rock dust below.

When they did that, Kelly knew he had a chance.

It was true he could not gamble on waiting for Sayapi to come up and join the powwow. But he was positive what would happen once the subchief took over the discussion. After a suitable round of argument in which every brave would take a different tack— that god-given Indian genius for delaying to debate in the face of action, which perverse trait alone accounted for the white man's survival on the frontier—all of them would fall in with their leader's orders, precisely as they had intended to do from the first. There was no doubt, either, that in his pain and anger, Sayapi would order them to spoor down the wounded Lone Wolf, run him to final cover, move in, and shoot him down like a crippled animal. With this certainty that his pursuers would follow wherever he led them, Kelly's heart leaped with a last wild hope.

If, in the excitement of their immediate hunting eagerness to run his blood-flecked track and be the first to count a coup on such a renowned quarry, he could draw all the Sioux away from the cabin, then double back—

He closed his teeth with an audible snap, cutting off the unfinished thought.

Reaching down, he seized the protruding arrow by its head,

pulled it forward through the wound until its feathers lodged at the shaft's entering channel in his back. He then broke off the bent, soft iron point, drew the headless shaft back through the wound channel, unclenched his teeth and was at last free of its seesawing pinion. He did not carelessly drop or throw the parts of the broken arrow but secreted them skillfully among the bushy needles of a hand-close clump of pine seedlings, leaving Sayapi's well-trained trailers no reason to suspect he was not still hampered by the bowman's shaft.

The ten-second surgery performed and its postoperative evidence disposed of, he turned swiftly into the deeper shadows of the forest, was gone from sight in less than a dozen soundless strides.

24

Now the chase had grown an hour old, and Kelly was mightily pleased with it.

His wound had bled just freely enough to cleanse itself and to leave exciting fresh sign on the broken snow patches through which he deliberately wove his tracks. Yet it had not flowed hard enough to weaken him seriously. He had lost a good bit of blood, it was true, but it was what he and his hardened hunting colleagues along the Yellowstone and the Missouri called "nosebleed" blood, the nice medium-colored kind a man could lose a pint or two of and never notice the drain.

Of course the trailing Sioux could read blood color as fast as he could shed it. They would know they were not looking at the dark blood of a viscera wound or the bright scarlet froth of a lung puncture. But beyond that they would have to guess whether he was carrying a surface scratch or a crippling deep muscle penetration. Meanwhile, the more red splotches among his moccasin prints, the better for the whetting and making careless of Sioux appetites for the big coup on Lone Wolf Kelly.

But now he had played with them long enough, had led them

far enough away from his meadow nest and helpless loved one.

It was time to open up ground. To get far out past the sound of their eager tracking yelps. To make his double-back and his straightaway run to reach the side of his beloved little Kangi Wicasi wife.

Reckoning as he limped along, he guessed he had brought his pursuers at least three miles east of the lookout rock above the cabin. This would have to be far enough. He could risk no more of this deliberate allowing of them to keep almost within shooting sight of him. He opened his stride with the decision, his head swinging from side to side as his eyes darted through the heavy growth seeking what he needed for the remainder of his ruse.

Presently, he saw it—a ninety-foot patriarch of a cedar deadfall free of snow and with its bark not yet rotted soft or turned punky. Beyond it lay a tiny creek foaming across the game trail he was following. The fallen cedar's rust-red length lay almost directly at right angles to the trail, its cleanly broken top-spar protruding a convenient foot or more into the trail's foliage-free tunnel.

Waste. Very good. Very good indeed.

He passed the deadfall without a break in stride. As he did, he reached into his war bag for the wad of trunk moss he had pulled from a trailside conifer some moments gone. Nearing the small stream, now, he plugged both entrance and exit holes of the arrow wound tightly with the absorbent lichen, stanching the telltale drops within the last stride short of the water.

Coming to the very edge of the brawling rill, he suddenly reversed, stepping meticulously backward in his own moccasin prints until he again reached the fallen cedar. Here he twisted his body agilely, not moving his moccasins a hair, planted his rump gratefully on the tip of the deadfall's broken spar, swung his feet free of the trail, peeled off his wet footgear so that no snow water would show on the dry red bark, leaped up, and ran along the rough trunk at full speed in his bare feet. He reached the upheaved root end of the big tree just in time to dive into the snow-filled crater torn out of the shallow earth of the mountainside by the old giant's sundering fall. Three seconds later, Sayapi led his string of anxious Sioux hunting dogs into sight along the backtrail.

As the Hunkpapa party split up at the creek, some to go up it, some down, looking for his emerging footprints, Kelly knocked the snow dust from his eyes, toed his wet moccasins back on, slid out of the snow crater, and swung westward in his high-shouldered, swift-going wolf gait.

Luther Kelly was well pleased with himself.

Given time, Sayapi's boys would unravel the knot he had tied in his trail back there. There was no question of that. But that time was all Kelly wanted or needed. Well within its tense span, he and Crow Girl would have picked the two top mounts out of the Sioux ponies at the cabin, shot the others through the head, taken off down South Pass at a High Plains gallop.

With the thought, the Irish scout allowed himself the luxury of the first flicking grin he had shown since glassing the innocent lower end of South Pass at sunup.

And why not, pray tell? he asked himself cheerfully.

Sayapi had fallen for his deliberate bait like a toothless, old, rheumy-eyed squaw reaching blindly for her tin cup of brown sugar at the post trader's store. When the young subchief came presently to measuring his own bitter cup of Luther Kelly brand sweetening back there at the cedar root crater, he would be very unhappy with himself for not realizing that Lone Wolf was no different from any other cheating white man when it came to weighing out the unsuspecting red brother's apparent fair measure—he, too, kept his big broad thumb deep in the cup!

Opening up his rolling lope, the black-haired scout laughed softly and joyously aloud.

It was good to know that a man could still give the red scoundrels cards and spades and beat them out of the big pot, regardless. Of course there was that old saw about the last pasteboard to be uncovered always proving the real blanket cleaner. But from where Luther S. Kelly loped along right now, it looked as if the luck of the Irish would hold good all the way downhill to Reed's Ranch. And, after that, on out through the lovely valley of the Yellowstone to the fabled Land of the Absaroka far beyond.

A panting twenty minutes later, he was standing at the northern edge of Crow Girl Meadow and was, for the second time that morning, hitting the soft snow on his startled belly. He had time, then, to recall another old saw much more apropos of life's realities at the moment than any happily laughed allusions to last cards or bitter cups of Sioux sugar. This one would be from the works of his old friend Bobbie Burns and would go as any fool but Luther Kelly might have remembered in time, thus:

> *The best laid schemes o' mice*
> *and men*
> *Gang aft a-gley;*
> *An' lea'e us nought but grief*
> *and pain,*
> *For promis'd joy.*

But he had not remembered in time, and his chance for doing so was just now gone with the rising morning wind which brought to his cedar-rimmed hiding place from across the intervening sweet-scented mountain grasses, the familiar acrid smell of sweated Indian horseflesh.

Down the meadow, winding up out of the ages-old weatherworn throat of South Pass, starting in toward the silent cabin, their ponies caked with old lather and stiff with the weariness of long hard driving, came Gall and a seemingly endless line of war-painted Hunkpapa braves.

It went very quickly after that.

The war chief came to the cabin, studied his missing nephew's abandoned horses, dismounted, and went inside. He was out immediately, carrying Crow Girl in his arms.

Kelly clearly heard the angry bark of his order to Black Fox—"Fire the signal shots. Bring that young fool in."

Then he saw, but did not hear him say, something else to Frog Belly. Apparently, however, it was a request for the latter to help him with the girl, for the big-paunched Hunkpapa swung lightly down from his mount, took down and unrolled from his saddle a beautiful cow buffalo sleeping robe. This he placed upon the ground in the strip of shade remaining along the cabin's west-facing front wall and, when Gall had lowered the unbound Absaroka girl gently to it, joined his chief in carefully chafing her slim hands and feet. Kelly grimaced and entered another debit in the mental credit ledger he was keeping on Gall's nephew. Although savagely passionate and persistent, Sayapi was clearly a brutally insensitive lover. He had bound the tiny, heavy-with-child Crow girl so thoughtlessly as to entirely cut off circulation to her extremities. But the white scout's attention could not long linger on his mistreated mate. Too much other movement was going forward in the meadow.

Black Fox now drew his Model 66 Winchester from its heavily fringed saddle scabbard, upended the polished repeater, and triggered off the Sioux bad medicine signal of five shots. As he did, Kelly's trained eye noted with alarm that at least half of Gall's big band of over one hundred and fifty braves were newly armed either with Model 66's or the earlier Henry sixteen-shooters.

The echoes of the signal shots were still being flung flatly back by the surrounding ridges when they were answered by a good medicine signal of four shots from Sayapi's band, meaning, Kelly figured, that Sayapi was engaged in important work and did not intend to be called away from it. He further surmised that the content of those labors, right now, would have to do with the young subchief having succeeded in backtracking him to the cedar's root crater and being once more in full bay along his track line. It was an uneasy proposition, but help came from an unexpected quarter.

At the sound of his nephew's negative return signal, Gall grabbed up his own Winchester to fire five more thundering shots in instant, short-tempered reply. This time, after a little proud delay and while Gall waited glaring eastward, Sayapi answered with five raggedly spaced shots and, half an hour later, trotted sullenly into the meadow with his eight followers.

The hostile tempo picked up at once.

First, the four Indians Kelly had shot were brought down from the outcrop behind the cabin. Two of them were able to walk with support from both sides and would probably live, the Indian animate force being what it was. The third brave was dead, the fourth dying. While the latter were being ministered to, Gall left Crow Girl's side, raised both long arms aloft, called for a council session of his principal lieutenants.

Kelly was able to make a nearly word-perfect translation of the following tableau through the twin media of his field glasses and a frequent wind-carried Sioux phrase. Between the two sources he was able to understand what was being said almost as well as though he had been squatting in the circle of subchiefs and leading warriors now forming around Gall. And as he read the flowing hand signs which always accompanied a Plains Indian speech of any passion, his scalp began to crawl.

First, there was Gall's lecture to Sayapi on his breaking of the Musselshell camp's march discipline to outrace his uncle to Crow

Girl Meadow.

But the arrogant youngster was the war chief's besetting weakness. Having no warrior son of his own, the wild-riding, reckless-willed Sayapi was the darling of his uncle's fiercely jaundiced eye. Kelly could make out that Gall, although he thought it was a great pity Sayapi's haste had lost them Lone Wolf, forgave his errant nephew once more. After all, he had recovered the Crow girl for Gall and she had been the whole reason the war party had swung thus far out of its course to the great rendezvous with Tatanka Yotanka and Tashunka Witko on the banks of the Greasy Grass.

The watching scout's eyes narrowed as these last signs carried clearly to him through the glasses.

Now Gall was sorry, the guttural Sioux phrases and fluent hand signs continued to tell him, that he had had to call Sayapi in off Lone Wolf's trail. But time would permit of no more delay. This was the last of May, and the great gathering along the Greasy Grass had been cried through the villages for early June. All must now put aside personal matters and devote themselves fanatically to Sitting Bull's Big Medicine Dream, his great vision of a vast wikmunke of the hated white Pony Soldiers and Walk-A-Heaps at the place of the rendezvous. It was known that Three Stars Crook was creeping cautiously up the Rosebud from the south. That Star Terry and Red Nose Gibbon were moving up the Yellowstone by boat to come down from the north. And that Yellowhair Custer was riding bravely out from Fort Lincoln to the east with his feared maroon pennants flying their big white "sevens" and his famous ripe-corn curls waving and tossing in the Dakota wind. Now it was Tashunka's war plan (of Tatanka's dream) to let them all come, let them all close in—on the greatest gathering of horseback Indians in the history of the High Plains. If all went as Tashunka had told it to Tatanka and if the Cheyenne and Arapahoe came in as promised, the unsuspecting mila hanska would ride, open-eyed, into a war-camp of no less than ten thousand heavily armed Shacun fighting men.

These unbelievable facts and figures came so fast, Kelly had to shake his head to clear it for reducing the incredible whole to an acceptable part.

What he came up with, finally, was that the hostile Sioux, Cheyenne, and Arapahoe had, under Crazy Horse and Sitting Bull, at last agreed to a united and coordinated effort to fight a major military action against the white cavalry which was pushing them to the brink of total surrender. The expressions and signs Gall used to inform Sayapi and the others of this closely held, intertribal decision left a man no other translation.

The "Greasy Grass" was the Little Horn River. A wikmunke was a trap. The mila hanska were the "long knives," another Sioux name for the Pony Soldiers, taken from the curved field sabers of the regular US Cavalry. The hand sign names for the four famous white officers referred to completed the hair-raising red jigsaw: Crazy Horse meant to set a trap for the combined forward forces of Crook, Terry, Gibbon, and Custer, somewhere along the banks of the Little Horn River early in June.

Now a man was faced with the toughest decision of his Indian-fighting life.

He was calmly resolved, on the one hand, to trail Crow Girl to the last breath of life in his body. But he was compelled, on the other, to break off that trailing long enough to detour into Fort Buford and apprise the military of what he had just seen and heard. It made no moral difference that in all actual likelihood the grandiose Indian scheme would never materialize. The identical rumor, in a dozen different forms, had been heard along the frontier ever since Red Cloud had stalked out of the Laramie Council in '66. But no matter for that. Who would want such guesswork on his conscience?

For a three-year regular army man like Luther Kelly, there was no real choice, of course. He would simply hang to the Sioux trail as long as it went toward the Yellowstone, leave it when it crossed over, cut east to the fort, alert the post commander, return, and pick up the hostile track on the south bank.

That settled with a grim clenching of his broad jaw, there was nothing for him to do but wait for the cross-meadow conference to break up. This it did almost at once.

Crow Girl was given a mount, the torch was thoughtfully put to the little cedar cabin, the Sioux caravan swung away across the meadow and was gone down South Pass, leaving Luther Kelly to watch in jaw-set silence as his impossible dream of happiness for himself and his gray-eyed Absaroka child bride went snaking skyward on the roiling, clotted smoke of three thousand dollars' worth of prime-baled wolf pelts.

BOOK FOUR
THE YELLOWSTONE

25

The Hunkpapa war party went southward toward the Yellowstone, bearing east to skirt the sunrise slopes of the Snowy Mountains, rather than following the regular Indian trail passing to the west between the Snowies and the Little Belt range. The Sioux were clearly in no hurry, which fact materially added to Kelly's temper and tension while at the same time considerably easing the physical chore of keeping pace with their ponies afoot.

It took them two full days to reach and ford the Musselshell where it bent sharply westward below the Snowies and another day and a half to cross over from the Musselshell to the Yellowstone. Here, at high noon of the fourth day, in the rich bottomland meadows of the Clark's Fork confluence, they halted. Turning their ponies loose and shaking out their blanket rolls, they gave every evidence of resting a few days or, since for the past twenty-four hours they had been moving through one herd after another of spring-grazing buffalo, more likely of organizing a major hunt before going on to the rendezvous. This latter idea had especial merit, because no Indian is so welcome in a big war camp or, for that matter, at any large tribal gathering place, as the one who comes bearing juicy hump ribs, sweet marrow bones, and fresh tenderloin fat. Kelly understood this; and prayed mightily, as he lay atop the closest small foothill north of the river glassing the Indian activity on the south bank, that it was indeed a hunt Gall's braves had in mind.

Presently, he began to grin and shortly put the glasses aside with a sigh of real relief.

Over there across the beautiful clear-bottomed Yellowstone, the plier-jawed, old-style bullet molds and the little lead-melting pots had begun to come out of the saddle-slung parfleches. Beaded elk and antelope and doeskin carrying cases had begun to be peeled from the precious Winchester and Henry repeaters, and from the older Spencers, Sharpses, Springfields, and smoothbore British trade muskets. The proud and lucky ones who had factory ammunition for the newer guns busied themselves counting out and inspecting their gleaming brass treasures, to the obvious envy of their less wealthy fellows.

There was no doubt about it now. It was going to be a hunt. And, more than that for Kelly, it was going to be the most timely stroke of fortune he had enjoyed in many a risky moon.

Cutting out and running just the right animals—fat young dry cows or second-year open heifers—then dressing them out, cleaning, preparing, and packing the meat for transport was a process which would not be completed tomorrow or the next day. The Hunkpapa, given good hunting, would be at the Clark's Fork camp at least a week and more likely ten days before moving on over to the rendezvous on the nearby Little Horn Fork of the Big Horn River.

In that time, providing he could cover fifty miles a day on foot, a man could reach Fort Buford, borrow a fast horse, turn him around, and run him to death back up the Yellowstone and be bellied down on this selfsame ridge again with the glasses once more safely on his captive bride and her Hunkpapa hosts, ready to follow them to the ends of the Indian earth if need be.

There developed only one slight flaw in the nearly perfect crystal ball of Gall's immediate future, and it was but a temporary one. Shortly after it became apparent that a hunt was in preparation, the Hunkpapa chief dispatched Sayapi and his surviving, still loyal little group of eight eager young men down the south bank toward the Big Horn Valley. Kelly, on the point of letting this unexpected maneuver spoil his afternoon, realized Sayapi's band had merely been sent ahead to the Little Horn rendezvous to report in to Sitting Bull or Crazy Horse that their fellow war chief would be delayed a few days killing meat up the river. With that supposition accepted, he dismissed the Sioux youth and got back to himself and the lad's dark-tempered uncle.

The passing-whim halt of Gall's war-painted cavalcade was more than a typical example of Plains Indian indirection. It was a rare piece of prairie luck with which Kelly did not intend to fool around. He had backed down from his skyline vantage point and was wolf-trotting toward the Missouri and Fort Buford before the first bright Sioux lead hissed into the rusted bullet molds across the Yellowstone.

He made good time—time comparable to that of a well-mounted horseman going an average, unhurried gait. It was no great feat for his iron-limbed kind, of course. The properly conditioned, inherently powerful plainsman could easily move four or five miles an hour over reasonable terrain such as he had under him at present. And, moreover, could keep it up hour after untiring hour. In fact, upon many of his most advertised travels, Kelly had gone afoot by preference. He insisted that a trained man enjoyed more "reach and freedom" if he did not have a "temperamental equine" to worry about, and it was only upon matters of the most urgent nature, such as his famed ride for the army to open the military mail route between Forts Buford and Stevenson, that he would condescend to seek the help of a horse. So it was that at present he had every confidence of his ability to make the necessary time toward the Missouri.

His course lay east by north up the north bank of the Yellowstone; a course he would continue to hold to journey's end, where the tributary Yellowstone entered the parent Missouri opposite Fort Buford. The going was open and level along the lazy sweep of the broad stream. The day was cool, clear, windless; made for jogging a long smooth piece of country. His only concern was to keep a constant eye out for possible war parties converging on the Little Horn rendezvous—if, indeed, there was actually going to be any such rendezvous. In any event, it was an active concern, or stood to be one, from the proximity of the gathering site. The Big Horn, with its Little Horn Fork, was the Yellowstone's next main tributary east of Clark's Fork. Business could pick up sharply at any time along this stretch.

An hour later, it did.

In the next sixty minutes, he saw ahead, and had to lie up in cover or detour in route to avoid, no less than three small and one sizable bands of Sioux. All were wearing the black charcoal paste and yellow ocher paint which were the Throat Slitter war colors, and all were bearing in toward the Big Horn crossing. There were two Oglala, one Miniconjou, one Brulé group.

The traffic was growing a bit heavy. Further daylight travel became a matter of very questionable policy.

When the fifth hostile band, thirty-six Wolf Mountain Cheyenne looking meaner than sin and twice as uncertain, loomed ahead, Kelly quit cold and quick.

He made, perforce, for the only cover momentarily available—a dense riverside stand of alder, cottonwood, and willow scrub too low and marshy to invite any Indian campsite consideration. Here he lay up until nightfall, pinned down by the continuously passing war parties and suffering the torments of Montana purgatory from the attentions of an early hatch of black deerflies swarming the swampy growth. Yet, he told himself, these were the unadvertised joys of scouting life in the Far West. A man endured them at the moment, left them out of his memoirs later on. Who would believe that a hatch of flies could break a man's mind? Or drive him beyond the endurance of a nervous system which would not quail in the least under hostile war whoop or feathered rifle fire? Obviously, no one. So you endured. You sat there, and you plastered your hands and face with slimy blue-bottom silt, and you endured.

Still, Kelly thought the lengthening spring twilight would never close. At last, however, its western rose and eastern turquoise horizons were gone, leaving only the velvet blue and silver of the young night. An hour later, Luther Kelly was another five miles up the Yellowstone.

With daylight, he had made forty more miles and was safely past the mouth of the Big Horn.

And here he got the pleasantest shock of his venturesome young life.

Just over the stony, brush-lipped rise upon which he lay hidden preparing to glass the country ahead, and idling brisket-deep in the fat grass of an unnamed creek coming in from the north, grazed the only voting mule in Montana Territory. Beyond him, alongside a little motte of misplaced cottonwoods, was displayed a prairie breakfast tableau beautiful past apt description.

Kelly laughed aloud, his dark eyes shining. He sprang up from his hiding place, his laugh startling the cross-creek camper into a blundering rise to his own unbelieving feet. Striding delightedly down the rise, rich voice rolling in a happy abandonment of his usual dependence upon the masters, the Irish scout brought forth a double couplet of his own, specially tailored for the occasion:

> *"Where feeds yon Phineas with*
> *mouth of brass*
> *Content upon yon creekside*
> *grass,*
> *Methinks a man is bound to*
> *find,*
> *His noble lord not far be-*
> *hind—"*

For his flabbergasted part, Big Anse Harper could do no better than stand staring across his clear-flamed little coffee fire, his spilling cup suspended in midair, his slack lips moving soundlessly around words of astonishment and joy too compounded for his simple tongue to utter.

The reunion with Anse was as brief as it was gladdening. Neither man was given time to fully unburden his heart. Necessity forced the parting as good fortune had guided the joining. The big southerner was enthusiastically agreeable to the abandoning of his interrupted return to Crow Girl Meadow, reluctantly so to Kelly's request of reversing his course and carrying the word about the possible hostile assemblage on the Little Horn to Fort Buford.

Frowningly, Kelly cautioned the drawling Georgia giant that he must make it clear to the troop commander at Buford that the hidden valley of the Little Horn was precisely the most likely place to look into. It was famous among the Sioux and Cheyenne for its good wood and water and especially for its wonderful forage conditions. Its very name, the "Greasy Grass," had come from the fact the ponies always took on such hard fat and high finish in its rich level bottom meadows and low treeless hill pastures.

When he was satisfied his huge friend understood the message, Kelly urged him on his way. They shook hands, the big man breaking down at the last minute to start pleading that his friend allow him to come back to join him in "shaggin' them red scuts which tooken the little Injun gal." Anse was "sure as tarnal sin not aimin' to set by fer any of them redskin sons to bring no more grief to thet pore little crippled up Crow gal, especially now that she was fixin' to have a young 'un by Mr. Kelly."

It was a crude and clumsy compliment but so clearly heartfelt that Kelly's sensitive Irish feelings were touched. He impulsively shook hands again, turned hurriedly away to busy himself hiding the evidence of Anse's coffee fire. The slow-witted Georgian swallowed hard but said no more. Heaving his two hundred fifty pounds up onto the groaning Phineas, he turned him away downstream. The last Kelly saw of them, sneaking the glance with his back turned to make the big mar think he had already put him out of mind, Anse had halted the mule at a river bend point of willows which would take him out of sight of his friend and was waiting for Kelly to look around and see him.

But Kelly did not look around and, presently, Big Anse, like an only child being sent off down the road on the first day of school, waved forlornly, swung Phineas around the point of trees, and was gone.

"*A-ah,*" grunted Whistling Horse, staring across the big river's swirling current and shaking his head uncertainly with the Sioux warning word, "I don't know if I would go over there or not, Sayapi. It is not what your uncle said to do."

"He-hau, that is true, Sayapi," said White Bear, another of the eight young Sioux sitting their horses on the south bank of the Yellowstone nineteen miles below the mouth of the Big Horn. "Your uncle told us to take his word to Tashunka up on the Little Greasy Grass. We should have been there with it last night. But no. You had to go chasing off down the Yellowstone because those thieving Cheyenne we met yesterday said they had seen many Pony Soldier smokes down that way."

The youthful brave elevated his hands helplessly.

"Now here we are, having seen the cursed mila hanska camp-fires, on our way back upstream still many miles even from the Big Greasy Grass, and you are seized with a new inspiration. Now you will go galloping off up north on a wolf hunt! What is the matter with you, Sayapi? Have you been chewing peyote again?"

"No, he does not need peyote to make him crazy," grinned a third young warrior, refusing the premise that Sayapi was addicted to the herbal drug so commonly used by the Plains tribes to work themselves up. "He has his hatred of Lone Wolf to make a *heyoka* out of himself."

Sayapi, who all this time had been looking scowlingly across the Yellowstone, now turned his thoughtful frown on his restless companions.

"Now, listen," he said quietly. "It has been hanging in my mind that Lone Wolf has been following us down from the mountains all the while. I think he may be hiding back there right now, watching my uncle's camp and that Crow girl we took back from him. Now I have sworn to take his hair, you know that. So all I want to do is circle around up that way and see if we can cut his trail, before he gets nervous and slips away."

"*A-ah,*" repeated Whistling Horse unhappily. "Someone should go to Tashunka with your uncle's word. You may be a big fool, Sayapi, but I am not. I am afraid of your uncle."

"I, too," agreed White Bear candidly. "And of Tashunka, as well."

"Then that is good!" barked Sayapi. "Someone *will* go to

Tashunka with my uncle's word. You and you!" He pointed disdainfully at Whistling Horse and White Bear. "You will be the ones! Your hearts are too weak for wolf hunting anyway. We are well rid of you. Tell Tashunka," he added loftily, "that I will bring him the long black hair of Lone Wolf Kelly by way of apology. Nohetto. Get out!"

"*Waste*," nodded the sagacious Whistling Horse, glad enough to be relieved of duty he had already had far too much of.

"*Wagh!*" agreed White Bear, his belly as full of chasing Luther Kelly as that of his friend. "Good hunting!" he grinned at the half-dozen braves who would accompany Sayapi. "We will see you six fools along the Greasy Grass. *Or*," he emphasized leeringly, "whatever small number of you Lone Wolf decides to spare."

His listeners, for some reason, had no ready answer to this sally. They sat silently with Sayapi, watching their young leader's two couriers to Crazy Horse ride off up the Yellowstone. Then they turned their horses, after his, northward into the swift shallows of the crossing.

Ten minutes later, riding over a low rise going east along the north bank, they drew their still wet-legged ponies to a hock-sliding stop.

Coming toward them, cheerfully whistling a melodious Wasicun marching song, which no Sioux could have been expected to recognize as "The Yellow Rose of Texas," and his huge moccasins almost dragging the ground despite the fact he bestrode the tallest mule in Montana, was a white man they remembered well.

And who remembered them well. But only after a tense moment of shading his widening blue eyes against the glare of the morning sun. By then, it was too late.

"It is the red-haired giant," said one of the Hunkpapa, vastly pleased. "Isn't that a fine axe he wears in his belt?"

"Aye, and that's a good mule he rides, too," nodded another.

26

Sayapi's band pushed their ponies relentlessly. The little horses were tired, hot, hungry, but their red masters were broodingly immune to their sufferings.

Sayapi's young men had other problems.

Or at least three of them did.

Of the other three, excluding always the dark-browed Sayapi who rode alone out in front of his six followers, two would never worry again, the third was unable to express his concerns by reason of being in deep shock and dying from loss of blood.

Glancing back at the sodden jounce and flop of the three slack bodies tied across the flyblown backs of the little pack line of led-ponies, Sayapi's scowl grew blacker.

Of course, in a certain grisly meter, there had been a measure of the malignant poetry of justice in the hurried departures of his friends for Wanagi Yata, the Sioux Land of the Great Shadow. But it was not easy to console oneself with that bitter logic.

True, Lame Elk, the brave who had coveted the huge one's belt axe, had gotten it—right to the haft through the frontal complexes of his skull. Also true that Antelope Boy, the youthful warrior who had assayed the big man's old Sharps bull gun as a weapon of sterling worth had had his judgment sustained—by a .50-caliber slug which had opened up his belly, shattered his spine, left his body frozen from the waist down, his life draining away through the ugly hole in his stomach. And true as well that Yellow-Eye-Wolf, the young man who had imagined the rangy mule to be an animal of desirable parts, had also had his evaluation vindicated. With his last breath and fading of sight, the giant white man had knocked the latter off his pony and in under the mule's flailing feet with his clubbed rifle butt. The tall mule's ironshod hoofs had pulpingly completed the work begun by the white man's gunstock. Not even Yellow-Eye-Wolf's mother would know her son now. Even by Hunkpapa standards, he was not a pleasant thing to look upon.

And so Sayapi was depressed.

And so he was more angry and more full of vengeance than ever against Lone Wolf Kelly and against all the Wasicun invaders.

Brooding thus, he did not keep his usual keen eye upon the trail, nor allow his superb instincts their ordinary rein or watchfulness. Glumly, he led his silent cavalcade of living and dead warriors westward along the north bank of the Yellowstone toward the mouth of the Big Horn. When, shortly before noon, he forded a lonely little creek coming in from the north but a few miles below the Big Greasy Grass, he did not even look at the small growth of yellow-pollened cottonwoods clustering its upstream bank. Instead, he splashed his black and white stud quickly through the limpid shallows, his burning eyes straight ahead, his handsome face darkening with each jarring shift of the runty stallion's sharp withers.

Behind him his three companions were as preoccupied and downcast. They did not look up and search the trees either.

And behind them their three companions, forever careless,

only bumped and bobbed along, trailing their dangling hands and feet in the cleansing waters of the little stream.

Thirty-five feet away, hidden behind a screening clump of buckbrush, just within the first straggly rank of trees but luckily up and across a stiffly quartering wind from the wearily grunting Indian mounts, Luther Kelly slumbered peacefully on.

He did not see the bloody axe in the first brave's belt.

Nor the oily rust-brown length of the old Sharps in the hands of the second.

Nor the balky shuffle of the tall, wise-eyed mule bringing up the rear of the pony pack-string led by the third.

Nor did he see, drying upon Sayapi's saddle horn and smearing the yellow-sweated white shoulder patch of his piebald studhorse, the clotting, fly-encrusted tangle of bright red human hair.

Twenty seconds after they had come upon it, the Sioux were gone across the little prairie creek. The reedbirds and redwings scattered by their approach settled back into the stream-mouth rushes, resuming their endless cheery argument of scolding raspy-filled and incredibly clear sweet bobolinking notes. The sun slid swiftly toward the tops of the Big Horns, the Little Belts, and the Bear Paws. Kelly awoke. The strength was back in him from his first full sleep in five day and four nights. It did not worry him that he had slept the sun up and down. He had yet plenty of time, thanks to Big Anse.

Cautiously, he made no coffee fire but ate heartily of the cold bread and cooked pork the good-natured southerner had left him, washing the meal down with dipped creek water. Ten minutes later he, too, was gone westward up the Yellowstone. The view behind him was open and straightaway, the lingering prairie twilight clear as good telescope glass. But he did not turn to look back again on the rendezvous he would never keep with Big Anse Harper.

Antelope Boy was still alive when Kelly found him in the

abandoned camp of Gall's Hunkpapa shortly after sunrise of the following day. The story the former told was as strange and startling as the deserted camp's echoing dead-still emptiness.

"Who are you?" asked the dying brave, as Kelly's stooping form loomed in the opening of the small buffalo robe tepee Gall had ordered constructed for him. "I can see your shadow there between me and my last sun. But your face is not clear. There is a blackness all about you there in the bright light. Is it you, Sayapi, come back to be with your old friend? You, Buffalo Child? Pesla? Broken Hand—?"

"It is I," said Kelly softly in Sioux. "*Lone Wolf.*"

"*Lone Wolf!*" gasped the brave. Then recovering from the effort of the surprised expletive, "You have come to kill me for what we did down there yesterday?"

He moved his hand weakly to motion off down the Yellowstone, but Kelly did not follow up the question, and Antelope Boy did not press it.

If Lone Wolf did not yet know what had been done down there, all the better. It was not a very proud thing. Not the sort of thing a dying man would want to talk about or admit his shameful part in. So the moment's fleeting opportunity slipped past. It was as close as the white scout came to knowing, in time, that his message was never delivered.

"No, I have not come to kill you." He shook off the Indian youth's query. "No one is going to kill you. You are already killed, don't you know that?"

"Yes," said the Indian youth bravely, "I guess that I do." There was an awkward pause, then he asked haltingly, "Could you come in, Lone Wolf? Sit here by me? Talk a little? Let me touch your hand, perhaps?"

Kelly slid into the little tepee, touched the young Sioux's hand. "I am here, do not be frightened."

"No, I won't."

"What is your name? How do they call you?"

"Antelope Boy."

"That sounds like the name of your childhood, as if you hadn't been given your full name yet."

The Sioux youth nodded imperceptibly, the trace of a shy smile flicking his tortured face. "I was to have received my manhood name after the fight on the Greasy Grass. It was to depend on what deeds I might do there."

Kelly patted his hand clumsily.

"Do not feel bad about that. You are too young—perhaps no more than seventeen winters."

"Oh, no!" Proudly. "I am nearly eighteen!"

Kelly touched his forehead gently, recoiled involuntarily at its clamminess, knew his time for questioning was short.

"You are one of Sayapi's band?" he probed quietly. "One of his eight young men who came back from my meadow?"

"Yes, but we are only five now. Soon it will be but four. There was a little trouble down the river, as I said."

"I see. About Sayapi now. Where is he? And the others too. Where is Gall? Where is the Crow girl, H'tayetu Hopa, where is she? Where are all the braves?"

Again, the young brave's wan smile flickered briefly.

"Was that her name? Beautiful Evening? How very soft and pretty it sounds when you whisper it. She was a fine girl, Lone Wolf. I liked her a lot. Brave. Strong. A good mate. Is that your child she was carrying?"

"Yes. Will you tell me what I ask now, please?"

"Gladly. What little I know. May I have some water first though?"

"It is here." Kelly uncorked the canteen, tipping it.

The brave gulped spasmodically. Kelly winced and set his

teeth as the water bubbled out of the bullet perforation in the youth's belly, down into his blood-caked breechclout.

"Thank you. Will you hold my head a little higher, please. The blood comes up in my throat when I try to talk to you, Lone Wolf."

Kelly propped him up, and the words came out between choking drinks, rusty gaspings for breath, rattly throat coughs, and low cries of impossible pain. It was a short story, soon done, and its teller with it.

Sayapi had ridden into camp from down the Yellowstone about two a.m. of the present morning. He had apparently sought his scarlet blanket and gone to rest with Antelope Boy and his other companions. But when the camp came awake in the gray dawn to set out for the hunt, Sayapi was gone.

And gone with him were Gall's two best buffalo runners, his famous iron-gray mare, and his matchless midnight-black gelding, also a fine pack mule lightly loaded with sugar, salt, pemmican, ammunition, and extra blankets and, oh yes—the pretty little Crow girl!

In a frothing rage, Gall had ordered the hunt abandoned and his warriors to follow him along his errant nephew's track away westward up the Yellowstone. The war chief had sworn his personal oath that this time Sayapi must die. He had taken out his knife and put his lips to its haft and said one fearful word— hinmangas! All had known the nephew was as good as dead in that moment. But in the very act of his uncle's touching the knife haft, the reckless youth had gotten a startling reprieve. Even as Gall flung up his arm in the signal to start after him, a rider had come in on a staggering horse from Tashunka Witko over on the Rosebud.

There was great news!

Tashunka had caught old Three Stars Crook camped in a

bad place over there and thought he could trim his famous red whiskers if he could get enough help. All who heard his call were to answer it at once. He, Crazy Horse, would wait as long as he could for them, but he did not think Three Stars would stay in camp more than another two weeks. He was shoeing his pack mules and that meant he was going to move soon, of course.

It was the kind of order no war chief could, or would want to, ignore.

Gall took his braves off Sayapi's fleeing track, swung them eastward and southward toward the middle Rosebud.

They had been gone about two hours now. Sayapi, before them, had been gone nearer five. He, Sayapi, had very fast horses and even the mule, tall on the leg and not too coarse in bone, looked like a fine mover, one which could get over a distance of ground with all but the very best of ponies. And Sayapi, of course, rode like a *Tshaoh*, a Comanche; he would be very far away by now.

Where to? Toward what exact place?

Who would know.

Sayapi was a little crazy, everyone realized that. There was simply no telling where his wild mind would guide him, or what it might make him do. Nohetto. There was no more anyone could say.

When he was sure Antelope Boy had meant his "nohetto," Kelly thanked him seriously, gently eased his flaccid body down onto the deep pad of blankets his departed companions had arranged beneath him. The suffering youth's own blanket, together with a liberal parfleche of food, salt, tobacco, and ammunition was fastened upon his war pony, grazing on short picket just outside the little death lodge. The stunted animal, a scrubby Nez Percé Appaloosa, had been left after the Plains Indian custom to bear his master along the steeply climbing trail into the endless buffalo pastures of Wanagi Yata. And it was of his horse—next only to his rifle, the dearest possession of any prairie warrior—that Antelope Boy spoke now.

"You will not take my pony!" he pleaded with Kelly suddenly. "You would not leave me afoot to go on the long trail—"

Kelly said nothing, only patting him reassuringly on the shoulder. The youth relaxed, moving his head and muttering gratefully. "You will give him a little water, too, before you go. And perhaps lengthen his rope. Already I have taken longer to start the journey than my brothers thought. I fear he has eaten all the grass within his reach."

Again Kelly touched his shoulder, and again the young Sioux nodded his understanding gratitude.

"His real name is Wanbli K'leska, the Spotted Eagle. But many times I call him little Ya Slo, the Whistler. He makes a funny little noise in his lungs when he is tired after a long run. Like an eagle-bone flute or like a small boy's green willow whistle. But he can go all day eating only the air and drinking the wind. He is truly *sunkele ska waste*, a good little spotted horse."

With the last words about his beloved pony, Antelope Boy closed his now unseeing eyes, sighed a final time, long and slow and heavy. Thinking he was gone, Kelly arose to depart. But he spoke again.

"Lone Wolf—"

"Yes, my brother?"

"Can you find it in your heart to do one more thing for your enemy?"

"You are not my enemy. When the Dark One hovers, all men are friends." Kelly came back to his side, knelt once more beside him, put his big hand lightly on his pallid cheek. "You see I am here. And I am your friend."

"Yes, yes! I feel that now, I feel that you are my friend, and I am glad. It is dark now and very cold, but I am not afraid, because you are with me. Surely you will grant me, then, this last favor, you who are my true friend and who stays beside me."

"You have only to name it," murmured Kelly, taking his cold hand and holding it in both his strong warm ones.

"Thank you, it is this. I may lie here a long while yet. My heart is strong, but in my belly the pain is very great. My gun is by my right hand, here, hidden beneath the blankets. It is a good Pony Soldier gun, shooting hard and close. I would consider it a—"

"Say no more now," muttered Kelly, reaching for the gun and rising noiselessly to his feet. "I understand that you would do the same for me. H'g'un, Antelope Boy."

"*Woyuonihan*, Lone Wolf," smiled the dying youth, gray-lipped. "I salute you …"

"*Woyuonihan*," said Luther Kelly softly, and eased back the hammer of Antelope Boy's old Spencer carbine to full-cock and shot him through the head.

27

Even the ugly death wound of Antelope Boy fell into the happy pattern of Irish luck Kelly imagined he had been enjoying in his trailing of Crow Girl. Had not the Hunkpapa youth been given that ghastly hole in his stomach—most probably by some chance cavalry patrol from Crawford's command, a man would guess—Kelly would not now be standing outside his lonesome last resting place in the confluence meadows of Clark's Fork and the main Yellowstone, looking over his prized Nez Percé pony and the treasure trove of supplies the latter bore against his master's journey to the Big Beyond.

Outside of a good blanket and settlement belt axe, there was a fairly decent saddle of double-rigged southwestern design (a man could bet that saddle had cost some Comanche wanderer his life and, before him, some Texas rancher his), two cross-slung parfleches crammed with pemmican, salt, flour, tobacco, dried larb leaves, ammunition, and even a little precious sugar and *pejuta sapa*, "black medicine," coffee beans.

Kelly threw a grateful glance accompanied by a wordless acknowledgment of help from higher up, skyward. And not simply because he was a devout Christian who accepted his God as a literal power, either. The actual truth was that a man could not have outfitted better for a long tough trailing job had he gone clear into Fort Buford or even Fort Berthold.

Coming to the horse, however, only time and doubtful trial would tell.

He looked like anything but the noble sacred bird of the Dakota Sioux after which his admiring master had named him. He might physically answer to the proud title of "Spotted Eagle," Kelly decided, but he could never qualify for it artistically.

He was, in a word, a true Appaloosa.

The rangy "leopard horses" of the Nez Percé were famed along the northwest frontier for their speed and endurance and, before these things, for their high intelligence, easy gait, and eagerness to work. They had been, in the opinions of the original mountain men, the "doingest" little horses to be had. These hairy-eared early comers had considered one Appaloosa worth six ordinary Indian ponies, and this high reputation was still fully intact thirty to forty years later, in Kelly's day. Still, looking candidly at Spotted Eagle, the puzzled scout allowed a man would have to incline to the uncharitable diagnosis that Bridger, Colter, Fitzpatrick, Hugh Glass, Jed Smith, Father DeSmet, and all the rest of them had been more than a "leetle teched."

Viewed dispassionately, Antelope Boy's equine pride and joy was a sight to make any compassionate horseman reach for his pistol. A merciful ball behind the ear was the only remedy for such a pitiful prairie rosinante as Spotted Eagle.

A rusty red roan with four high white socks and a big blaze, he looked as if he had been hit across the haunches with a five-gallon drum of white lead and linseed oil in the middle of a March blizzard. He was, in hideous truth, a leprous splatter of bursting white spots from tail root to mid-barrel and back again.

But "for a' that," as Burns would say, he was a horse.

And Luther Kelly needed a horse.

He wedged his empty Winchester into the blanket roll behind the saddle, slung Antelope Boy's Spencer in the fender-guard scabbard, gentled the little beast for a brief moment, stepped up on him, and gave him the knee to go west.

Spotted Eagle spun around and went.

By sundown that night, some ten hours later, Kelly had made a surprising seventy miles up the Yellowstone along the clearly marked trail of Sayapi and Crow Girl. He had come, with the rose and saffron skies of that long-ago twilight, to the sweeping "big bend" of the river, where it angled southward to enter the roughening country of its canyon and to enter, too, some forty miles farther along, that arcane northwest corner of Wyoming called in the old days Colter's Hell or Gardner's Hole, but newly christened and set aside by the government only four short years ago in 1872 as "Yellowstone National Park."

It was a sacred area forbidden to the white man by Indian legend, and one of surpassing interest to the peripatetic Kelly. For all his wanderings up and down the Yellowstone, he had never been inside the Park itself. But he had long cherished the ambition and intent to one day explore its every wild nook and eerie cranny. Now, gazing intently through the gathering dusk at the fading track lines of the two barefoot Sioux ponies and the shod pack mule, he knew the hour of actuality drew close.

At this point on the Yellowstone, the main north-south travel route of the High Plains tribes—called by them the "Great Trail"—came down out of the buffalo pastures above the river to follow its banks southward into and through the Park and on to Colorado's famed mountain-fenced South Park buffalo range. Kelly had scouted the trail north but never south of the river. Nor had, for that matter, over a dozen single-traveling white men before him.

But now the prospect lay immediately ahead.

Studying it, boring deep through the sinister stillness which seemed suddenly to lie all about him, his dark eyes narrowed yet further.

The tracks of Gall's two best buffalo horses and those of the long-striding pack mule led straightaway down the Great Trail toward the distant twelve-hundred-foot-deep maw of the Fourth, or Grand Canyon, of the Yellowstone.

There was no doubt remaining. Red Paint and Beautiful Evening were heading for the many-mysteried, Indian-worshiped "Land of the Smoking Waters."

28

The Great Trail, in places as wide and sweeping and clearly delineated as Washington's Pennsylvania Avenue, in places as narrow and crooked and hard to find as Carondelet Street in old St. Louis, bore away westward from the river as the rearing rhyolite walls of the stream's First and Second Canyons began in roughening earnest below the Big Bend.

Some miles later the wandering track passed through a towering gap into a secondary canyon which it followed southward to open out into a region of spectacular rockfalls of bright rusty red detritus. This area Kelly believed to be the fabulous "Devil's Slide," long thought to be composed of virtually pure cinnabar ore, albeit his own present, passing examination convinced him the decomposing mother material was but ordinary stone brilliantly stained with red hematite ores and containing no least trace of mercuric sulphide.

In any event a man had little time to wonder about the mineral content of the slides. The important thing about them was that they marked, less but two or three miles, the northern boundary of the Park.

The ex–Lima Academy student was, among his other accomplishments, something of an amateur cartographer. He had made maps of his own of practically every mile of the uncharted Montana Territory he had traversed. And had copied, in addition, all the available Government Survey and military maps of the country to the south of the Yellowstone's outer valley, including the one rather sketchy plot of the Park then in existence.

But at the present moment, Yellowstone Park was a complete new world to Luther Kelly. Every stride of the little Appaloosa stud was moving him deeper into the virgin unknown. Indeed, since leaving the Big Bend country early that morning, he had been traveling through a land familiar to him only by white hearsay or red legend. Yet, after all, it had been up to this point a type of High Plains topography with which he was at least somewhat comfortably familiar.

Now, suddenly, he had an eerie feeling of having just lost contact with reality.

Ahead of him, as he rested Spotted Eagle beneath the sunset flaming palisades of disintegrating rhyolite and feldspar towering above the Devil's Slide, lay a two-million-acre mountain wilderness whose plunging canyons, crenelated peaks, gemstone lakes, lofty timber, lush meadows, rock crystal streams, thunderous thermal fountains, and brilliantly mineralized formations were as incredibly fantastic to the unwarned discoverer as would have been the cratered, unlit backside of the frozen moon.

Kelly was stunned.

The brooding, unbroken silence hovering over the deserted trail bore down on him like some great invisible hand.

Shivering, he clucked to Spotted Eagle, and the little Nez Percé horse took him forward again. Refreshed by the brief blowing out and still showing life after ten hours on the trail, the wiry mustang wanted to go. Kelly let him stretch, wanting to "get across the line" and commit himself to the "Land of the Smoking Waters" before full sundown. In a place like this, a man felt the compulsive need to make camp and secure himself ahead of nightfall, no matter how foolish the notion of his being afraid of the dark might strike him.

Shortly, again following the Yellowstone briefly now before it entered its Third Canyon just south of the Park's north line, he struck a fork where a beautiful stream came in from the south, as the main channel itself veered sharply off to the east.

From the fact that the Great Trail crossed over this entering tributary above its junction with the Yellowstone, to continue paralleling that stream by passing behind seventy-nine-hundred-foot Mount Everts and going on to cross present-day Blacktail and Tower Creeks down to the Great Yellowstone Lake, he judged correctly that the smaller stream was the Gardner River, leading of course to old Johnson Gardner's celebrated "hole."

Excepting only for the word "Yellowstone" itself, "Gardner's Hole" was the oldest place-name in the Park. Its lovely meadowed basin, lying between the Gallatin and the Washburn Ranges, had been the old free trader's secret rendezvous forty-four years before when, in 1832, Gardner had stumbled across it while trapping out of Fort Union for the American Fur Company. Its rich history was as well known to Kelly as his own poor small biography, and it was with heavy regret that he realized, having come so close, he was not to see its legendary beauties.

Still, it was not to be. The Great Trail, bearing away from the Gardner to follow the Yellowstone as it did, would take him many miles west of the old mountain man's reported paradise, beginning with tomorrow's earliest daylight.

He made a fireless camp, putting on Spotted Eagle's shaggy forelegs the set of Sioux hobbles which Antelope Boy's thoughtful comrades had laced to their dying brother's saddle before racing off to cut back Crook's carrot-red muttonchops over on the Rosebud.

He used the hobbles rather than the picket rope—also thoughtfully provided by the dead youth's lodge brothers—for a good hard High Plains reason.

Any spooked yearling colt could snap a braided horsehair rope and run off beyond recovery. But a four-year-old stampeded bull buffalo could not break a set of Hunkpapa foreleg hobbles, nor get far enough from camp in a whole night's hopping to take more than a pleasant morning's stroll to round up again. And in his position at the moment of his cautious cold supper of rancid last-winter's pemmican at the forks of the Gardner and Yellowstone Rivers the night of June 4, 1876, Luther Kelly figured he could not afford to take a great many liberties with the uncertain laws of Sioux chance.

The fact was that he had made up a great many miles on Sayapi and Crow Girl in the past forty-eight hours. Gall's nephew, apparently expecting immediate and hot pursuit in strength, had clearly been thrown off guard by his uncle's failure to appear in force along his backtrail. Especially during the second day, just past, had the Hunkpapa youth's pony tracks shown him to be slowing carelessly. Now, safely within the tangled vastnesses of the Park, he was moving entirely at ease and completely without suspicion that he was being followed within fifty miles. Much less that he was being followed, according to Kelly's grim guess as the sun sank that fourth day of June, *within five miles!*

With the jade-green mountain twilight fading peacefully and with Spotted Eagle contentedly cropping the verdant Gardner River grass not thirty feet away, and with the murmuring, passing swirl of the stream's smooth-bouldered current soothing his weary nerves, Luther Kelly found life good again. Wrapping himself gratefully in Antelope Boy's worn Three Point blanket, he sighed deeply and lay back upon the fragrant meadow hay. Within thirty seconds he was dreaming of Crow Girl's calm gray eyes and curving, soft-lipped smile.

But from a weathered eagle's-nest lookout spire perched atop the gaunt stone flank of Gardner Canyon high above his grassy campsite, the glittering Indian eyes which looked down upon him were not calm and gray.

Nor were the cruel knife-thin lips below those eyes, soft and smiling.

With daylight the morning of the fifth, Kelly was moving. He did not move far. He had no more than forded the Gardner to pick up Sayapi's tracks on the far side than he sat the surprised Spotted Eagle on his haunches.

Turning him, he cut to the right, coming off the main thoroughfare of the Great Trail to halt where a dim sidetrack led off up the Gardner toward that stream's canyon issuance. This latter track appeared to be no more than a game trail, grass-grown and little used. But there was one big trouble with that last assurance. What little use it had been getting had been given it within the past twelve hours.

Kelly could have read that triple line of fresh prints leaving the Great Trail and starting off up the Gardner goat path in his sleep.

They belonged to Gall's two top buffalo runners and a very tall, shod mule. And if they had been cut into the firm clay of the riverbank trail more than thirty minutes before his own arrival at the forks last night, Luther Kelly could not tell a bighorn biscuit from a buffalo chip.

Flinching to the thought, he threw his eyes nervously upstream toward the weirdly oxidized rock fangs arming the weather-rotted jaws of the canyon ahead.

Nothing moved.

Not a lizard stirred, not a pack rat scurried, not a deerfly droned to break the orange– and ocher-stained stillness of the crumbling canyon walls. The only movement within anxious eye's reach of the Gardner and Yellowstone forks was the lazy swing of a mated pair of osprey eagles soundlessly circling the blue air over their rock-spired nest fifteen hundred feet above the river's canyoned exit.

Kelly ground his stumpy white teeth, fingered his blue-bearded chin, studied the ground, and scowled darkly.

He had made a bad mistake with that five-mile guess last night. He was very lucky to be alive this morning to realize it, too. Actually, he must almost have run Spotted Eagle's soft pink nose up the lathered crupper of Sayapi's borrowed black gelding late yesterday afternoon. He could not have missed him at the forks by more than two miles, and it might as easily have been less than one.

It must be the cursed spell of the Park that did that to a man. Stunned his senses. Overcame his ordinary cautions. Dulled his painfully sharpened instincts. Made him unaccountably careless as he, Kelly, had been the night before.

Be that as it may, the last of his Irish luck had been used up in saving him from stepping on Sayapi.

The dangerous youth had only spotted him, then cut and run like any wolf-shy Sioux. He could just as well have hung around to night-sneak his camp and slip a knife between his blanketed ribs, Pawnee style. But saved or not, the hump-fat was now in the fire. Kelly had overridden his big luck in a tomfool way worthy of a Yellowstone yearling running his first hostile trail. He had galloped right up his quarry's unsuspecting back as stupidly as a Pony Soldier sergeant on his first Sioux patrol assignment. He had wantonly thrown away the tremendous advantage of surprise which had been his up until sunset last evening.

Now there was the Indian piper to pay.

The moody, unpredictable Sioux youth was alerted. And six feet three inches, a hundred and ninety-five pounds of forewarned, mentally unstable Hunkpapa subchief was something to sweat about.

Would he turn and fight proudly by open challenge? Would he set an ambush and strike from cover?

Would he whip up his tiring mounts and run straight away, slowing himself to suit the necessarily laggard gaits of an ungainly pack mule and a woman eight months heavy with child, yet still hoping to lose his white shadow by superior trail craft?

Or would he cut the mule's throat and put a bullet through the burdensome squaw's head, taking both ponies to make good his own escape by relay riding?

Only one answer was certain in the white scout's desperately turning mind. Now that the issue was committed, the chase clearly joined, Sayapi would never abandon Crow Girl alive. If he could not now win through and have her for himself, he would kill her as surely and naturally as dark follows daylight.

But which of these perilous choices the unpredictable young Sioux would make, no man could foretell.

Only God knew that and, as usual, God was not talking.

A man would have to gamble now with the girl's life. To pit his own wilderness skills against Sayapi's. To hunt down the dangerous Sioux and kill him like a rabid dog. No mercy shown. No quarter considered. Crow Girl's precious life and that of her (and his!) unborn child at stake every chancy step of the way.

Either that, or he conceded the game to Gall's nephew. Refused to risk his Absaroka mate's dear life. Gave both her and their baby over to the hunted life of a Hunkpapa hostile's squaw. Turned around right now and went back to the outer valley and his old free, uncluttered life along the Montana game trails.

It was question enough to set the jaw and blacken the scowl of any man's Christian charity of decision.

Yet, as he sat there staring off up the Gardner, Kelly's frown faded. The quick trace of his pawky grin picked up his mouth corners. He gathered the single-plaited rawhide reins of Spotted Eagle's Indian hackamore, clucked to the little horse, and gave him the indicating knee-squeeze.

Spotted Eagle stiffened his flopping ears, shot them forward, then back, blew out softly through his flared nostrils, glided off on a left-foot lead into his ten-hour trail gait. Aboard him, his new white master sat to the swinging single-foot as fluidly as any Sioux, his dark eyes fastened on the rocky flanks of the rising trail ahead, his wide lips still touched with the strangely eager little smile.

Luther Kelly was pleased enough.

He was going to see Gardner's Hole after all.

29

Despite the need for extreme care not to crowd up on Sayapi or to blunder into any traps he might set, Kelly could not keep his naturalist's eyes from wandering the wonders of the trailside. This was as it would be with his nature-worshiping kind, for, since leaving the forks five miles back, the canyon track had climbed nearly a thousand feet, opening up vistas undreamed at the lower elevations at which the Great Trail entered the Park.

Now, spread all about him were scenes such as would subdue the senses of the dullest clod, let alone the acutely tuned feelings of a wilderness lover like Luther Kelly.

Behind him and to his right, across the Gardner, loomed the ninety-five-hundred-foot funeral crest of a tremendous mountain shaped like a sepulcher. Immediately below the grim peak began a remarkable mile-long "sliding hill" apron of moving foothill earth being pushed forever forward and downward into the river to assuage the insatiable land hunger of its predatory current and to replenish the resultant never-ending crumble of its eroding banks.

Behind him, to the left, rising more than two thousand feet above the already mile-high bed of the Gardner, was a second towering behemoth. This monstrous Cretaceous relic, more cliff than mountain, whose somber three-mile facia of alternate glistening black coal seams, dove-gray andesite extrusions, and colorful rhyolite porphyry caprock, had been a Great Trail landmark for more centuries than the white man knew, was even more humbling than the snow-crowned immenseness of the tomb-shaped peak to his right.

Guarding the canyon trail above and below him were perpendicular walls of heavily fossilized marine rock, stained and emblazoned with every possible oxide-of-iron pigment from palest cream through fiery orange to deep blood red. Contrasting brilliantly to the rufous earth, yellow rock, and aquamarine river water were the shadowed green of the Rocky Mountain red cedars, silver gray of the sage, dusty olive of the greasewood, mellow chartreuse of the bankside willows, flaring purple and saffron of the prickly-pear cactus blossoms, and the rare golden haze of the night-blooming stickleaf thistle.

Kelly rode on, entranced. The miles, with their weird and wonderful markers, fell silently behind. There was first the eight-foot-wide, scalding-steamed channel of a boiling hot river. Then, the roaring hundred-and-fifty-foot plunge of the Gardner over a falls where dozens of osprey eagles wheeled and screamed.

Next, the dizzying two-mile rampart of Sheepeater Cliffs, where the Indian tribe of the same name had reputedly lived in ancient times. And westward, the sky-high, unbelievable steam clouds hanging over some nearby and immense hot springs. There was literally no end to these continuing wonders. But the peculiar suspended stillness of the Park, that strange sense of God's great quiet which no Yellowstone visitor ever forgets, was once more getting to Kelly.

As early afternoon set in, his dark eyes left the trail ahead less and less frequently.

He became abstractly absorbed in Sayapi's track line.

A restless depression began to grow upon him, a feeling of premonition not warranted by the sparkling sunlight and cedar-scented air bathing the tranquil Gardner game trail and the clear-cut Sioux pony prints.

Shortly after one o'clock, Spotted Eagle halted of his own accord. He stood flicking his coarse ears first west, then north, then south, his pale eyes walling to follow their changing point.

Kelly let his own puzzled gaze join that of the wise little Appaloosa. The Nez Percé pony was right. There was indeed a matter of direction to be guessed at, of decision to be gambled upon.

They were at a blind crossroads.

In from the right at this juncture, running due north and south to cross the Gardner where it left Sheepeater Canyon, came a well-marked Indian trail, no doubt an important division of the Great Trail itself. From its bisection of this trail, the river bent sharply northwest to begin its last steep climb into old Johnson Gardner's Hole.

Kelly gritted his teeth, took down the glasses which he had unslung and focused but the moment before. As far as he could scan along both the Gardner's Hole track and the north-south Indian path, the surface of both trails lay across dry bare rock. A herd of ironshod elephants could have taken either route and the best tracker in the world could not have told you which way they had gone. Not, at least, without wasting precious, perhaps irretrievable time, running out all three options.

At the point of giving Spotted Eagle the knee and leaving the choice of trails to his Indian-bred instinct, Kelly straightened suddenly in the saddle.

Flat and many-echoed with altitude and intervening rough terrain as it was, the distant sound was nonetheless as familiar to him as the tone of his own voice. Its origin was equally clear and identifiable.

That rifle shot had come from a new model .50-caliber Springfield trap-loader, fired not over five miles to the Northwest. *Sayapi's gun!* The Lord be praised. The Sioux had gone on across the Indian trail, up the Gardner!

There could also be, Kelly told himself excitedly, but one interpretation put upon the fact the fleeing Indian youth would chance his shot being heard by his white pursuer. His supplies must have given out in some way—most likely lost in a river crossing—forcing him to kill game to keep going. Now, with proper care, a man had him. He had him right where he wanted him. Position located. Distance known. Direction definite. All he had to do was go and get him!

He nodded to himself, spoke to Spotted Eagle, sent the little Appaloosa across the Indian trail.

There was still an hour of good shooting daylight remaining when Kelly topped out on the low pass which dropped the river trail into Gardner's Hole. It was high up here, a good thousand feet higher than where the Gardner had come out of Sheepeater Canyon to cross the Indian branch trail. Where he sat, up there in the notch, it would have to be well over seven thousand feet. Yet, nevertheless, the sun was already gone behind the Gallatins, shielded thus early even from this elevated vantage point by the ten-thousand-foot upthrusts of a set of huge twin peaks immediately to the west.

Below him the Hole spread in all its staggering immensity, running from a long ridge to the east between him and an unnamed peak, westerly to the base of the Gallatins. To his right lay a beautiful large lake he could not place in his memory of the Park Expedition's charts. To his left lay two smaller lakes, completely uncharted. And everywhere the delighted eye might reach was the bright running water and waving blue-green mountain grass of Gardner's three-forked upper drainage basin.

The Hole was alive with grazing game.

Mule deer, pronghorn antelope, moose, bighorn sheep, wapiti, and buffalo all came under the passing turn of Kelly's glasses in their first thirty-second sweep of the great sunken pasture below him.

Surely it was a sight to let a man die happy, having seen. And which he could know not over fifteen or twenty other lone white wanderers had gazed upon before him.

Suddenly, Kelly froze the glasses, all thoughts of living game driven from his mind.

Down there, a mile out across the floor of the Hole, near the yellow sand beach of the smaller of the two lakes, the buzzards were circling. Below their wheeling arc lay what he sought— Sayapi's kill.

It was a big, long-yearling buffalo calf, a bull to judge from the dark head curls and light cape beginning to show their rich contrast. It lay back-to to Kelly's vantage point, so that all he could see of it was that the hump ribs had been hacked out. As to why the buzzards were not down upon it long ago—it had been all of four hours since he heard the shot—a man was left with two guesses.

Sayapi was ambushed somewhere down there covering the kill, visible to the vultures but not to Kelly. Either that, or the Sioux youth had risked lingering at the kill to eat and rest, had gone on only now, perhaps bare minutes before Kelly's arrival.

Of the two ideas, the first was palpably impossible.

There was not within one hundred yards of the slaughtered bull a solitary stick nor upthrust stone large enough to hide a five-year-old boy with a blunt-arrowed rabbit bow. Let alone to screen a six-foot buck with a Pony Soldier Springfield. And by Plains

Indian ambush standards, one hundred yards did not constitute anywhere near a proper wikmunke.

If you were a Sioux setting a trap for a white foe of Lone Wolf Kelly's rifle-handling abilities, you simply did not take hundred-yard chances. Ten yards, yes. Fifteen, maybe. Five preferably. Never over twenty. Otherwise, you were gambling on giving the second shot to a man who had already—in Sayapi's case—shown you he could knock a gun out of your hands at seventy feet firing from the hip.

No, Sayapi was not laid up down there covering that kill. Your second guess was the right one and, depending on how fresh you found his pony tracks when you got down there, might put you anywhere from twenty minutes to a short hour behind him. Kelly nodded to himself, grunted to Spotted Eagle. Ten minutes later the little horse had him down out of the pass gap, across the Hole meadow, and up to the stiffening carcass of the dead bull.

He swung down, letting the Appaloosa's reins slide.

Moving toward the bull, he kept Antelope Boy's Spencer hipped and on the cock. There was always the crazy chance that Sayapi was hidden behind the big body. His pony tracks led on past it, around the sandy shore of the little lake. But he could always have taken the ponies on, hidden them and Crow Girl in the stand of red cedars at the head of the lake, come back across the grass afoot, and lain up behind the young bull. Stretchy as the idea was, Kelly heeded it. Nothing was too quirky for Gall's hotheaded nephew.

But Sayapi was not behind the buffalo.

When Kelly moved cautiously around the huge black-bearded head, the ground beyond the sprawling brute was innocent of any foreign tenant, save the flyblown pile of viscera Sayapi had pulled out of the bull to get the liver.

Kelly relaxed with an audible sigh. Propping the Spencer

against one of the bull's up-hooked black horns, he turned to find a ground-stone upon which to whet his skinning knife. He was six or seven days sick of rancid pemmican, and where Sayapi had taken the hump ribs and liver, he had thoughtfully left the tongue, and a man could not ask for any better fare than—

It was then that Kelly's narrowing eyes noticed that Sayapi had *not* taken the liver. It was lying right there under a thick loop of intestine, not a foot from the whetstone rock for which his suspended hand was reaching. In the same second, he heard the little noise behind him and saw, above him, the sudden flare of the circling buzzards. He spun around in time to see Sayapi, slimed from head to foot with stringing buffalo innards, rise up and out of the disemboweled belly of the yearling bull.

"Hohahe!" barked the tall Hunkpapa youth. And closed the blood-smeared crook of his forefinger around the trigger of his Springfield trap-loader.

As Sayapi's fingers pressed inward, Kelly's were not the only eyes which went wide. The young brave's did too.

There would have been no normal chance to escape the murderous pointblank blast. The muzzle of the Springfield, as Sayapi stepped from his ambush in the buffalo's carcass, was no more than four feet from the white scout's face. Kelly should, by all honest rights of superior stalking craft, have been dead in the next half breath.

Instead, he got a reprieve and a second chance all in the same following moment of futile sound—the leaden, plunking, lifeless snap of a released firing pin biting into a bad round. Ensued, the little percussion-cap "pip" of the primer discharging without igniting the defective powder-load. Then, the weak fizzling run and muffled "chock" of the barely released bullet lodging midway in the barrel, the delayed compressive whiff of acrid gray smoke leaking from the locked breech—and, finally, *dead silence.*

Sayapi's brand-new Pony Soldier carbine and its handsome brass cartridge had malfunctioned in a grimly prophetic rehearsal of the same weapon's and its issued ammunition's coming failure to perform in the far more famous scene so soon to be played out on the banks of the Little Big Horn.

The dreaded, sickening "pip" of the misfire was as acutely familiar to Kelly as to any man alive. It was a sound which could mean life or death, depending on how fast one reacted upon hearing it.

Kelly struck back with the reflex speed of a prowling silvertip, surprised at a blind turn on a one-way mountain ledge and knowing instinctively he had but one way to go. He came up out of his half-crouched turn as he drove in under the plugged barrel of Sayapi's carbine. The Sioux, recovering an eye flick later, reversed the weapon to drive its ironshod butt into the charging white man's face.

But, save with the knife, the North Plains Indian was never the frontiersman's equal at infighting. Particularly and obstinately did he fail and refuse to understand that the clenched fist can be a deadly weapon.

For the second time in ten days, Kelly's hard-knuckled right hand smashed into Sayapi.

This time, however, it could not be to the jaw and did not end the encounter. It only caught the powerful young Sioux giant in the ribs, breaking three of them, exploding the breath out of him, and forcing him to drop the Springfield. Growlingly, he went for his knife, flashing it out of its sheath, whipping it back for an undercutting drive into his enemy's unprotected belly. But as the glittering blade hesitated at the outer limit of its backswing, Kelly's knee, blunt and brutal as a splitting maul, drove up and into the snarling Sayapi's loin cloth.

Strangling with pain, the Sioux youth clutched instinctively at the bursting torture in his groins. The forgotten blade fell from his spasming hand, his tall body jackknifing forward in uncontrollable agony as it did. Kelly caught him coming in with a hooking left to the mouth, the jolting blow straightening his head for the crushing right hand which followed instantly and flush upon the jaw.

At this point the mortal memories of Sayapi, Red Paint, youngest of the hostile Sioux subchiefs, beloved chosen nephew of Gall, war chief of all the Hunkpapa—ceased.

He died as quietly as had Antelope Boy before him and by the same merciful method—the bullet placed carefully just behind the left ear. But he did not die as well. Looking down upon his slowly relaxing form, the flat echo of the Spencer's single shot still slatting off across the surrounding ridges, Luther Kelly grimaced bitterly and turned away.

There was no peace upon Sayapi's handsome face in death, as there had been none within his wild heart, in life.

30

The next two weeks began as a dream and ended as a nightmare for Kelly.

He found Crow Girl bound and gagged but otherwise unharmed, hidden in the cedar grove at the head of the lake. There also he found Phineas. And, upon the scarred pommel of Sayapi's saddle, he found the knotted red grotesquerie which had once been Big Anse Harper's hair.

The latter discovery put a cruel curb upon the joys of the reunion. Even while his sobbing Absaroka mate was still kissing and clinging to him, Kelly's dark eyes were staring over her trembling shoulder, his black brows painfully knit in deep hurt and despair.

He had found his beloved, but at what cost!

Big Anse was horribly dead, butchered alive by Sayapi and his renegade band, sent to his Sioux slaughterers like a big dumb faithful ox by Kelly's own thoughtless selfishness. And worse, far worse than that. His brave death had been in pitiful vain. The message he carried for Kelly—perhaps an empty warning, perhaps a true alarm which might save uncounted soldier lives—had failed to reach the white troops. As a result, with his Crow love just returned to him and what should have been a time of great happiness ahead, Kelly was faced with a decision which could have but one answer. An answer which could mean nothing but misery to the slender child-mother in his arms.

There might still be time to reach some troop commander in the field between Fort Buford and the Big Horn. While there was any shred of reasonable chance to do that, or, failing that, to go on to the fort itself, any white man's instant duty was clear.

He tried in vain to explain his need to Crow Girl. The latter's unwaveringly hostile Indian viewpoint had not been weakened by her ten days with the wild Hunkpapa. She was, if anything, more set than ever in her determination to despise all Wasicuns, save Lone Wolf Kelly. That would be Gall's influence, Kelly thought, filling her simple mind full of war talk and the endless list of woes brought unto the red man by the white. He knew his gray-eyed bride openly admired the great Hunkpapa. How much or to what extent this admiration had grown in the days just past, he could not know. But the very thought of it was enough to send a sickening wave of jealous anger through him. He fought the feeling down with difficulty, and its lingering suspicion was not wholly destroyed at that. Yet there was no time for personal concern. A man must go on the best way he knew.

Failing to make headway in his attempts at putting forward reasonably his moral need for reaching the Pony Soldiers, he bluntly asked Crow Girl if she had been in the Park before. She at once answered that she had, many times, and knew its every trail like a brother, or at least a cousin. He then asked her if she was aware of any shorter way to return to the branch trail than via the Gardner River route.

Again she replied that she did, although her affirmative

this time came only after an appreciable hesitation to check the northwest skies where an ominous bank of thunderheads had been building all day.

Kelly should have caught the little pause and the object of its study, but he did not.

He left off questioning Crow Girl at once, satisfied with her allegations. There was yet a little time before they had to go. Kelly wanted the most of that moment.

They camped that night by the unknown lake, both full-fed with fresh buffalo ribs and drowsily content with the fragrance of the cedar fire and the arm-locked hour of happiness borrowed against tomorrow's rude awakening. During the night the wind came up, driving the northwest cloud bank down over the Park.

Kelly slept nine hours, was up and packing Phineas with the misting five o'clock daylight. By six his little caravan, following Crow Girl on Gall's gray mare, was on the move up and out of Gardner's Hole.

The rain began in earnest an hour later. By eight o'clock Kit Carson himself could not have told north from south without a compass and some weatherproof matches to read it by. Shortly it became necessary to pass a picket rope between Crow Girl's mare and the Appaloosa stud. It was literally so dark and the rain so driving that Kelly could not see distinctly Crow Girl's small form ten feet in front of him.

It was as well that he could not. He would neither have liked nor understood the soft smile curving her full lips.

But despite his trusting blindness, Kelly was beginning to worry by nine o'clock. They were in a region of no timber and the most weirdly gigantic artemisia sagebrush he had ever seen. Where the average bush of this omnipresent western shrub seldom exceeded three feet in height, many of the surrounding specimens shot up to ten feet and the average was over the head of a mounted man. There was no other plant life in appreciable number, save the familiar white-flowered umbrellas of the wild buckwheat. It was utterly impossible to guess their direction, yet his repeated anxious queries to Crow Girl brought only further soft smiles and quick assurances that she knew exactly where she was going.

She did, too, but Kelly never realized it.

When they had not cut the Indian branch trail by ten o'clock, he suspected his tiny companion of whistling in the dark, at the very worst. By high noon, with the trail still unlocated, he was only sure she had been bravely bluffing and was in no way suspicious of any more devious motive. He thought simply that they should have found the north-south Indian trail two hours ago and that whether or not Crow Girl would bob her dear stubborn little head and admit it, she had lost them. It did not occur to him then, or at any later time, that his Indian sweetheart had deliberately led him astray.

It was not in Crow Girl's uncomplicated mind to think of her act as anything but natural. Kelly's concern with the Sioux gathering on the Greasy Grass meant less than nothing to her. All she knew was that her time was very near and that she did not want to have her baby in a Pony Soldier camp or at Fort Buford, where Kelly had said they would have to go if they did not find some of the mila hanska on the way there. It was further in her heart that this Land of the Smoking Waters was a sacred place and that any man-child born here would walk tall and strong and carry very big medicine for all of his life. It was in her heart, too, that she wanted Kelly to be with her when the little one came and to stay with her until journey's end in her Absaroka homeland.

In the whole of this civilization-shy Indian thinking, she was fatefully abetted by a high-country summer storm which is still remembered by a handful of ninety-year-oldsters on a certain Montana reservation to this day.

For thirteen days and nights, the sun was not seen over the Land of the Smoking Waters. The winds blew first hailstone cold, then silver-thaw warm. The remaining snowpack melted downward into the east-west draining rivers, rendering north-south travel impossible. And for thirteen days and nights, Luther Kelly wandered the flooded canyon and river trails of the drowned Park, now lost by reason of the rain's increasing torrent, now found by the deluge's slackening or momentary cessation—only to be lost again in its returning violence or trapped in its brief thinnings by the thundering streams and inundated lowlands he must cross to get north with his message to Fort Buford. As best he might have salved his tortured conscience with the unguent that such a tremendous storm would be pinning down the Sioux as surely as it was him. Meanwhile, history had it written otherwise. The freakish downpour was not falling east of Clark's Fork nor north of the Big Bend.

But on the morning of the fourteenth day, the sullen clouds broke away unexpectedly to show Kelly, immediately ahead of and below the dripping ridge upon which he sat the Appaloosa, the clean sun dancing on the unbelievably blue-green waters of an immense sheet of water which could only be the great headwaters lake of the Yellowstone itself.

An hour later he and Crow Girl had made camp on the lakeshore, hung out their molding blankets to cure in the hot breeze, and were themselves stretched naked upon the packed sands, letting the June 19 sun bake the bone-chill and trail-damp out of their aching, exhausted bodies.

They rested forty-eight hours, compelled to take the extra day and night not only by their own fatigue but by the poor condition of the ponies after two weeks of bloating, water-coarsened feed.

Repacking their sun-dried blankets on the morning of the second day, they started north along the lake toward the Yellowstone's seven-mile-distant outlet at about eight o'clock. A little over an hour later they reached the head of the lake. Here they came once more upon the Great Trail where it followed the west bank of the river northward. Another half hour and three miles along, they rounded a blind turn in the travois-rutted track and pulled their snorting ponies to a rearing halt.

Fifty yards ahead, their lathered mounts drawn up and blocking the trail from side to side, their expressionless silence so thick you could have sliced it with a stone tomahawk, waited Gall and two dozen picked Hunkpapa braves.

Kelly was thunderstruck.

He had completely dismissed the war chief the minute he had seen him gallop off down the Yellowstone in response to Crazy Horse's summons. Now, here he was in the Park, big as life and twice as ugly. *Wagh!* What a shock!

What in the Lord's good name could have happened to Tashunka's intention to hit Old Red Beard on the Rosebud before going into camp over on the Greasy Grass? It was impossible that the plan to bluff Three Stars out of the big fight could have been carried out so soon. Gall must have backed out to come looking for Sayapi and Crow Girl.

But for all his years along the Yellowstone, Kelly still had a little something to learn about what was impossible for High Plains hostiles.

It was June 21. On the 17th Gall and Crazy Horse had caught Crook starting up the Rosebud, and it had gone exactly as Tashunka had predicted.

Three Stars was driven clear back to his base camp and, for all his big Apache reputation, so badly scared that he refused to leave it again. He deliberately ignored the projected rendezvous with

Gibbon, Terry, and Custer, thereby insuring the latter's date with destiny. By the later admission of his own troopers, had it not been for the inspired fighting of Washakie and his Utah Shoshone scout corps, the Battle of the Rosebud would have been Crook's last command.

As it was, he was alive and would fight again.

Also as it was, Gall and twenty-four Hunkpapa friends had ridden from the Rosebud to Yellowstone Park in something like seventy-two hours, and were waiting now to have a little talk with Lone Wolf Kelly.

31

"Where is Sayapi?" asked Gall quietly.

"Dead," said Kelly, as quietly.

"You killed him?"

"Of course."

"Over the woman?"

"Why else?"

"Then you will fight for her."

"Have you ever thought otherwise?"

"No, your heart is strong."

There was a long pause during which the ponies shifted hips, pawed restlessly, shook out their hackamores.

Kelly had no idea where the conversation was leading but knew it was not aimless. Gall, unlike so many of his brother chiefs among the Sioux, was not enamored of his own voice. When he said something, you had better listen very hard.

"Well?" he demanded at length, unwilling to wait Gall out and impatient for his decision.

"Well," echoed the latter simply, "then I will fight you for her."

Kelly was taken completely aback. "You will *what?*" he gasped.

"Fight you for the Crow girl," repeated Gall patiently. Then softly shrugged. "Hinmangas, naturally."

Kelly was looking at Crow Girl when the Sioux chief added the sibilant qualification, and he saw the rich color drain away from her dark face. He remembered, too, the looks of fear on the faces of the Hunkpapa braves many moons before when their leader had threatened them with the word.

"Why hinmangas?" he asked, suddenly dry-throated.

"You know hinmangas? You have heard of it?"

"I have heard of it but do not know it. It is some sort of traditional duel, is it not? I understand the word itself means 'you and I tear at each other with a knife,' but that is all."

"You have noticed perhaps that it makes men uneasy to hear it spoken?"

"Yes. Why is that?"

"Because it is a duel of manhood. The loser is deprived of his male pride."

Kelly paled.

"That is a monstrous thing!" he declared angrily, his Christian mind and civilized mores revolted by the pagan thought. "It is a thing which is done to animals! An atrocious, barbaric thing!"

"Yes," agreed Gall, not unpleasantly and clearly serious. "It is indeed a drastic law. But can you think of a more effective way to settle permanently a question of disputed love between two men for the same woman?"

Again the white scout was stunned.

"Do you mean Crow Girl?" he cried unbelievingly. "That is impossible! Do you deny that she is already my true mate?"

"She was another's before she was yours."

"That is a lie! She told me she had not yet taken the ceremony of living outside and alone when you captured her."

"I believe that."

"Then what are you saying? Are you blind? Can you not see she is carrying my child? That she is happy to be with me and to stay with me?"

"Perhaps she was not unhappy with me," said Gall. "Why not ask her?"

Kelly looked around at Crow Girl, but to his amazement she dropped her eyes and would not look at him. He could not ask her then and got no later chance.

"But the child—" he resumed lamely with Gall.

"The child," rumbled the war chief, "is no more yours than it is mine. Has she not told you that it will be an Indian child, that she wishes to rear it as a Shacun?"

"Yes, yes, we have talked of that and agreed. But the child is mine! That I know."

Gall shook his head regretfully, and Kelly, for all his own confused excitement, could not help but note the shadow of sadness which passed over the great warrior's face. "Let us say no more about it, my brother. We shall fight for her, hinmangas. That is all. Nohetto."

When Gall said nohetto, that was truly the end to the matter. The grim preparation for the manhood duel over H'tayetu Hopa, the gray-eyed child squaw of the Absaroka, went forward with deadly quietness.

While others of the braves were marking out a twenty-five-foot circle in the dust of the Great Trail, Frog Belly came over to Kelly and explained to him the rules of the Hunkpapa hinmangas. They were short, sinister, uncomplicated.

A single ceremonial knife was driven to the hilt into the ground in the middle of the circle. The contestants were stripped to their breechclouts, placed facing each other on opposite edges of the circle, the knife exactly between them. At a given signal and with the starting word, hopo, the fight was on. The entire simple idea was to get to the knife yourself or to keep your opponent from getting it.

Once possession of the knife was gamed by one of the fighters, the duel's motif became a little less basic, far more artistic. The purpose of the knife-wielder then was to weaken and wear down his adversary by a classic, difficult series of minor wounds to the point where he could be brought to a weaving, helpless stand or fixed in any other posture of defenseless exhaustion for delivery of the inhuman hinmangas coup de grace; the entire mold and intent of the skilled passage being precisely the same as the matador's in debilitating the bull with cape and dart before placing him for the moment of truth with the espada.

The unarmed fighter could use any ruse or tactic, while staying inside the circle, to wrest from his enemy the vital knife. Yet if either fighter mortally wounded the other with it, rather than using it in the traditional method of literally "cutting the other to ribbons" without killing him, then that fighter himself must face the death penalty from the duel's impartial judges. It was a necessary safeguard, Frog Belly explained seriously, to assure a classic hinmangas and not a common ordinary knife fight. It made the duelers honest, put them to their best and most artful efforts, guaranteed the impartial ends of hinmangas justice being served in place of any personal vengeance.

With a bobtailed nod and half a dozen eloquent Sioux grunts, Kelly signified that all this was clear to him. All clear, that was, up to the point where the victor had possession of the knife and the vanquished was fixed and helpless, waiting for the unspeakable climax. *What happened then?* What about the "manhood" part of the thing?

Frog Belly looked puzzled for a moment, then brightened.

Eh? What was that Lone Wolf wanted to know?

Oh, yes, the manhood part. One almost forgets that. It is

merely a matter of form after the real fight. Like paying a gambling debt after a pony race. Nothing more. Six or eight braves hold the loser down while the winner uses the knife on him. And in that respect, Lone Wolf was going to be especially fortunate. Gall had expected to fight Sayapi hinmangas for stealing the girl again. So he had brought along the medicine kit to seal the wound after the cutting.

Lone Wolf could surely see, the fat brave concluded, that the way it was fought, the hinmangas was essentially a contest of animal strength without the artificial equality of weapons; a mating battle between rival human males, based on bone and muscle and primeval brute cunning—as of course such a thing should be.

Kelly looked at Frog Belly, his dark face pale but composed. He shook his head, level black brows contracting in helpless, angry repugnance.

"It is a heathen, wicked, inhuman thing," he said, white-lipped. "God forgive me my part in it …"

They faced each other across the circle, crouched motionless as two carved marble statues awaiting only the touch of the magic word to spring them into animate, terrible life. Off to one side, Black Fox held the plummet of eagle feathers fastened to a small stone, which he would drop to the ground with the starting word. Meanwhile, the combatants had to watch him while at the same time watching both each other and the all-important knife.

The Hunkpapa braves stood ranked behind their chief, adding their hostile, slant stares to his. On the edge of the circle opposite Black Fox, Frog Belly now stood guard over Crow Girl. The tiny Absaroka squaw was huddled down beside a large boulder, trembling hands covering her face, thin shoulders racked repeatedly by the convulsive nerve shudders she could not repress. Kelly looked at her again and again—pleading, demanding, desperate looks, begging unashamedly for acknowledgment and return of the deep love he bore her. But there was something beyond understandable nerves wrong with Crow Girl. She would not look at her erstwhile white lover. Either she did not see his silent entreaties, or she was deliberately refusing to admit that she did. Kelly called out to her, urgently, compellingly. She did not answer him or even indicate that she had heard him. Yet he *knew* she had. His heart turned and writhed within him. He grew literally sick with the hurt of the rejection and the jealous fear of its meaning in relation to Gall's dramatic reappearance. Perhaps it was a blessing that he had not followed the war chief's quiet advice to ask the girl how she felt about being with him and the wild Hunkpapa, compared to walking with Kelly in the white man's way. Perhaps it was—

But the time for such torturing doubts was suddenly run out.

Across from the sobbing Absaroka girl, Black Fox was raising aloft the lean hand which held the starting token. In the little moment remaining now, a man would never find out the answer to the questionable loyalty of Crow Girl's love. And he had better forget about trying. Kelly made a wordless, deep-hurt sound. He tore his eyes from his Indian mate's slender form, swung them, narrowed and glittering, back upon Gall his mind cleared and concentrating upon but one thought—the hinmangas.

He had no idea whatever how this brutal duel would be best fought by one such as himself, completely unfamiliar with its traditional techniques. But its rules held one apparent hope— *anything went, so long as you stayed inside the circle.* If that were true, it gave him a chance. A lone, lethal, long-odds chance to be sure. But a chance.

It was simply to keep Gall from ever getting his hands on the knife: to gain and retain possession of the terrain which held the blade, beating the Hunkpapa to death or into utter senselessness as he strove to come to it. That way—

"Hopi!" shouted Black Fox, and dropped the eagle-feather plummet.

The order, for all his nerve-strung anticipation, caught Kelly unready. His crouched limbs uncoiled smoothly but a fraction of a second slower than Gall's. The Sioux chief had hurled his powerful body across the intervening space and seized the knife's protruding haft a full second before the white scout's delayed leap carried his lean form to the center of the ring.

But the lethal blade never left the ground.

Gall's hand was still on its haft when Kelly's cruelly malleted fist came down between his tensed shoulder blades with a blow that would have separated the vertebrae of an Oregon Trail ox. Yet all it brought from Gall was a surprised grunt, a stubborn headshake, a momentary reflex slackening of his grip on the knife. Kelly asked no more.

The bottom of his bare foot, callused into a sole of oaken density by eight years of western wilderness trails, smashed into the side of Gall's huge neck with the force of a hand-swung fence post.

The Sioux chief was driven bodily back away from the knife, face down into the dirt beyond it.

Kelly did not follow his advantage. He did not dare to.

He was afraid to get within hand's reach of the Hunkpapa Hercules and was forced to let him regain his feet unmolested. Gall did so, to find his adversary waiting for him, feet widespread over the contested knife. Followed a five-second lull—a brief moment's silent checkmate while the fighters looked again and more carefully at one another.

What Gall saw was encouraging. Lone Wolf, in the naked flesh, was a strong man. He had very long arms, big hands, a good flat belly and shoulders so wide they made him look deformed.

But even for that, he was not nearly as strong or big or experienced a man as Gall. *Waste*, it was a good thing.

What Luther Kelly saw was demoralizing.

Gall, though not as tall as his nephew, was a tall man. He may have been just over six feet, Kelly thought, and built like a burnished dark bronze reproduction of the drawing he could remember in his geography book of the black African Congo gorilla. Thick legs short and bowed, trunk long, heavy, flat-torsoed, chest broad and deep, shoulders and arms enormously boned and muscled; he was a tremendous man, weighing at least thirty pounds more than Kelly's lean, dry one hundred sixty-five and moving every ounce of that awesome physique with the deceptive celerity of a ninety-pound prima ballerina.

But the fleeting instant of mutual assay was past.

The die of the contest was irrevocably cast in its first movement. It was to be the skilled white boxer against the immensely strong Indian wrestler. At stake was a grisly trophy. Dearer than a scalp, if not so deadly. A trophy which would not cost the vanquished his life but would only make him wish that it had. Gall came back for Kelly like a hurled buffalo lance. He left his feet at the last moment, throwing a vicious savate kick at the latter's head. Missing their intended mark, his murderous feet slashed into the Irish scout's chest, ripping open the white skin and red flesh to the rib-ends of the prosternum and knocking him flat upon his back.

He recovered his feet barely in time to drive Gall away from the knife with a crushing series of lefts and rights into the bones of the face. Gall did not go down but staggered backward, allowing Kelly once more to take foot-spread possession of the precious ground over the hinmangas knife.

Again and again Gall came in.

Again and again Kelly's slashing fists drove him back.

They fought without a sound or more than ten seconds

surcease for thirty-five minutes, and when that time was gone, Gall was down on his face in the dirt, and Kelly sagged to his knees over the unremoved knife.

The white man's hands and the Hunkpapa's face were alike broken and bloodied beyond human recognition. The Sioux could scarcely see, the scout barely move. It seemed, then, that the fight was over and sheer animal exhaustion the only winner. Yet in that last moment, Gall tottered once more to his feet, groped stumblingly forward toward Kelly.

The latter tried to get up and could not. Gall's reaching hands found him. Gathered him up. Raised him high overhead. Flung him down and away and into the sodden ground. He fell with the jarring, loose-limbed laxness from which there is no further rising.

Gall, swaying, fumbled for the knife, found it, drew it from the trampled earth.

He felt with his feet painfully along the ground until he found Kelly's sprawled body. Behind him there was no sound from his followers. No man moved to help him. There was no need. Lone Wolf would not require any holding.

Gall stood over him with the knife, staring blindly down. He stood like that a long, quiet time.

And then he did a thing unheard of in all the legend and tradition of the hinmangas manhood duel.

With his last strength, he threw the knife far out and away from him, into the passing current of the Yellowstone. He touched the fingertips of his left hand to his blood-caked forehead, waving them weakly downward toward Kelly. "Woyuonihan!" he croaked hoarsely. And, turning away from the motionless body of his enemy, took two faltering steps and pitched forward, unconscious, into the puddled dust of the Great Trail.

BOOK FIVE
TONGUE RIVER

32

When Kelly came awake, the sun was standing straight overhead.

The stillness of the mountain midday lay like a fragrant benediction over the drying red and yellow earth, pungent meadow grasses, and tall dark cedars. The puzzled scout let his eyes study his surroundings, holding his head motionless after his ingrained Indian habit. Presently, it came to him where he was and how he had gotten there, and that the Sioux who had left him there were gone. He made no effort to move with the discovery.

He was still lying flat on his back where Gall had flung him. It felt quite warm and pleasant there in the centuries-old dust of the Great Trail. Behind him the murmuring splash of the Yellowstone was a compelling sedative. All about him the bright twitter and whistle of the Park's songbirds bubbled through the clear champagne of the June sunlight. Nowhere in this peaceful summer noontime was there any least hint of human urgency for Luther Kelly. Then he tried to move.

Instantly, his wandering mind leaped back to reality.

He sat up, the effort bringing a stifled cry as the pain it induced knifed through his dorsal muscles. Gritting his teeth, he rolled to his hands and knees, staggered to his feet. He stood a moment, swaying.

His legs were all right. His hands would heal. But the pain in his back was enormous. Every movement shot a wave of sickening hurt from sacrum to shoulder blades. He refused the dread thought of a spinal fracture. Forced himself to move, told himself that only time and tooth-set trial could say whether the injury was muscular or vertebral. The thought of what tortures might lie ahead made him wince with its direct reminder of his present strange escape from the grim disfigurement usually meted out to the loser in hinmangas.

Why had Gall spared him? Why had the Sioux band left so soon? How long had they been gone? In which direction? At what pace? Toward what destination?

These answers lay in the downstream line of departing Hunkpapa pony tracks or might lie there if a man were purely lucky. Starting to limp toward the Sioux pony sign, Kelly was startled to hear behind him a familiar high-pitched mustang whistle. Turning painfully, he was astonished to see, watching him curiously from across the Yellowstone, the outlandish, flop-eared figure of Spotted Eagle. Now, by thunder! This passed belief. But a man in Kelly's moccasins was in no position to deny a gift horse.

At first he was only glad to see the friendly little Nez Percé scrub, as a man would be glad to have a faithful lost dog turn up unexpectedly. Then his awakening brain began to work.

The Appaloosa was barebacked and bridleless, his saddle, headstall, and Kelly's precious Winchester stripped from him by the voracious Sioux. But from his stringy neck dangled a shred of frayed Hunkpapa horsehair rope, and there was your suddenly hopeful clue. Add to it the fact Spotted Eagle was on the other side of the river and you might have the story of the Sioux retreat.

If you did, it would read close to this:

Somewhere downstream between you and the heading of the Yellowstone's grand canyon was an Indian crossing not shown on the white charts of the Park. From that crossing, undoubtedly, led a northeast Indian trail which had allowed Gall to get into and out of the Park despite the high water. Naturally, your only proof of this was the hank of Sioux rope on Spotted Eagle's scrawny neck. But if the little Appaloosa stud had not broken indignantly away from being led off by some rough-handed Hunkpapa buck and made his way back upstream to the gentle white master who had replaced Antelope Boy in his dumb brute heart, Luther Kelly had completely lost his touch for interpreting telltale Indian signs.

The fact the homely rascal was across the river proved he had been taken across. That in turn established beyond doubt where the Hunkpapa had gone, and let a man know, as quickly, where he must follow.

Gall was across the Yellowstone heading for the Little Big Horn.

He traveled slowly and under great pain at first, his course taking him down the west bank toward the distant booming roar of the Fourth Canyon's upper and lower falls. Spotted Eagle, whickering querulously, kept pace with him along the far shore. Gradually, as he forced himself, his hurt back began to loosen. By the time he found the Sioux crossing several miles north, he was trotting a little.

The Indian ford was created by the nearly twin junctures of opposing streams coming in from the east and west. The cross currents of these tributaries had created a submerged half-moon sandbar from bank to bank, quieting the river above and making the crossing safe for a strong swimmer even in high water. Kelly plunged in without hesitation.

Minutes later he was clambering out on the east bank, calling to Spotted Eagle who was watching him from a grassy rise above with intent interest. When he whistled and waved him in, the little stud whickered happily, slid down the bank, trotted up to him arch-necked and proud of himself as a pomponned circus pony.

Kelly laughed at him, then gave him a bear-hug squeeze of welcome, swung up on him, and gave him the heel. They cut the emerging Sioux trail a hundred yards north. Kelly studied it a moment, nodded, pressed the Appaloosa with his right knee to turn him along it. The little horse snorted his understanding, took out along the Hunkpapa pony tracks, due northeast.

The Irish scout's long gamble against beating Gall back to the Big Horn was on.

If he could short-cut the distance to the goal—any major troop concentration moving on the Little Horn would most likely be coming up the Big Horn—he might yet have time to turn in his warning about the trap on the Greasy Grass. In any event, one thing was as sure as the fact that every stride the little stud took was grinding his rider's teeth with back-pain: if it cracked every vertebra in his ailing spine and broke every blood vessel in Spotted Eagle's stout heart, he and that little Appaloosa studhorse were going to give Gall a run for his red money.

They left Yellowstone behind with twilight of that first day. The trail, going east by north across the high country of Mirror Plateau, was a good one. Crossing the Lamar River at its Soda Butte Creek fork, it followed the latter stream up Ice Box Canyon and out the northeast corner of the Park between Mineral and Amphitheater Mountains. But after that, time became meaningless, the trail murderous.

Day and night were as one. Rest was taken when it had to be, without regard to darkness or daylight. Water and grass for the Nez Percé pony came in the same harsh category. Of food for his broad-jawed rider, there was none. When the horse was fed and rested, the man went on, that was all.

By the third night, Kelly was becoming confused.

The Hunkpapa trail began to fade on hardening ground, and in the darkness and drainage of a hard thundershower, he lost it altogether.

After sunup the fourth morning, he traveled by the snow-crowned compass of the Big Horns' ragged peaks. Weak from hunger and heat fatigue, half-crazed by the pain in his grating spine, he was talking to himself by the fifth night. But it showered again shortly after dark, turning the night cool and returning reason to his tiring mind.

The following morning fortunately continued cool. Kelly drove the Appaloosa on without mercy, carried forward now by that last bright burst of clearheaded strength which immediately precedes final collapse.

As midday approached he began to pick out familiar landmarks—a patriarchal tree here, a bizarre rock there, a particular rising climb of prairie, a certain lay of high tableland, a fall-off of drainage slope to valley below, and the like. In another hour he knew where he was and an hour after that he rode the staggering Spotted Eagle squarely into an advancing scout patrol of General Alfred H. "Star" Terry's command coming up the lower valley of the Little Horn from its previous night's bivouac on the banks of the Big Horn twenty-five miles above its junction with the Yellowstone.

The startled patrol sergeant sent the heavy-bearded, staring-eyed apparition back down valley with a mounted trooper on either side to hold him on his wind-broken horse. Half an hour later, Kelly was confronting Terry and his unshaven staff, his cracked lips forcing out the story of Sitting Bull's big-medicine dream of a great wikmunke of mila hanskas along the Greasy Grass.

The weary officers heard him through in stony-eyed silence.

When he was done, they bit their lips and turned away.

It was two p.m., June 26, 1876.

Twenty-four hours earlier on the barren treeless slopes above the Miniconjou Ford of the Little Big Horn River, the last of Lieutenant Colonel George Armstrong Custer's gallant Seventh Cavalry had been martyred to the dashing "boy general's" incredible military ignorance and political ambition.

The next two months were the hardest, most dangerous in Luther Kelly's life, calling for the expenditure of every last ounce of physical endurance, tracking skill, hunting prowess, and Indian scouting ability at his command. Yet in the end, he had to admit the wily Sioux had dealt him a defeat as crushing and total, if not as fatal, as Custer's.

For sixty-one days he followed Gall and the Hunkpapa of Sitting Bull. In a classic of plains scouting not surpassed by Bridger, Carson, Meeker, Smith, or any of the earlier mountain immortals, he hung on the trail of the moving Sioux from the first mile of their flight from the Seventh Cavalry's tragedy toward the Big Horn Mountains to the last somber days of that 1876 summer when Sitting Bull knew beyond final doubt that the hour of his people grew short.

For nearly the whole of that time, Gall knew he was being followed and strove constantly to ambush his white shadow. Yet so wary was Kelly and so determined that this time he would not be denied Crow Girl short of death, that in the entire eight weeks of his herculean hunt, not one hostile Sioux came within rifle shot of him. More than that, he went the whole time without seeing or speaking to a fellow white man, making all his few contacts for food and information with the chance bands of friendlies who were in part trying to emulate his own course—avoiding the post-Custer hostiles with which the tributary valleys of the Yellowstone were literally acrawl through these desperate days of July and August.

Still, at the end of that time, Kelly was no nearer Crow Girl than he had been at its beginning.

No chance had developed for him to even get close enough to the Hunkpapa camp to so much as see her, so watchfully had Gall kept his flankers out along the backtrail of the retreating band.

Thus, it was that the most the Irish scout received for his perilous sixty days in the Sioux wilderness was a detailed addition to his former knowledge of the unexplored lands north of the Yellowstone. These were the same lands which history, even at that moment, was leading George Crook's erudite adjutant, John Bourke, to label terra incognita. And they were the same lands whose blankness on the existing military maps was at that identical August hour causing Colonel Nelson A. Miles to dispatch up and down the river his historic summons for Luther Kelly to join him in his camp on the banks of the Yellowstone at the mouth of Tongue River.

Thus it was, also, that on the murky hot morning of August 25, the latter, coming back down the Big Dry Creek Range from below Fort Peck on the Missouri, having lost the village trail of Sitting Bull's and Gall's band twenty-four hours before in the charred ash and clotting smoke of an Indian-lit prairie backfire, rode his little Appaloosa stud up out of a blind draw to collide, dead on, with a disreputable old friend from his Fort Buford days.

"Liver-eating" Johnson was in that era and place as celebrated a sobriquet as "Yellowstone" Kelly. And it was so largely for the same reasons of its owner having successfully kept his long hair from being shortened while poaching the sacred game preserves of the Hunkpapa and Oglala Sioux. Thereafter, however, all resemblance between the two delighted white scouts ceased. While they "howdied and shook" and slapped one another thunderously on the back, a hidden observer would have found it difficult to believe they followed the same profession.

To match the Irish scout's clean-shaven chin, carefully trimmed mustache, and respectable buckskins (albeit they were torn, faded, and alkali-stained now), Johnson presented a picture from another day and time.

Ragged leather shirt and leggins unbeaded and black with the grease and soot of a thousand cook fires, wild hair frizzled and sun-faded, unkempt beard dirtied by chaw spittle, tobacco-ruined teeth rotted to the gum-line, illiterate, unwashed, profane, roving-eyed, raucous; he was the remaining classic chromo of the last of the Big Horn beaver trappers.

But it was not the way his friend looked, nor his raw language, nor even his gamy odor downwind, which unhinged Kelly's jaw. *It was what he had to say.* And what he had to say brought to Kelly a suddenly leaping new hope to replace the waning one which had just died out in the ashes of the Hunkpapa grass fire.

But Liver-eating made him wait.

First off, knowing the hunger of a lone white man long weeks away from the river for news of his fellows, he brought him up to date on the general situation.

The army had just sent Crook a new commander from clean down to Fort Leavenworth in Kansas, Johnson began. This latter was only a full colonel, but he had hell's own reputation as an Indian fighter. Kelly would likely recall having heard of him. Fellow named Miles. Nelson A. Miles. Same Miles that had knocked the liver and lights out of the Comanches down south in '74.

Well, anyways, Liver-eating went on, this Miles' orders were to "set on" the hostiles that had "done for" idiot-child Custer over on the Greasy Grass. He had been campaigning with Crook and Terry the past weeks getting the "feel of things," mostly down around the Rosebud, Tongue, and Powder. Then Crook had been sent on southeast into the Black Hills, virtually out of the

Sioux campaign, and a couple of important things had happened. Just before old "Three Stars" pulled out, General Wesley Merritt had broken up a big Cheyenne column moving out from Camp Robinson to hook up with Sitting Bull, weakening the Hunkpapa plans aplenty. Then that young heller Anson Mills had caught poor old American Horse trying to join his Oglala up with Crazy Horse's and had completely routed them, killing American Horse and cutting the Oglala strength in half before the big fight ever got started.

Miles and Terry had then marched north to the Big Dry and right back south to Glendive Creek on the Yellowstone. Here Terry had loaded his boys on the *Far West* and four other steamers and "gone south for good," leaving Miles' Fifth Infantry with orders to "build a cantonment on the Yellowstone and occupy the country during the coming winter."

But it looked as though "Bear Coat," as the Sioux called Miles, had other ideas than just "occupying" the country.

He wanted to go after the Indians and reckoned he had a ring-tailed good chance to catch up with them and give them a little northern dose of Palo Duro and Adobe Walls. There was just the one little hitch. None of his scout staff knew the Yellowstone country well enough to shag hostiles through it with the snow up to a tall horse's belly and the mercury stuck in the bulb at sixty below.

At that point, Liver-eating claimed proudly, he himself had thought of "Old Yellowstone."

It was what came then that dropped Kelly's jaw.

Miles wanted him to come in and talk about taking over his scouts and guiding the command after Custer's killers in a full-dress winter campaign the likes of which had never before been planned or put on by white troops in Montana or Dakota Territories.

It developed, via Liver-eating's excited insistence, that this was not a mere suggestion. It was a concrete offer. With no strings whatever tied onto it.

All Kelly had to do, apparently, was go see Miles.

After that it would be squarely up to him whether he kept on chasing the Hunkpapa all by his lonesome, or gave in and let the US Army back him up with somewhere around six hundred Comanche-trained troops of the Fifth and the Twenty-Second Infantry.

Having delivered himself of the Colonel's "gelded edge" invitation, Johnson eased back in his saddle to await his companion's reaction. He did not get eased very far back. The Irish scout took less than ten seconds to reach his decision. After that, they both "got down and sat a spell," risking a fire to boil up a fresh can of coffee and bake a hasty batch of frying-pan bread, the first of either civilized delicacy Kelly had tasted since leaving Terry's column two months before. They then shook hands again and went their careful, separate ways.

It was well within the hour of his chance meeting with Liver-eating Johnson on the Big Dry Creek Fork of the Missouri that Yellowstone Kelly started south to keep his date with destiny and Colonel Nelson A. Miles on the south bank of the Yellowstone at the mouth of Tongue River in Montana Territory.

33

In his ride south, Kelly saw no Indians. He struck the Yellowstone in good time and without incident. Crossing over, he turned east for the few remaining miles to the Tongue cantonment.

A short while later, he heard several shots downstream.

Slowing Spotted Eagle, he went ahead with considerable caution. It was a favorite tactic of the Sioux to harass military construction crews. The gunfire could well mean the hostiles had some of Miles' wood or hay-cutting details pinned down and cut off from the main camp. This did not prove to be the case. However, the wary scout had good reason to be glad of his precautionary alertness.

Had he not been keyed up by the shots, it is very likely he would not have seen the bear in time. Even so, it was one of the closest scrapes a man would want to make light of in his memoirs.

He came around a sharp bend of dense bottom growth—in those days the Valley of the Yellowstone carried much cottonwood timber and willow brush along its rich alluvial meadowlands— the battered Winchester he had acquired from one of Terry's teamsters in trade for his famous fifty-dollar beaver hat poked out in front of him on full cock.

The bear, a tremendous cinnamon, the largest bear Kelly ever saw, including silvertips, came out of the blind brush not twenty feet ahead of him. He reared upright as he came, squealing in desperate hurt and anger. It was at once clear to Kelly he had been hit by the shots heard downstream. This deduction was blended by an act of natural fright on the part of Spotted Eagle, which very nearly killed the helpless scout before the bear could even attempt to do so.

At the first sight and sound of the cinnamon-colored monster, the little Appaloosa simply blew up. He went sideways, backwards, and up into the air all in the same moment of squalling terror.

Kelly came unglued from him about midway in the wild three-way pitch. He hit the soft dirt of the trail without injury and still something like ten feet away from the swaying cinnamon. The bear at once dropped back to all fours and came for him.

He had only one shot—a very bad one—skull-on and trying to center the little shoe-button eyes.

Kelly pressed the trigger, and the god who had not seemed to be much with him of late obliged by opening the monster's mouth as he did. The .44 slug plowed upward through the back of the exposed throat, blew away the base of the pale-colored brute's skull, dropped him stone-dead with his great outstretched right paw crashing like a felled pine across Kelly's chest.

He was still lying there, pinned down by the animal's enormous arm, when the two hunters who had wounded the bear (a pair of packers from Miles' camp) came thrashing up through the willows.

They at once rushed to Kelly's side and began pouring shot after shot into the dead beast.

Only faintly amused and fearing one of the bullets would find a livelier mark than listless bruin, the scout hastened to pour a little Irish oil on the brave nimrods' enthusiasm by assuring them that he was prepared to issue an affidavit over his legal signature of Luther S. Kelly that the poor animal was long since done for and that, furthermore, if they did not at once abate their violent attentions to same, he would be forced to fire back in self-defense.

The packers of course ceased their excited fire in the face of this fey objection and were hence able to clearly hear and understand Kelly's laconic self-identification.

"*Yellowstone* Kelly?" they gasped in unison. Then they answered their own query before he could accommodate in kind: "By God! It's him!"

Kelly agreed that it was and, the formalities dispensed with, allowed them to pry him out from under the bear and guide him triumphantly toward the nearby cantonment. Before departing, however, and in the lackadaisical act securing another whimsical bit of Kelliana for interested posterity, he cut off the bear's right paw and slung it to the recaptured Spotted Eagle's saddle. Twenty minutes later he was shaking hands with Miles' quartermaster, Captain Randall.

It developed that the "General" himself was off in the timber supervising logging operations for the camp's ambitious construction program. (Though he was a colonel not made brigadier until 1880, Miles' officers and men invariably deferred to his Civil War brevet rank in addressing or referring to him. The same courtesy was afforded him by his civilian employees; packers, stock handlers, scouts. In fact the only one to call him consistently by his regular rank was old Liver-eating Johnson, who would not knowingly defer to the Devil or "grant one inch of undue credit to Jesus Christ himself," as his leather-clad companions put it.) It further developed that Captain Randall did not expect Miles back for some time.

"He doesn't ordinarily return until late afternoon," the quartermaster advised Kelly. "However, I'm sure he will want to see you before then. We had best send up, right off, and let him know you are here."

"I suppose you had," agreed the scout, "but wait a bit now—"

He broke off to finger his jaw and stare contemplatively at the outsized bear paw dangling from his saddle horn.

Randall's eyes widened as he noticed the huge appendage for the first time.

"Good Lord, Kelly, I do believe that's the biggest bear paw I ever saw. Do they come much bigger?"

"Not a great deal," agreed the other laconically. "This one will measure over twelve inches without the claws and the unfortunate brute who furnished it will, in my opinion, scale close to as many hundred pounds. Here—" He waved the paw to the courier who was starting off to notify Miles of his arrival. The man came up, and he handed him the grisly trophy. "My card," he grinned. "Please present it to the General with my compliments."

When Miles got the bear paw, nothing would do but that its sender should come up at once to see him at the wood-cutting site. He had been quietly despairing of hearing from Kelly, and the celebrated scout's "calling card with claws" struck just the right note of rough frontier humor, as well as realistic military relief. Miles, too, as Kelly was soon enough to learn, had a gift for prompt action not shared by most of his more famous fellow Indian fighters of the regular army. Completely without Custer's headlong, suicidal haste, he possessed at the same time an eagerness to get on with the job which was all too apparently lacking in Crook, Terry, and Gibbon.

He had, also, that rare gift for spot decision and full commitment which distinguishes the competent field commander.

Five minutes after he entered the General's tent at the cutting site, Luther S. Kelly emerged with the official appointment which guaranteed him his unique place in the dangerous history of US army scouting.

As of the moment he let the flaps fall behind him to start toward the sun-drowsing Spotted Eagle, he was "Chief of Scouts, District of the Yellowstone, Colonel Nelson A. Miles Commanding."

Kelly's impromptu commission as head of Miles' scout corps brought to a head his whole life on the northwest frontier. In four short months, his storied career reached its strange climax. In sixteen brief weeks his own unreported personal tragedy played itself out against a backdrop of officially documented military triumph. In a hundred and twenty dark winter days of relentless army pursuit, the proud Sioux Nation was forever driven apart and destroyed.

In all of this, Luther Kelly played the paramount guiding role for the long delayed forces of white frontier retribution.

The part cost him, in the end, more than its fleeting fitful day upon the stage of public acclaim could hope to repay him in a lifetime of such empty applause. Yet, easing up on the dozing Nez Percé pony that baking hot afternoon in the woodlands south of the Yellowstone, he had no least inkling of what lay ahead. His only thought was that now, at last, he had found the means and method, brutal as they might prove to be, of running down and cornering Sitting Bull's Sioux. And, trapping with them, of course, Gall and Crow Girl.

How, in that final moment when the Hunkpapa war chief turned at bay, he, Kelly, proposed to deprive him of Crow Girl, could not at present be predicted. But a way *would* show itself. That was as sure as the good Lord was watching from above. When that way did show itself, Luther Kelly would be ready.

34

Luther Kelly's days upon the northwest frontier were now numbered. Within the first twenty-four hours of his arrival at Bear Coat's camp, they began to telescope with confusing speed. Nelson A. Miles was at work.

The very next morning, the General was up with the last of the starlight. He did not go to the woodcutting site but instead sent an orderly for Kelly. It was still dark when the sleepy soldier tapped the scout's blanketed shoulder and told him, "Beg pardon, Mr. Kelly, but the General would like to see you right away. He says to come along up to his tent and have breakfast with him."

Kelly reported as requested, to find Miles waiting for him politely.

"Sit down, sir," he greeted him, waving to the camp chair opposite his, across the field ambulance tailgate which had been nailed to a sawlog stump to provide the General's mess table. "You will find the accommodations severe but the food superb."

Kelly thanked him and sat down. For all of Miles' quiet courtesy, it was not a comfortable moment.

The General was one of the most impressive men Kelly

had ever seen. He was an absolute soldier's soldier; tall, broad-shouldered, strong, flat-bellied, erect, bold-faced. In the prime of middle life, he had about him that unmistakable "look of eagles" which the Prussian militarists so proudly ascribe to those rarest of war's aristocrats, the born field commanders. Seated within three feet of him, while four orderlies served the fried blacktail tenderloins, sourdough flapjacks, dried apple pie, and black coffee which were his standard morning fare, the embarrassed scout found it impossible to think of himself as "Yellowstone" Kelly, Chief of Scouts, District of the same name. A man just couldn't make the thought come, sitting that close under the ice-blue eyes and haughty, highbred nose of a full colonel and brevet major general. Not, at least, and (plague it all!) with three years in the regular army showing in his own service record.

Thus, feeling exactly like Corporal L. S. Kelly, late of Company G, 10th Infantry, and nothing at all like the reputed "best Indian scout west of Fort Lincoln," he kept his head down awkwardly, his ears open alertly, while Colonel Nelson A. Miles talked on.

Surprisingly, he was kept in that attitude quite a spell.

The General had fooled him with his informal brevity of yesterday. That had been an occasion of purely social pleasure; this was a matter of strictly military business.

"Now then, Kelly," he nodded, easing back and waving in an orderly with more coffee, "let me bring you up to date. Afterward, I shall be glad to hear from you, and I am satisfied you will be able to provide several worthwhile advices. Meanwhile, I have found the quickest method of communicating a military situation is for chief to talk while staff listens."

"Yes, sir," grinned Kelly stiffly, pleasantly surprised at being considered "staff." "As my Sioux friends say, General, 'my ears are uncovered.'"

Miles only bobbed his head again, not returning the smile.

Kelly froze his own expression, deciding quickly enough that his new employer was not the smiling type. He was not, either, the beloved thoughtful father to his endlessly marched but seldom engaged men that Crook was. Nor the disliked, tooth-flashing, glad-handing politico that Custer was to his cynical, hard fought command. Nor, again, was he one of the foot-dragging, wait-for-explicit-orders-in-triplicate book followers that Gibbon and Terry were. Miles was a man of but one passion—professional soldiering.

"It has been contemplated by my superiors," he told the uncomfortable scout, "that my troops should build a cantonment here with a permanent fort to follow, but not that they should do more than occupy this country until next spring, when it is expected that they and this base should form the springboard for another season of summer campaigning.

"Now, sir, this does not suit my purposes at all, even though the orders are Sherman's own. Still, I have my problems past Sherman.

"He promised me fifteen hundred troops, including a full regiment of cavalry. You can see my cavalry. We have procured, I think, something like thirty spare horses. As for the actual number of effectives I have here now, they are less than five hundred. All infantry, of course.

"I have determined the main enemy to be two thousand strong, composed of five tribal elements in the main; the Hunkpapa under Sitting Bull and Gall, the Oglala under Crazy Horse and American Horse, the Northern Cheyenne under Dull Knife and Two Moon, the Miniconjou and Sans Arc Sioux under their various leaders.

"Now, as to Sherman's plan for another summer operation, we are coming to you and to my need for you."

Kelly quit fooling with his empty coffee cup, looked up quickly. Miles was waiting for him. He caught his eye and held it.

"Judging from my experience of winter campaigning down

in the southwest Indian Territory, I am satisfied that the winter is the best time for subjugating these northern Indians as well. At that period it is commonly regarded as utterly impossible for white men to live in this country and endure the extreme cold outside the protection of well-prepared shelters. But I am satisfied that if the Indians can live out there, the white man can also, if properly equipped with all the advantages we can give them, which are certainly superior to those obtainable by the Indians." An expression of quick annoyance crossed Miles' handsome face. "I remarked to General Terry that if given these proper supplies and a reasonable force, I could clear the Indians out of this country before spring. Do you know what he said, sir? Of course! The same weary old story. That it was impossible to campaign in this country in the winter and that I could not possibly contend against the elements.

"I have had no doubts of my own contrary opinion, you understand, Kelly. But up to this moment I have been handicaped and held up in my plans by the lack of proper eyes and ears. I have, of course, employed the usual agency spies. Those people proved invaluable to me down south. They go constantly between the agency and the wild camps, and their morals are as cheaply bought as a lame pony or the services of a sick squaw. I have found them to mean more to the astute troop commander than perhaps a regiment of promised cavalry, shall we say.

"But, their limitations are critical. You can only guess at the accuracy of their information, evaluating it and correlating it with your own hard facts. You cannot, in any case, put implicit faith in it or base a troop movement blindly upon it. However, what I have lacked for, and what I now trust I have found, is a person who knows this northern country, the Indians in it, the trails through it, the campsites the hostile bands will most likely inhabit in hard winter, and the most direct, feasible routes by which white troops on foot may press these sites when the time comes.

"Now, what I want to know from you, is this:

"One; do you know this country as well as you are reputed to? Two; can you find the main hostile encampments for me? Three; can you guide me to them in any weather?"

He stopped abruptly, his pale eyes fastened on his new chief of scouts.

"Yes," was all the latter said.

"Good. When do you think we should start after them?"

"Not until the weather turns off dead mean. They'll keep moving till the drifts get too deep to pass a travois."

"What about meanwhile?"

"Meanwhile, use every minute scouting them and nailing down their whereabouts; that is to say the exact whereabouts of the big winter camps of the main bands."

"That would be the five groups I mentioned."

"Not quite, General."

"How's that?"

"I'm going to speak out, General. I understand that's the way you would want it."

"You understand exactly right, sir. Go ahead."

"You can forget the Miniconjou and Sans Arc. I have just come from eight weeks in the field trailing the Hunkpapa for personal reasons. I have found out a few things. The Sans Arc and Miniconjou are pretty well out of it. Oh, you will always find a few strays of any band in the camp of any other band. But as tribes they've largely backed off into the Black Hills, or so I heard."

"Yes, I had heard as much myself from the agency Sioux, without being able to confirm it. Anything else?"

"Yes, I think you can forget the northern Cheyenne too. The

Indian rumor is that Two Moons and Dull Knife are tired of war and will come in next spring if unmolested this winter."

"That," Miles shook his head sharply, "I will not believe. What else?"

"Crazy Horse and Sitting Bull are at odds. Some say Crazy Horse will follow the Cheyenne in or even beat them to it."

"And Sitting Bull?"

"He will never come in. They say he will go to the Land of the Grandmother first. That's Canada, sir."

"We'll see about that. All done, sir?"

"That depends, General."

"On what?" Miles stiffened perceptibly, and Kelly did not miss it.

"Whether I get to make straight-out suggestions."

"I did not hire you to make any other kind, sir." The ramrod was still shoved up the back of the rebuke. "If you have a specific recommendation, out with it."

"All right. In my opinion, General, your main troublemaker is Sitting Bull. Get him, and Crazy Horse will come in. If Crazy Horse comes in, the Cheyenne will follow. But to get Sitting Bull, you don't go after Sitting Bull, you go after Gall."

"Gall?"

"Yes, sir. Cut him out and corner him, and you've got Sitting Bull."

Miles frowned quickly.

"Well, sir, I should like to cut him out and corner him, for he has been killing my couriers to Fort Buford and burning my wagon trains from Camp Glendive. But I am afraid I do not follow your logic. I had not imagined Gall was more than another petty chief; certainly not to be compared with Sitting Bull as a prime mover of the Sioux rebellion."

Kelly shook his head, trying hard to say the right thing,

knowing well the difficulty he faced in convincing Miles of his point.

"Sitting Bull is a medicine man, General. He is a prophet, a dreamer, a politician, a speechmaker, if you will. But Gall is the man who fights for him. He is his strong right arm, as surely as Crazy Horse used to be his savage left. Now, amputate the right and you have him helpless, for the left has already begun to wither and fall away. Get Gall, and the entire Sioux tribal complex will start to come apart. You may well say that Sitting Bull is the hostile arch, but you must know that Gall is the keystone of that arch. Pull him out, and you will have brought down the whole red building."

Miles let him finish. He looked at him searchingly and steadily. At last he shook his head, the refusal inviting no further rebuttals.

"I'm sorry, Kelly. It's still Sitting Bull I want. After him we will take the others as we are able to come up to them. But first I want the man who killed George Custer."

He paused, chopping the words out from under his campaign-faded mustache, his light blue eyes showing their cold fire, his back as stiffly braced as an angry dog's. "There's only one Indian who answers that description, Kelly. And you have been hired to do just one single solitary thing in regard to that Indian. *Find him.*"

35

Kelly did not know if Miles' biting charge had been meant for a dismissal or not. But he sat still.

Torn between his honest belief that Gall was the logical primary military objective, and his knowledge that Crow Girl's presence with the Hunkpapa war chief might easily be contaminating that belief, he hesitated, confused by Miles' continuing silence and his own reluctance to push a questionable conviction.

Of the two concerns, the aloof, aristocratic officer came first.

Miles was an enigma to many men. But Kelly had to assay him and assay him fast, or miss his chance to make his difficult point, perhaps for good.

First off, a man could see that the famed Comanche fighter actually did not like to talk. Accordingly, when he had to, as with Kelly now, he liked to get it done in uninterrupted bursts. This suggested that his ordinary modus operandi was action. Quite clearly he suffered neither from Crook's fussy infatuation with delaying logistics, nor Custer's fatal mania for blowing Garry Owen before his support came up. His military philosophy was apparently quite simple; seek, find, destroy. But before putting this philosophy into active effect, to judge from Kelly's short contact with him, he was a man who would want to make sure his men understood the dangers ahead.

This line led you to what the Indians thought of him.

The Sioux, of course, feared him because of the word which had come up to them from the south plains via the Southern Cheyenne; that Bear Coat wanted to fight first and talk afterward. Kelly realized that, literally, this was not true. What the Indians meant was that once the talk was over, once both sides had been given equal opportunity to express their viewpoints, that was the end of the discussion. To the red men, who felt a fight was no fight at all unless it started and stopped at least a dozen times for oral argument, Miles' policy of refusing to treat once the action was joined amounted to what they feared in him and accused him of—all fight and no talk.

Sneaking an eye-corner glance at him now, Kelly still could not determine whether his own talk with him was over or not. He decided in quiet desperation to risk reopening it along the lines of defending his opinion of Sitting Bull and hence his possible last chance at rescuing Crow Girl.

"But, General—" he plunged back into the awkward silence, "I know full well I'm right about Sitting Bull! Did you know it was he, sir, who saved Reno after Custer was gone?"

"No, nor does anyone else to my knowledge," said Miles.

"I do!" averred Kelly, plowing recklessly ahead. "I got the story from some Crows who got it straight from old Paints Brown, who was within ten feet of Yellowhair when the end came. The old man swears that Sitting Bull went to the warriors who were cutting Reno to pieces the following day and told them to stop. It was just before noon of the twenty-sixth when he came up shouting, 'That's enough. Let them go. Let them live; they are trying to live. They came against us, and we killed a few. If we kill them all, a bigger army will be sent against us.'

"Now that was Sitting Bull, sir. But do you know what Gall said? He raged like a wounded grizzly and said to kill them all, that the big army would come anyway. 'Let nothing live!' he cried. 'Not a man, not a horse, not a mule!' That was Gall, sir. He is your real white-hater and your real war leader. Sitting Bull may stir it up, but Gall is the one who carries it out. If the Sioux had listened to him rather than Sitting Bull, sir, there would, indeed, have been no survivors up there on the Little Horn. But for this old medicine man you say must come first, Major Reno for sure and most likely Captain Benteen with him would have gone under the day after their CO did!"

Miles rewarded the impassioned plea with a shrug.

"It makes an interesting story, Kelly. Perhaps even a plausible projection of the tactical situation. But it is scarcely admissible as military evidence. Anything else?"

"Yes," said Kelly.

He knew his Irish temper was beginning to fray under this typical display of ironclad army opinion, but put out his jaw and went ahead quietly.

"Why is it that the army will never consider the Indian viewpoint? Will never listen to the way *they* see things? I am giving you the results of two months' intensive scouting of the Hunkpapa, divided by the sum of eight years' experience with all the northern plains hostiles, multiplied by personal acquaintanceships with both Sitting Bull and Gall. And all you are ready to say is that it makes an interesting story or a plausible projection. I submit it's a little more than that, sir!"

"And I, sir, submit that it is nothing more than that." Miles' rejection was unheated, but his pale eyes darkened with intensity as he went on. "If you want to speak in mathematical paraphrases, you are forgetting that we have a common denominator here which cancels out all ordinary rules of red arithmetic. You are forgetting Custer, sir!"

"No sir, General, I am not!" denied Kelly. "But Custer was a fool, sir. You know that. Even General Grant said so!"

"Yes," said Miles softly, his fierce eyes far away. "But Grant had not been to Fort Lincoln this summer. Nor, for that matter, have you, sir."

"Well, no, I haven't," agreed the latter tentatively, warned by the others' distant gaze to go slow.

"Well, Kelly," said Miles, still quietly but eyes going even darker with the recalled thought, "*I have*."

"Yes sir," muttered the scout, and had sense enough to leave it there and wait.

"I saw over thirty widows there, Kelly, including Elizabeth Custer. I talked to every one of them, and I will tell you that no experience of war can equal the suffering I saw there. To see and talk to those women would have broken the heart of a Tartar. And do you know the only Sioux name we heard at Fort Lincoln, sir? *Sitting Bull*." He paused, jaw tightening, muscular throat moving. "I don't know about your information, Kelly, but mine tells me that he had the original creative idea for this massacre and that he sat upon the bluffs above the river all morning, directing its completing details in action. To me, as to those thirty-odd women at Fort Lincoln, that makes him *my* Indian and *our* number one campaign objective. Kelly, if you can make me see it any other way, I want to hear it."

Kelly shook his head. He knew he could never make himself understood now. Miles had swallowed the Sitting Bull bait like everyone else who read the newspapers. The white press said Sitting Bull was the Sioux monster who had murdered the gallant, brave, and noble General George Armstrong Custer. You could parade Indian eyewitnesses to the contrary all fall, and it would not change the army's opinion one whit. You could prove beyond any reasonable doubt that the real butchers were Gall, Crazy Horse, Hump, and half a dozen other Sioux and Cheyenne war chiefs. And that the only thing which had put old Tatanka up on top of that bluff while the fighting was going on was the fear that he might get hit by a stray bullet if he stayed down below. All it would get you from the military would be a sneer and the nasty frontier label of Indian-lover.

And then, in all inner honesty, even when you had advanced your best arguments, was not Sitting Bull still the primary villain that public opinion said he was? It did no good for a man to feel in his heart that killing Gall would start the Sioux disintegrating when all the real evidence pointed to Sitting Bull as the ruling leader of the warlike Hunkpapa.

"General," he said defeatedly, "I'll have to admit it. It *was* Sitting Bull's vision that started the whole thing. Without that there would have been no Custer Massacre. I only ask that once we get into the field—and if any good chance to cut him down presents itself—you remember what I've said about getting Gall. I know he's the present head of the Sioux sidewinder. Cut him off the main body, and your Hunkpapa snake won't live past sunset. Don't ask me to prove it, sir, for I can't. But you asked me for my opinion, and that's it."

Again, Miles regarded him with that lingering, unhurried, penetrating look which was his thoughtful specialty. And, again, he gave his decisive nod when he had finished the examination.

"I will make a deal with you, Kelly." He smiled faintly, showing his first and last trace of humor at the conference. "You *find* me Sitting Bull, and I will *give* you Gall."

Kelly stood.

"That leaves only one small question of permission, sir."

"Which would be?"

"May I start looking first thing tomorrow?"

Miles stood up, then. He eyed him quickly, nodded, turned

away into the tent, asked curtly back over his disappearing shoulder, "What's the matter with today, Mr. Kelly?"

The sun was less than an hour older. Kelly stood again in front of Miles' tent waiting for Captain Randall to finish some supply business and be gone. Presently, the quartermaster departed, and Miles looked up, cocking a cold eye at him.

"Don't tell me you've found him already?" he challenged, straight-faced.

Kelly could not read this man, took no chances with what sounded like good-natured sarcasm. "No sir, I was about to leave and needed a couple of things you will have to authorize for me."

"All right, what's first?"

"A horse. My Indian pony is done in. I've turned him out, and I'll need as good as you've got in exchange."

"And you shall have it, sir. How about my own Belshazzar? He is a thoroughbred but not too hot-blooded to handle smartly. He will go a mile or ten miles until he drops, without forcing. Will take swift water, can be hobbled, picketed, or stood on his reins. Will carry double or pack an injured man or any game and is absolutely gun-sound. What do you say to him, sir?"

Kelly wanted to inquire if this blue-blooded wonder could also gut a deer, sew moccasins, pitch a tepee, and boil up a mess of hump ribs, but only grinned and said, "Thanks, General," and got on with it.

"I'll need a packhorse too, sir."

"Good Lord! Tell Randall. Don't bother me about packhorses, man!"

"Yes, sir. One more thing, sir. I'll need a friend."

"I trust you're serious, Kelly?"

"Never more so, General. No man should go alone into that north country right now. I want another scout to go with me, and I want a good one."

"Agreed, agreed. Who will you have?"

"Vic Schmidt."

"Impossible. He's Colonel Otis' best man."

"And mine," said Kelly flatly.

Miles' head moved negatively. "Otis needs him down there at Camp Glendive. He's been getting our supply trains through where the others couldn't."

"I need him too. You don't go up against Gall and Sitting Bull with second-rate help, General."

"All right, take Schmidt. I'll give you a note to Otis." His pen moved quickly and he handed the scrap of foolscap to Kelly, adding as an afterthought, "By the way, speaking of Otis and our supply trains, I didn't show you this—" He fumbled among his papers, came up with a well-thumbed piece of ruled agency school paper, handed it across to Kelly, who took it curiously.

It was Sitting Bull's famous note to Otis demanding to know the meaning of the wagon line from Fort Buford through Camp Glendive to the Tongue River cantonment.

I want to know what you are doing on this road. You scare all the buffalo away. I want to hunt in this place. I want you to go away from here. If you don't, I will fight you again. I want you to leave what you have got here, and turn back from here. I am your friend.

sitting bull

I mean all the rations you have got, and some powder. Wish you would write me as soon as you can.

Kelly handed the pitiful document back to Miles without comment.

But the latter pressed him at once. "Well, sir, what have you to say to that?"

"Just one thing, General. Sitting Bull didn't write it."

Miles' eyebrows went up.

"I suppose you know who did?"

"Johnny Brughière. I recognize the hand."

"That's the half-breed Sioux they call Big Leggins. The one who runs with the Hunkpapa."

"Sitting Bull's interpreter," amplified Kelly. "And the greatest scout on the plains."

"So I've heard. I've asked him to come in and see me, with an eye to alienating him from the Sioux. But he hasn't shown up. Afraid to, I suppose."

"Yes sir, but I might be able to get him to come over to our side, General. I know what he's afraid of. It seems to be an old law charge back in the settlements. He's a wanted man, they say. Now if you could manage to get that charge quashed and—"

"I don't think we need Mr. Brughière at this late date," Miles interrupted. "Why bother with getting an amnesty for him? I hadn't caught up with *you* at the time I was looking for him."

"That's not the idea, General. You don't want him for the same reason you'd want me at all."

"So? Why do I want him then, pray tell?"

"Because," said Kelly slowly, "if getting Gall is cutting off Sitting Bull's right arm, getting Johnny Brughière is putting out both his eyes."

For the third and final time, Miles gave the Irish scout his intent, searching appraisal. Then he nodded abruptly.

"Go find Sitting Bull," said Miles, "*and bring me his eyes.*"

Kelly and Vic Schmidt were gone some five weeks. They were back in Miles' mouth-of-the-Tongue cantonment in early October, having covered all the country north of the Yellowstone from Camp Glendive to Milk River to Missouri River to Fort Peck to Big Dry Creek Fork and back down the latter's buffalo trail to Camp Glendive again. In all the wary miles of their three-hundred-mile compass-arc of the closed Sioux country north of the Tongue cantonment, they saw not a single hostile Hunkpapa, Oglala, Miniconjou, Sans Arc, or Cheyenne.

They reported their failure to Miles, who interrogated them exhaustively but without result and who then put Kelly to work on his famed filling-in of the blank spaces on the military maps north of the Yellowstone and south of Fort Peck. In this tedious manner, a week or ten days went by, Miles betimes working around the clock outfitting and organizing his pursuit column against the inevitable break in the hostile silence which he continued to predict would occur by mid-month at the very latest.

History made a superior prophet of him by a scant six hours. It was nearing sunset of October 15 when the courier came in from Camp Glendive.

The news was nothing less than galvanic under the tensely anticipatory circumstances.

A strong force of Sioux, vanguarding a very large village on the move, had attacked one of Otis' supply trains north of the river, between Glendive and the Tongue. The clash had occurred that same morning. Identifications had been unquestionable. Gall, Low Neck, and Pretty Bear had led the raiding outriders. The big mixed village which followed them was predominantly Hunkpapa, was apparently moving northeast to hunt buffalo on the Big Dry and was under the leadership of Sitting Bull.

These were the Indians. This was the camp. *The big camp.* The one Miles had been waiting for.

In the frosty dawn of October 17, 1876, he crossed the Yellowstone with Luther Kelly and four picked scouts far out front and 394 riflemen, a long train of winter-rigged supply wagons and an artillery piece, trailing behind.

On October 19 Kelly found the Hunkpapa village.

On the twentieth, while holding it under surveillance to make dead certain of its identity, he had the rare luck to see Johnny Brughière come in from the east, spend an hour in Sitting Bull's big black lodge, come out, mount up, and ride back in the direction from which he had come. Moving back and around the camp in a big circle, he lay up on the trail for Brughière and nailed him, open-mouthed. With the rifle snouts of his four companions keeping the surprised half-breed honest, Kelly took him off a way and talked to him like a Pennsylvania Dutch uncle. Albeit, one who could speak very fluent Sioux.

At first the big breed was wild-eyed with suspicion, fear, and dislike. But Kelly had a rare way with red men, one which seemed to work as well with half-red men. Big Leggins began to talk. Yes, Gall still had the Crow girl. Yes, she was all right. Not too well, mind you, but all right. There had been some trouble bearing the baby. It had been a boy, very big in the shoulders, like Kelly himself, and it had come breech-to. But it had lived, and the Absaroka squaw would, too. Yes, Gall treated her fine. Even with great love. Everybody talked about how he had lost his head over the Kangi Wicasi snip.

When he had gotten what he could of personal information out of Sitting Bull's big interpreter, he put Miles' offer of amnesty before him, urging him strongly to accept it and come over to the Pony Soldier side.

Brughière said he would think about it, looking away evasively when he said it.

Kelly was satisfied. He was sure he had seen the signs of hesitation and doubt, yes, and of fear, in the renowned half-breed's face. Shortly, the latter confirmed the suspicion.

Johnny Brughière had decided. He would come in, he said, but first he would have one more try at convincing Sitting Bull to do likewise. Lone Wolf would surely understand that. He must know that Tatanka had given Johnny sanctuary and had been like a father to him. Kelly had heard the story and nodded his agreement to and understanding of the half-breed's loyalty. Brughière went on quickly.

He himself knew the true strength of the white man, he assured Kelly. He had lived in the eastern settlements. He realized that the numbers of the Wasicun were as the leaves of all the aspens, sycamores, willows, and cottonwoods along all the waterways in all the hunting lands of his red half-brothers. Sitting Bull knew that, too. But he would not believe that Bear Coat would be any different, when it came to the last minute, than Three Stars or Red Nose or Star. He would not believe that Miles meant to kill him, where Crook and Gibbon and Terry had only chased him. Johnny would try once more to make him see that; to make him see the truth. After that, he promised he would come and talk to Miles.

Kelly left the matter there, freeing Brughière after enjoining him to impress upon Sitting Bull the fact that Miles was already too close for the village tepees to be taken down and moved away again. If Tatanka would not now take this last chance to talk, there would be no other. Once Bear Coat started to fight, he would not stop.

Brughière said all the Sioux knew that and that he would give Sitting Bull the warning exactly as Lone Wolf had said it. They shook hands and parted at four p.m.

Kelly reported in to Miles at eight o'clock that night. The following morning, October 21, no word having come from Sitting Bull, the advance upon the Hunkpapa village was begun.

36

Brughière must have been watching the column's bivouac, for no sooner had Miles begun to move his troops out of it than the half-breed appeared. With him were two agency Sioux bearing a white flag of truce. Sitting Bull, it appeared, wanted to talk after all.

Kelly, who had been riding with Miles, saw through the situation and so informed the latter. "They've been watching us all night, General, waiting to see if you really meant to come after them. Be very careful talking to this Brughière. He is quite intelligent and may have had others with him who have already been sent to warn Sitting Bull while Big Leggins delays us. We have about ten miles to the village."

"All right, Kelly. Come along. Let's see what they want."

Miles, Kelly, Captain Snyder, and Captain Frank Baldwin, Miles' principal subordinates and prime camp favorites, rode forward. What the Sioux wanted was soon enough discovered. Sitting Bull wanted to talk to Bear Coat. He asked Bear Coat to come and see him right away. He would wait for him. He hoped Bear Coat would give him an answer as quickly as he could. He the two agency Sioux were back with the flag of truce but without Johnny Brughière. This time they had a concrete proposal, making it clear that the crafty Sitting Bull had foreseen all contingencies.

The Hunkpapa leader would meet with Miles between their commands. Each would bring six companions; an officer and five men for Miles, a chief and five warriors for Sitting Bull. What did Bear Coat say to that? Was he afraid, or would he come?

Kelly saw the danger in the proposition, but Miles would not listen to his suspicions of a trap. The officer of course saw the risk involved but belonged to the school of white thought which believed that "face" was everything in treating with the savages. Kelly argued briefly that face with a man like Gall was indeed everything and with a Siouan Machiavelli like Sitting Bull precisely nothing. Miles would not have it that way. Kelly thereupon suggested the only insurance which came to mind. Would the General permit him to be one of his five men?

"Why not?" agreed Miles, not displeased with the idea. "After all, he has his interpreter. Please ride back and tell Lieutenant Bailey to pick his four best riflemen and mount them up." He turned away, calling up his first sergeant. "Meyers, please inform Captain Snyder that Lieutenant Bailey and myself are going forward to meet with the Sioux. He and Captain Baldwin are to retire upon the camp, secure it, and be ready for trouble." The noncom saluted, following Kelly down the halted line. The little truce group was formed up and ready in five minutes. Kelly waved to the waiting agency Indians in guttural Sioux. "*Hookahey, tahunsa.* Hurry up now, cousins. Get out of here fast. Go tell Tatanka we will meet him as he has suggested. And tell him we will then see who is afraid and who is not afraid."

The truce-flag bearers swung their runted ponies and were gone. The seven white men took a community deep breath, started their mounts forward. Behind them, Captain Snyder's sergeants were already barking the "about face and fall in." A bend in the trail quickly cut off both sight and sound of the retreating column. The stillness of late October lay over the sere and russet land. The only sounds were the grunts and snafflings of their horses, the squeak and jingle of their saddle leathers and bit chains. One dead-still mile fell behind. Then two. Still nothing. The silence became menacing. The trail began to narrow and grow bad. Mile three was walked under by the growingly restive horses. Noting the swing and prick of his own mount's ears, Kelly wetted a finger and held it up. The wind was into them. The next moment Miles' thoroughbred flung up his head and neighed challengingly. Instantly, Kelly checked him and dropped him back. "Hold up," he said to Miles. "Yonder they come." The white group spaced its horses instinctively across the trail. Miles and Bailey loosened the flaps on their belt holsters. The four troopers looked to their Springfields. Kelly watched the trail ahead and the ridges flanking that trail. It was not a good spot to meet Sitting Bull, but scouts could only suggest, they could not command.

Kelly pulled his Winchester, threw its lever half down, partially opening the breech to check the loading chamber. The cartridge's dull brass winked comfortingly in the pale October sun. He closed the action.

As he did, Sitting Bull's group rode into view.

The Hunkpapa leader had chosen well. Black Fox, Frog Belly, Buffalo Child, Whistling Horse, and Yellow Hand were his warriors. His chief was Gall.

It seemed to Kelly as though it took the Sioux an hour to ride over the hundred yards of trail separating them from the white men. Probably it took them thirty seconds. To which had to be appended the additional thirty seconds they sat with their horses' muzzles not six feet from those of the white truce group, staring at Miles and his men through the eternity of an intentional stillness which would have cracked the nerve of nine out of ten frontier officers, before ever a word was said.

Miles, however, had sat and been stared at by a good many tough Indians in his time. He knew exactly what to do and did it. He kept his mouth shut and his eyes open.

It was Sitting Bull who said the first word.

"What are you doing here? Why are your troops remaining in this country? Why do they not go back to their posts or into winter camp somewhere?"

"We are here to bring you and your people in. We do not want to do this by war, but you cannot be allowed to continue roaming over the country, sending out war parties to devastate the settlements." Miles broke off, giving him time to accept this, then went on. "If you insist on war, such a war can end only one way for you. Do you know of a single war which the Indians have won when the last rifle has been fired?"

Sitting Bull frowned and spoke rapidly to Gall in Sioux. The latter barked his reply angrily, and Sitting Bull nodded.

"This country belongs to us and not the white men," he told Miles, apparently repeating Gall's sentiments. "We have nothing to do with the white men and wish only to be left alone in peace."

"What do you mean by that?" demanded Miles.

Again Gall growled his guttural comment to the Hunkpapa leader, and again the latter nodded scowlingly.

"I mean you must leave the country entirely to the Indians. The white man never lived who loved an Indian, and no true Indian ever lived that did not hate the white man. God Almighty has made me an Indian, and he has not made me an agency Indian either. Neither will I ever be one."

The talk went on a little way from there, while Kelly watched Sitting Bull closely.

The Sioux messiah had aged greatly since Kelly had seen him in the camp of the Red River half-breeds nine years before. But the powerful squat physique, huge head, great bony nose, sunken glittering eyes, uncompromising mouth, and prognathous jaw were still cast of the same indestructible, belligerent red iron. And the shifty, unsure, wild mind had not been stabilized a single degree through those intervening years. A man could tell that by the swift, dangerous drift the talk was suddenly taking.

"How did you know I was here where I am?" Sitting Bull asked Miles sharply, breaking in on the white officer to put the apparently innocent question.

"Be careful of that one, General," Kelly muttered quickly. "I don't like the way this is going."

Miles acknowledged his comment, but ignored it.

"All the Sioux are not our enemies. I not only knew you were here; I know where you came from and where you are going."

"Tell me," said Sitting Bull quietly. "*Where am I going?*"

"Watch it, General—!" hissed Kelly, but Miles again overrode the warning.

"You intend to remain here three days and then move to the Big Dry and hunt buffaloes."

The change in Sitting Bull was incredible. The words turned him from a quiet-spoken human being to a dumbly furious brute. As it would any commander, the thought of spies and traitors in his own camp sickened him, the resultant nausea poisoning his good judgment. Kelly saw him throw up his arm in an apparently prearranged signal and advised Miles that they had best begin getting out of there at once.

The latter was by now alerted, but it was a little late in the morning. Singly and by twos and threes, armed warriors began to appear along the ridge-sides behind the meeting place and to drift silently in toward it. Behind these converging few, the ponies of at least two hundred braves began to silhouette themselves against the raw blue of the ridgetop sky. It was a very bad time in a very bad place. And it was transparently clear by now that Sitting Bull had planned it exactly that way.

Miles calmly warned the latter that he must either stop the inward movement of the near warriors or the talk was at an end for all time.

Kelly, thinking furiously, knew that it would take more than that. Even as Miles was threatening war, a young brave slipped up to Sitting Bull and brazenly handed him a carbine, which the latter made a patent show of hiding beneath his buffalo robe. For a moment, the Irish scout thought of trying a cold bluff—saying, perhaps, that the ridges behind them were as acrawl with soldiers as were those behind the Sioux with warriors—but Sitting Bull had at least one thousand braves and it was no time for begging him to prove it. No. Their one chance lay with Gall. And with Kelly's knowledge of the war chief's savage pride in race and person.

He touched Belshazzar with his heels, jumping the thoroughbred forward. The big horse stopped with his shoulder a foot from that of Gall's roan. Kelly kept his voice down. He made no impassioned accusations or appeals. He merely said, "This is treachery, my brother. I know it is not your doing and that you will not be a party to it. We are going to turn around now and go back to our camp. We ask to go in peace. Woyuonihan."

Gall returned his salute of respect without a word, then, unexpectedly, called softly after him. "She is well, my brother, and not unhappy; the child was a fine boy. Woyuonihan."

Kelly did not turn but rode straight to Miles. "Don't hurry and don't drag your feet either," he muttered, side-mouthed, to the latter and young Bailey. "Just salute them as though we lad an honorable understanding, turn your horses and ride but slow. Do you men hear that?" he queried, standing a little in his stirrups to catch the troopers' attention. They nodded that they had, and he finished tersely. "All right, let's go. And for the love of God, whatever you do, don't look back once we've started."

Miles and Bailey saluted Sitting Bull as Gall rode up to him growling out some Sioux gutturals and tapping the breech of his rifle meaningfully. The Hunkpapa leader glared at him a moment, then wheeled and flung an arm-signal up toward the backing ridges. At once all Sioux movement ceased. The white officers turned their mounts away, followed by the four troopers and Luther S. (for *scared*) Kelly. They rode slowly and with good straight backs. In all the long way it took them to travel beyond the Sioux eyesight, not one of them looked back. And in all the long time of watching them go, not a solitary red man nor shaggy Indian mount moved to follow them.

Gall was still the war chief of all the Hunkpapa.

Miles was a man of his word. With dawn of the next day, October 22, he had his column on the move again. This time he did not halt it until its head was within a mile—and plain view— of the Hunkpapa village. At this point Sitting Bull rode out with a flag of truce. He came alone and Miles stopped long enough to hear what he had to say. The commander of the Fifth Infantry was no squaw-killer like the late head of the Seventh Cavalry. He clearly meant, as he had told Kelly at the start that morning, to clean out the village. But if Sitting Bull had meanwhile decided to come in peaceably, he would still be given the opportunity, with honor.

Such was not the Hunkpapa's intent.

His sole conception and condition of peace was that all white works and settlements, including military posts, railroads, wagon trails and telegraph lines, be abandoned at once and the entire country, save for selected trading posts, be turned back to the Indians. This pathetic defiance was delivered with savage hauteur and positive hostility. Miles let him finish his threatening tirade, then said quietly. "You will either accept our terms of government and place your people under our laws, as the other Sioux have, or I shall pursue you until I kill you or you kill me, or until one of us has driven the other out of the country."

Sitting Bull was stunned. He could not seem to grasp Miles' meaning and asked to have his words restated.

The General obliged.

"I will give you fifteen minutes to surrender. At the end of that time I shall attack your camp," he said, biting off each word now as though he were angry at it. "I am tired of talking to you."

Sitting Bull blustered darkly. He was much stronger than Bear Coat. He had a thousand men, Bear Coat only a few hundred. Bear Coat had better not talk to him that way. He had better be nice. Say something peaceful.

"You have fifteen minutes," said Miles.

Now the ill-famed Sioux leader understood. He put on no more. He dropped his mask of reasonable negotiator and revealed the true face of the incorrigible white-hater beneath it. As with the day before, when Miles had hinted at his agency spy system, Sitting Bull's speechless reaction of black anger ended the meeting. Without another word he spun his spotted war pony about and raced toward the watching circle of braves which had formed behind him while he talked to Miles. The whole group immediately wheeled and ran for the village. Within seconds of the first hoarse cries of warning, the huge camp was in an uproar. Warriors by the hundreds began to stream out onto the plain between their lodges and the white troops, riding furiously back and forth across the enemy front to mask the miraculous panic of the retreat beginning behind the towering dust thrown up by their desperate galloping camouflage. Squaws screamed, little children wailed, dogs yelped, horses neighed and squealed, war cries echoed everywhere. And somehow, despite the apparent wild confusion, the lodges were emptied, pack ponies run up and loaded, riding mounts secured, and the general evacuation of women, children, and old ones which any plains warrior will secure, to the death if need be, before looking to his own safety, was begun, coordinated and carried out in something less than Miles' seemingly impossible fifteen minutes.

For his part the white commander sat his mount, calmly dividing his attention between the activity in the Sioux camp and the movement of the minute hand on the fine double-cased hunting watch which he held in his left hand, the while quietly discussing the developing situation with Luther Kelly, Clubfoot Boyd, Liver-eating Johnson, Charley Bass, and half-breed Billy LeBeau, the five-man elite of his large scout corps.

Neither Kelly nor any of the others had taken part in that second morning's meeting, save as spectators. Now they all agreed with their Irish chief, in response to Miles' query as to their opinions of his decision to attack. "Well, General," Kelly had said, "when it comes right down to it, I agree with Bill Cody. He always said that in treating with Indians, the whole secret is to be honest with them and do as you agree. Now it looks to me as though you've agreed to run Sitting Bull out of the country. I'd say you'd best go right ahead and start running him the minute that big hand hits the mark."

Since Captain Snyder and Captain Frank Baldwin had already set up the skirmish line for the advance and since his scouts were ready and eager to lead it in, Miles could now give his whole attention to the inexorable creep of the minute hand toward a quarter after ten a.m.

Precisely upon the moment of its arrival, and not an instant before, he raised his yellow gauntlet.

It was 10:15.

An advance of highly trained infantry against wild-riding, disordered native cavalry can be a devastating thing. Miles' troops were highly trained.

Nothing the hostiles could do deterred them. They fired the grass entirely around the white command. Miles' men marched straight ahead. They ate the smoke, jumped the flames, stomped through the cinders. And they kept coming. In twenty minutes they had taken the village. In thirty, the skies were black with the greasy smoke of burning cowhide lodges. In an hour they had driven the Indians several miles north. In twenty-four hours they had pursued them fifteen miles, and in forty-eight hours had driven them forty miles, all without allowing them stopping time enough to even water their horses. And that was the end of it. Another desperate half hour and two more demoralized miles of white rifle fire and artillery pounding broke the spirit of the Border People. Nohetto. They could do no more. Bear Coat had won.

A third and final flag of truce came forward.

In the following terse interview, Nelson Miles accepted the surrender of two thousand Hunkpapa, Miniconjou, and Sans Arc Sioux, over four-fifths of Sitting Bull's entire war strength. Five well-known chiefs were given up as hostages against the faithful execution of the agreement. Within the hour these chiefs were on their way south to the reservation under armed guard of Lieutenant Forbes and a strong force of Fifth Infantry.

There proved to be only one flaw in the merciless brilliance of the forty-eight hour operation.

It came apparent when the last of the surrendering hostiles had been identified and checked off against Kelly's list of the important Sioux in Sitting Bull's big camp as of October 20, two days before the battle.

Three large red fish and some four hundred faithfully

following smaller fry had slipped through Miles' hastily flung Hunkpapa net. The four hundred were fingerlings and could be forgotten. The three were something else again. They were:

Pretty Bear.

Sitting Bull.

Gall …

37

Eight days of hard marching and hot fighting had worn the Fifth a little thin. When the weather turned severely cold on the twenty-sixth, Miles took a good look at his shivering men and ordered the column back to the Yellowstone. Here he put in the rest of October and the early part of November doing something no other white commander in the north had done before him—properly outfitting his troops for winter campaigning in the dread cold of the Montana high country.

Within a matter of days, and while Kelly and his four picked scouts were maintaining contact with Sitting Bull's escapees, he was ready. When the Irish scout returned to report the Hunkpapa fleeing up the Big Dry toward the Missouri, he was completely amazed at the scope and detail of Bear Coat's preparations.

Miles had indeed equipped his command as though readying it for an arctic expedition. This was not an idle comparison on Kelly's part, either, but an exact description tallying with Miles' own later personal recollections.

"In respect to climatic effects," wrote the General, "the record during that time and since has demonstrated that the severity of the cold of winter there was nearly equal to anything encountered by Schwatka, Greely, or other explorers. During the winter campaigns of 1876 and '77 all the mercurial thermometers we had with us were frozen solid. The following winter a spirit thermometer registered between fifty-five and sixty degrees below, and the lowest record was on Poplar Creek where the command crossed in 1876, and where the thermometer subsequently registered sixty-six degrees below zero; which was equal to the cold of the Arctic regions."

Continuing, Miles states tersely, "that temperature is simply appalling. Even when the air was perfectly still and all the moisture of the atmosphere was frozen, the air was filled with frozen jets, or little shining crystals."

Kelly and his four case-hardened cronies had to laugh, even so, at the extent of the commander's cautions and concerns over the thermal welfare of his troops. To men of their own Indian-like indifference to exposure, the appearance of the Fifth Infantry on the eve of its November departure northward from the Tongue cantonment was nothing less than "downright comical." As half-breed Billy LeBeau put it, "By Gar, him look like heap damn Eskimo!" and here again the opinion of one of his rawhide-tough scouts coincided almost precisely with the General's own eventual erudite summation.

"Both officers and men," remembered Nelson Miles, some twenty years removed, "profited by the experience they had been through in the winter campaigns in the Indian Territory, and applied themselves zealously to their equipment in every possible way. In addition to the usual strong woolen clothing furnished for the uniform, they cut up woolen blankets and made themselves heavy and warm underclothing. They were abundantly supplied with mittens and with arctics or buffalo overshoes, and whenever it was possible, they had buffalo moccasins made and frequently cut up grain sacks to bind about their feet in order to keep them from freezing. They made woolen masks that covered the entire head, leaving openings for the eyes and to breathe through, and nearly all had buffalo overcoats.

"This command of more than four hundred men looked more like a large body of Esquimaux than like white men and United States soldiers. In fact, with their masks over their heads, it was impossible to tell one from another."

But for all Miles' imaginative precautions and his chief of scouts' good-natured enjoyment thereof, Montana's winter hell very nearly had the last laugh, at that.

The mercury continued to plummet.

Three days later, when the column moved out of the cantonment, it crossed the Yellowstone—heavily loaded supply wagons, field ambulances, horse-drawn artillery, et al.—*on solid ice*. And from that moment until the fateful 18th of December, and the discovery of Sitting Bull's fugitive camp at the head of the Red Water River, the thin bright line in the army thermometers did not again climb beyond flat, dead zero.

The frozen days glittered with sun frost. The subarctic nights groaned and cracked and exploded with the expanding deepness of the cold. The weeks went by, and the snows came and the winter march went on. One hundred miles north up the Big Dry to the Missouri. One hundred miles west to the Musselshell, after crossing the Big Muddy. And one hundred and fifty miles southeast from the Musselshell, after recrossing the narrowing "mother of waters." Closer and ever closer upon the flagging heels of the Hunkpapa.

Miles' men did not remove their buffalo coats after leaving the Yellowstone. They slept, fully clothed, in the dry snow by blazing cottonwood fires, careful to keep their rifles near their bodies beneath their blankets, so that the actions would not freeze solid and fail to function. Food ran low. Wood and water were in desperate scarcity. For one seventy-two hour period, crawling across the barren spine of the high divide between the Missouri and the Yellowstone, there was no wood at all and no fires; and no water to drink, save that melted from snow in a mess kit held hard against a horse's hot and acrid belly. But no man dropped behind. No man deserted. No man died of the cold. And ever harder, ever more desperately close, they drove in upon the starving Hunkpapa.

At last the stark signs of disintegration began to appear along the Indian trail. A thinly clad old woman. A young squaw heavy with child. A boy of ten. A warrior who was young when Meriwether Lewis came west with William Clark, forty years and more now gone. A cradleboard babe, hours old, still swathed in a cloth showing the blood of the broken umbilicus. All mercifully dead. All grotesquely frozen. All huddled and blind and blankly staring, where the black frost had struck them down.

In his great wolfskin winter coat, Kelly shivered and felt sick. This was not war. This was not high excitement. This was not carefree adventure. Nor was it any of the romantic things he had persistently pictured in his own portrayal of the dashing frontier scout. This was a far different, less pretty, grimmer thing. There was nothing of drama, nor excitement, nor adventure in it. *This was murder.*

From the hour the pitiful Hunkpapa dead began to appear along Sitting Bull's backtrail, Luther Kelly knew that, for him, the eight-year happiness of the Yellowstone Dream was forever done. It died with the first small Indian child that gray, long-gone November afternoon in the twilight dark of the Montana winter.

The snows had been incessant since they had left the Musselshell. The one hundred and fifty miles marched southeast from that point to strike the head of the beautiful Red Water

Valley had been put behind entirely by compass needle. Day became scarcely distinguishable from night, yet so acute were Kelly's tracking abilities and so infallible his knowledge of the fierce terrain that not once in those terrible last ten days had the column been held up by loss of contact with the hostiles. But now, with the freshness of the trail telling Kelly the Sioux were almost in sight, the "wind turned upside down," as the Indians put it, and what had been merely a run-of-the-winter Montana snowstorm became a high-country blizzard.

In the half-hour lull before the big wind struck, Kelly and Billy LeBeau, feeling ahead through the stale breath of the old storm, perhaps three miles in front of the following troop column, ran the Hunkpapa track to a dead halt. They sat their horses staring down at the grim story not yet covered by the shifting snows, neither saying anything, both knowing what must come now. Sitting Bull had made his terminal move. Kelly and LeBeau were looking at the historic Hunkpapa "parting of the ways"; that now-forgotten, exact spot high up on the West Fork of the Red Water where Tatanka Yotanka, Pizi, and Mato Hopa smoked their last pipe and said goodbye: where the trails of Sitting Bull, Gall, and Pretty Bear went away from each other and did not meet again.

"You had better," said Kelly softly to his companion, "get the General up here right away. I'll sit on this sign till you get back. Best hop to it, Billy. This lull won't hold long."

The other nodded quickly. "*Wagh! No waste!*" he grunted uneasily. "Pretty quick him snow blow every which way same damn time."

It was a good enough description of a Montana blizzard. Kelly did not argue it. "Tell the General to hump his tail," he said. "Tell him," he added, with a peculiar intensity of emphasis, "*that I've found Sitting Bull for him.*"

The dark-faced scout bobbed his head again. He took a last

peering look along the fading track line of his Indian brothers, shook his head slowly. "Him poor damn devil," murmured half-breed Billy LeBeau, and sent his shaggy pony on the gallop to bring up Colonel Nelson A. Miles for the keeping of his forgotten bargain with Luther S. Kelly.

Miles came forward in a matter of minutes. He had been but a mile behind Kelly, two ahead of the column, riding with Liver-eating Johnson, Clubfoot Boyd, and Charley Bass. Now he studied the three diverging lines of Sioux pony tracks, turned on Kelly, and demanded bluntly, "Well, what do you make of it?" As bluntly, Kelly told him.

"They left here within the hour. The main bunch, about two hundred or so, went straight ahead, down the Red Water. The second bunch, less than one hundred, went east across the Fork. Third bunch, no more than thirty or forty, split off northwest, back toward the Big Dry. It's their last gamble; you've got them, General."

"We'll push on at once," said Miles, excitement beginning to light his pale eyes. "Baldwin's the best Indian fighter in the army; we'll give him the big band. I'll take the bunch that went east, and Snyder can take the handful that headed northwest. What do you think they have in mind, Kelly?"

"It looks to me, General, as though the second bunch is pulling out and will quit. But the other two are heading north and will likely reunite. Now we know Sitting Bull has always said he would go to Canada before he would stay here and surrender. We also know that Gall is not the kind to quit." Kelly paused and Miles was at him instantly.

"Well, well, man! Go on, go on!"

"There's hardly a doubt, General. Your big due-north bunch is Sitting Bull's. Your east-turning quitters are Pretty Bear's. Your little band of northwesterners is Gall's."

"Good, good," cried Miles, in a rare show of feeling. "Now as for scouts, Johnson and Bass can go with Baldwin, Boyd, and LeBeau with Snyder, and you can stay with me. That way, we can—"

"That way," broke in Kelly, low-voiced, "we can forget."

"What the devil do you mean?" snapped Miles, scarcely accustomed to being countermanded in mid-stride.

"I mean," said his chief of scouts levelly, "that we made a deal. With all due respects, General, I intend to hold you to it."

"Well!" huffed the latter, staring down his high-bridged nose at his wolf-skinned guide. "I must say your Celtic insubordination is exceeded only by your Irish optimism. However, a deal's a deal. What was it I promised you, sir?"

Kelly pointed north along the trail of the main Sioux band. "You said if I would *find* you Sitting Bull, you would *give* me Gall. Yonder goes Tatanka's track. Baldwin will be up to him before this blizzard blows itself out."

Miles' searching look picked the pockets of his mind with a single deft glance. His familiar decisive head-bob cemented the brief inspection.

"All right, Kelly, you go with Snyder. Who do you want along?"

"Only LeBeau, sir. And thanks, General. I'll never forget it."

"Don't thank me, man!" snorted Miles. "I only hope you know what you're doing—that you've picked the right bunch of redskins to go after."

Kelly's dark eyes narrowed as they flicked again to the faint track line veering northwest. And narrowed yet further as they singled out the peculiarly twisted left forefoot print of a certain blue roan gelding a hundred and forty-four days familiar to him since the great silence along the Little Big Horn. "Don't worry, General," was all he said to Miles. "*I have.*"

38

Kelly led Belshazzar very carefully up the night-dark, rocky gorge into which Gall had turned in a despairing final effort to dodge or outdistance Snyder's relentless riflemen. The scout had lost all track of time in the blizzard which had broken away but the hour before, to leave the dead-still blackness through which he presently moved upward along what must almost certainly be the last mile of the war chief's retreat. It might have been three days or three weeks since they had left Miles and Baldwin. It did not matter to Kelly, and he did not care. That was all behind now, left there with the many other things which had come too fast in these past weeks to bear individual remembering and which had no real remaining importance in the life of Luther Kelly, anyway. (Like finding Johnny Brughière at the Tongue cantonment when they had gotten back from the abortive talks with Sitting Bull, ready at last to "walk the white brother's road," but deathly afraid to let Old Tatanka catch him at it!)

Now all that mattered, or was important to what was left of the Irish scout's life, lay directly ahead.

Pulling up the tall thoroughbred, Kelly let him blow out

while he scanned the narrowing way ahead. As he did, his thoughts leaped instinctively beyond the limited range of his rock-trapped vision.

What was waiting for Luther Kelly up there?

Life or death? Love or hatred? Happiness or bitter disillusionment? Would his final reward be the murmuring caress of Crow Girl's soft lips, or the whispering kiss of an ambushing Sioux bullet? Had Gall turned at bay, or was he still staggering onward? Would the implacable white-hater surrender or die fighting? Had he alienated the love and loyalty of the hero-worshiping little Kangi Wicasi girl? Or was she still, and fiercely, Lone Wolf's woman? There was but one way to find these answers: go on up the gulley.

Kelly glanced behind him.

Back there somewhere, at best no nearer than thirty minutes, Billy LeBeau was leading Snyder's men upward. Ahead, Gall had either halted or was going on. Above, the black belly of the blizzard was beginning to moan again. Even as Kelly hesitated, the first hard flakes came whistling down the draw. He hunched deeper into his wolfskin coat. If a man had been waiting for an answer, here it was. In considerably less than thirty minutes, in such a deep cleft, the returning wind could wipe out Gall's track completely. He could go up any one of probably a dozen side-draws and be well on his way to Canada before you could get Snyder's men turned around and worked out of the gully. If you meant not to lose him now, your choice was quite simple—if somewhat spine-tingling.

Kelly spoke softly to Belshazzar. He dropped the reins in the snow, and the cavalry-trained gelding did not move to follow him by more than the curious flick of his pointing ears. He had moved up the precipitously steepening throat of the gorge perhaps three hundred yards, just scaling a ten-foot rock shelf to top out on a level, snow-free surface above its drop-off, when the well-remembered bear's growl rumbled out of the inky darkness closing off the trail ahead.

"Hohahe," said Gall, "welcome to our wikmunke, my brother. We are glad to see you. It has been a long hunt, and we are very tired."

Kelly could say nothing. When Gall had mentioned a wikmunke, he had meant it. The flat rock upon which the scout stood was the floor of a cave. The war chief's last turning had taken him into a blind-box, dead-end canyon. *He was trapped.*

Kelly kept staring, his startled eyes adjusting to the cave's gloomy light as his mind struggled to do as much for its contents. With Gall on the thirty-foot half-circle of the roofed-over rock shelf were thirty-three other Indians: thirty-two Hunkpapa men, women, and children; one sixteen-year-old Absaroka girl.

When he saw Crow Girl's gray eyes burning at him through the December darkness, all rational thought ceased. He made an instinctive move toward her, arms opening, lips parting, halting cry of glad relief and recognition welling in his tightened throat. But the cry died abuilding. Its formed words never left his mouth. Crow Girl turned on him like a cornered animal, shrinking behind Gall to crouch against the cave's rear wall and bare her teeth at him for all the savage world like some senseless wild thing caught and held and driven crazy by brute fear. Her once-beautiful lips, now blackened and cracked and bleeding with frostbite, writhed and curled like a she-wolf's warning back an unwanted male. Her slender hands, so soft and lovely but a dream ago, were clawed and twisted into swollen painful talons which she held drawn back, as though she would sink them blindly into the first thing that moved or came near her. Her tiny feet, only short moons gone tripping with such light fantasy and pure delight at his side, were shapeless bundles of frozen flesh wrapped in bloody butcher's packages of torn blanket, lichen moss, and pack-saddle canvas. Her face, the home of angels five months before, was a devil's mask of hell endured past human sufferance. It was not the face of a young girl or even a matron of the middle years. It was the skull-tight, parchment-wrinkled face of an old, old woman. And from that face stared the final heart-sickening evidence; the empty, tortured nothingness of the luminous gray eyes, once the very light and meaning of life itself to Luther Kelly and now the gaping, vacant windows of a mind which no longer remembered him.

"I would have spared you this, my brother," said Gall, breaking the long silence as Kelly stepped back and away from Crow Girl, "but there was no way. After we had eaten the last pony, after we had turned away from Tatanka back there on the Red Water, that was when it happened. She has been like this these past ten days that you have pushed us so hard. She knows only me, trusts only me. Soon we would all have been the same way. Like animals and not men. Now we can rest. Now it is over. That is why I said you are welcome, and we are glad to see you."

Ten days, thought Kelly. Good Lord, it must be nearing mid-December! No wonder the poor devils were ready to quit; were crowded to the very edge of sanity and far past the will to fight back; were driven beyond even the ability to any longer hate and were capable only of the blank-faced apathy of surrender by starvation.

Of them all—the two subchiefs, five able-bodied warriors, ten old men and women, twelve younger squaws, and small children— only Gall retained his full pride and self-possession. Even the fierce Black Fox and the ebullient Frog Belly squatted on their wasted hams and waited for the soldiers to come up like old women whose day of youth was long gone, and whose only remaining worries were to fill the stomach and find a warm place to sleep.

"Why did you not kill me just now?" he asked Gall, low-voiced. "You know the soldiers are well behind me, that they will not be up here for some little while yet. Why did you not do it?"

"We thought of it."

"What did you think?"

"Many things."

Outside the cave's warm shelter, the thickening drive and slash of the snow cried off down the canyon. Its gusting, growing wilder by the moment, rose suddenly to the full hideous crescendo so familiar to Montana ears. Kelly glanced over his shoulder at the outer blackness, peered back at Gall again. The first impossible seed of the thought began to germinate in his mind as he did. It was monstrous, his conscience told him. A thing beyond all frontier law, counter to all settlement sympathies, alien to all white interests. And yet—

"Do you hear that?" he said to Gall.

"Aye, Wasiya has returned. Perhaps he wants to cover the shame of his Hunkpapa children."

"*Or their tracks,*" said Kelly softly.

Gall's fierce eyes narrowed.

"What do you mean, my brother?"

"A life for a life," said Luther Kelly. "It is a law written in the old book of my people's god."

"I am waiting."

"Many moons ago it was within your power to take my life—or worse."

"You mean the hinmangas, my brother?" Gall shrugged self-deprecatingly. "It was a moment of weakness. I could truly not help myself. You fought too well." The least trace of a grim smile lit the Hunkpapa's savage face. "My people were very unhappy with me, Lone Wolf." The smile was gone. "They said that I was no longer fit to lead them. That I was become an old fool. That because I fought for the love of a woman half my age and honored a white warrior for a great fight, I was no good anymore, that they could not trust me to lead them as before." He paused, his mind weary with remembering, then asked with the unaffected guile of a child hoping to find parental agreement or approval of some minor sin of omission. "Do you believe that, Lone Wolf?"

Kelly grimaced, nodded slowly. "Yes, I believe it, my brother. Your people are right. This can happen to a man. Love and war do not sleep well in the same lodge."

"You walk in circles, as if you were going around a trap. What is it you are saying?"

"That my people, too, are the same. That if they were to know what is in my mind now, they would never trust me to lead them again. And they would be right."

"What *is* in your mind, Lone Wolf?"

"As you said yourself—many things."

Gall only nodded. Like all Indians he knew the golden rule of silence and practiced it with a chief's pride.

"I have heard that Tatanka will go to the Land of the Grandmother. Is that true?" said Kelly.

"Yes."

"And also that you will go with him?"

"We were to meet beyond the mouth of the Musselshell if we escaped Bear Coat and could come together again."

"Would you still do it?"

"With the last breath of life that is in my body."

"Do you think you could do it? That your people, here, have the strength and the courage to go on from this place if they were free to do so?"

Gall's mouth straightened. "That is a cruel thing to ask, my brother. You know we are not free to do so and cannot be set free to do so. We are in your trap."

The minutes were speeding now. What he would do, Kelly must do quickly. His own mouth grew hard.

"Do you have any guns left? Any powder and lead?"

"Three guns, but no more bullets."

In the floor of the cave to Kelly's left was a foot-deep crevice. He moved to it, not looking down as he dropped his Winchester and cartridge belt into it. "Perhaps you can find a gun and some bullets," he murmured. "Then it is only a day's march back over to the Big Dry. There will surely be a few stormbound bulls wintering there as always."

By now, even Black Fox and Frog Belly were coming awake. They and the five warriors moved up behind Gall, their combined black eyes beginning to burn with a last excitement.

Beyond them the women, and even the children, closed in, sensing rather than understanding what it was Lone Wolf had done and what he meant to do. Only Crow Girl remained crouched against the back-wall rocks, her thin arms tenderly clutching to her wasted breasts the crudely bundled form of the hungrily nursing five-month-old infant. Her tortured face was strangely composed and at peace now, as the blessed sedative of motherhood worked its never-ending miracle. In the aroused stillness which followed his depositing of the rifle and pointed reference to it and to the buffalo in the Big Dry, Kelly could clearly hear the greedy suckling of the child and the eerie, toneless crooning of its demented mother. He caught Gall's dark eyes upon him and was grateful for the look of compassionate sympathy which showed in their slant depths. He returned the look and hurried his remaining words.

"You will be good to her? And to the little one?"

"Do you need to ask that, Lone Wolf? You know that I have loved this Crow child even as you have loved her."

"Nevertheless, I ask it."

"Then I shall tell you. Though I have not touched her as a man touches his woman, and will never do so, now, she shall be as a daughter to me and her son as my grandson. From this day forth, she shall know no want which is in my power to prevent. Nor will the child lack for any love that a man may give his own blood."

He put a deliberate emphasis on the last statement, and Kelly asked quickly. "*Your* blood, my brother?"

"Aye. It is best that you know, Lone Wolf. I am not proud to tell you, but it is a matter of honor within my own lodge. The child is not yours."

Kelly caught his breath with a short, hissing intake, but Gall raised his hand to signify he had not finished.

"My nephew had his way with its mother even as she first lay in torment from the wound he had given her. It is Sayapi's son she suckles, my brother, not yours. She herself has told me this in shame. I am sorry."

Kelly bowed his head silently, accepting it.

It was more of a relief than an added pain, and somehow it seemed to bring together and tie off the last open artery of the deep injury Crow Girl's unexplained Indian disaffection and pitiful end had left in his sorrowing heart. Suddenly, it was not so dark in the cave. His six months' search for his Absaroka mate was over, his half-year hunting of her Hunkpapa captor done. His love for the one and his hate for the other had died within the same span of tragic yet healing moments. He understood them now where he never had before. And there remained within him, finally, only a great feeling of loneliness and brotherhood and wordless kinship with them both, and with all of their desperate, hunted kind.

When he raised his head to Gall again, the last doubt of his decision had left the mind of Luther Kelly.

"Go in peace, my Sioux cousins," he said to the still-eyed

group behind Gall. "The soldiers will not follow you beyond this place. Woyuonihan—!"

With the parting expression of respect, he touched his forehead after the Hunkpapa fashion, but Gall did not return the traditional gesture. Instead, he touched his own dark fingers to his left breast, then held out his hand. Kelly took it, and the silent grips closed hard.

"From this time that my hand touches yours," said Gall softly, "I will fight no more. I will lay down my gun and go to the Land of the Grandmother. I will not again paint my face against the white man." He took his hand away from Kelly's, stepped back, concluded yet more softly.

"Go in peace, my brother, and do not look back. It is not a good thing for men to look back. It only tightens the throat and makes the chest ache a little longer."

Kelly turned away. He lowered himself over the drop-off to the trail below, began sliding and stumbling downward through the darkness. Within seconds he was lost in the building howl and yammer of the blizzard.

He did not look back.

Ten minutes later he told half-breed Billy LeBeau of his rotten luck in the rocks above; of first losing his rifle and cartridge belt down a deep crevice in a bad fall, then coming upon a pitchforked divide in the draw where the Sioux could have gone any one of three ways and where the returning wind and fresh snow had already wiped out the old trail and buried the new. It was the devil's own piece of heathen good fortune for the Hunkpapa, of course, but there was no help for it from their standpoint. With the hostile track clean gone and the cursed blizzard blowing sixteen ways at once, they had better forget about Gall and concentrate on getting those soldier boys back out of the canyon before the snow was four feet over their frozen ears.

LeBeau agreed, and Captain Snyder did not argue.

The column was ordered about, sent double-time down and out of the gulch.

In its van, rifle-spined, head erect, broad chest squared to the December blast, Luther Kelly broke the trail. The wind had the bite of a rabid wolf. The temperature was past the last line below zero and still skidding. It was bitterly, gallingly, unbelievably cold.

But Kelly did not feel it.

He felt only the growing warmness in his quieting heart and was finally content.

His romancer's view of the frontier and of his own fabled near-decade upon it were no more. The frontier itself was no more. With the breaking of the Sioux power and the surrender of their fierce High Plains pride, an era was ended. Gall had fallen, Sitting Bull must follow. And, after him, Crazy Horse. Then, as surely as the weary moon will set when the fierce stars grow pale, Dull Knife and his battered Cheyenne.

Whatever he, Kelly, had done that was wrong, or had failed to do that was right for these Indians, must be resigned to the long years ahead. In the context of his own time, no man could hope to know the rightness or wrongness of his small personal part upon a stage so vast and poorly lit as that encompassing the death struggle of the Dakota Sioux and Northern Cheyenne. But he could know that in the latter cruel weeks of that fateful winter of 1876, he had left behind, forever, something that was precious and young and impossible and could never come again.

It was time to grow up and go home.

To abandon boyhood and its golden dream.

To bid goodbye and godspeed to a time of magic which can come to a few men—the brief vintage years of a virgin land— those incredible, sometimes legendary years which he himself had known so fleetingly and yet so well.

Kelly smiled softly and looked ahead.

How was it Omar Khayyám had put it in the *Rubáiyát*?

> *The Moving Finger writes;*
> *   and, having writ,*
> *Moves on: nor all your Piety*
> *   nor Wit*
> *Shall lure it back to cancel*
> *   half a line,*
> *Nor all your Tears wash out a*
> *   Word of it …*

BEYOND THE
YELLOWSTONE

The end of the last major Indian resistance in the American West came to pass exactly as Luther Kelly had predicted it would and almost in the identical sequence he had foreseen.

With the pulling out of Gall, the hostile house of cards came down, never to be rebuilt. Within the same fateful span of days that saw Snyder run the Hunkpapa war chief to his final earth, Baldwin caught and routed Sitting Bull's main band, Miles forced the surrender of Pretty Bear's followers and Ranald Mackenzie, moving up from the south in independent command, trapped and smashed the last of Dull Knife's Northern Cheyenne. Wesley Merritt had already broken up the Camp Robinson Cheyenne, Anson Mills had done for American Horse and his Oglala. It remained only for Miles to track down and destroy Crazy Horse, which he did on January 8, 1877, but a few brief days after his December '76 defeat of Sitting Bull's Hunkpapa. Catching Tashunka Witko's main Oglala band on the headwaters of the Tongue, in the snowbound fastnesses of the Wolf Mountains less than eighty miles from his cantonment on the Yellowstone, Bear Coat, with full artillery support, literally hammered the last of the big Sioux bands to pieces. Completely routed, the remaining Oglala fled deeper into the mountains.

Miles did not go after them. Instead, at Kelly's behest, he sent Johnny Brughière in with the surrender terms. Crazy Horse was beaten. He came in. His simple reply to Miles—the real funeral oration of the High Plains hostiles—was delivered by his friend Little Chief. Facing Miles, the proud Cheyenne dropped his buffalo robe to the ground, drew himself erect, spoke without humbleness or arrogance.

"We are weak, compared with you and your forces; we are out of ammunition; we cannot make a rifle, a round of ammunition, or a knife; in fact, we are at the mercy of those who are taking possession of our country; your terms are harsh and cruel, but we are going to accept them and place ourselves at your mercy …"

It was the end. In the swiftly following weeks, the various independent bands came in, their chiefs repeating to Bear Coat Gall's prophetic promise of "fighting the white man no more from that day on." Little Hawk, White Bull, Two Moons, Hump, Little Big Man, He Dog, The Rock, Horse Road; the list read like a veritable Who's Who of the Dakota Sioux and Northern Cheyenne high commands; and with the stoic surrenders of their chiefs came upward of another two thousand fighting Indians of the plains to add to the like number of Sitting Bull's brokenhearted followers already in transit to the reservations. With the news of Crazy Horse's decision, Gall and Sitting Bull, with the pitiful remnant of the Hunkpapa, made good their vow and fled to Canada. The Sioux and Cheyenne wars were over.

Kelly, at last free to do so, requested of Miles a leave of absence and left the country in redemption of the pledge made following his failure to report his final grim meeting with Gall. He later returned to serve the government in several field capacities, including his classic trailing and bringing to bay of Chief Joseph and his desperate Nez Percé, after General Howard and upward of four thousand troops from three commands had been unable to effect the same end in fifteen hundred miles of army cat and Indian mouse maneuvers. But something had died with Gall's defeat and the breaking of Crow Girl's mind. By his own admission, these later days were never the same for the romantic scout as those earlier ones along the Yellowstone.

Luther Kelly went on to a full life of continuing adventure. He rose to be a major in the regular army; a confidante of two Presidents; governor of a Philippine municipality; agent of a great Arizona Indian reservation. Surveyor; cartographer; Indian Bureau troubleshooter; Alaskan adventurer; California rancher. There will probably never be a full accounting of his incredible life. He himself has made sure of his. Any reader of his personal memoirs will understand that statement.

Major L. S. Kelly may not have invented modesty, but he should have been granted a patent on it.

He writes graphically and beautifully about everything and all things relevant to the wonders of the northwest frontier in the 1870s, excepting "Yellowstone" Kelly.

One must go to such obscure sources as the following (from a rare issue of the *New Northwest* for March 8, 1878) to see him in relationship to his beloved fosterland.

> Kelly, you may know [the yellowed paper states dramatically], is the man of the Yellowstone Valley Who-Never-Lays-Down-His-Gun. The Indians also call him "Lone Wolf." He has traveled up and down that valley for eleven years, and has challenged death in a thousand ways. He

has gained one of his names by the accuracy of his aim, and the other by his lone life. He orders up the Indian hand and goes it alone every time. He is held in high esteem by Miles and his staff, and by them regarded as their best card in playing cutthroat euchre. He is not like the average scout and frontiersman. He is a man of education, soul, and manners as exceptional as those of an "old school gentleman."

Kelly has not been demoralized by the life of the hunter. He has no bad habits and not even the swagger and general bearing of the frontiersman. The secret of his life is in his ambition to know and be somebody, and he has taken this way of realizing his ambition.

He is what might have been called a surveyor in George Washington's time, and he has one of the rare accomplishments of a certain surveyor of that time—he cannot tell a lie. When the Yellowstone Valley is settled up, Kelly will be one of the permanent men, and it is not improbable that his beautiful physique will be seen in the halls of the Montana legislature, or in those of congress, as the "gentleman from the Yellowstone District." He is only twenty-eight, is the oldest settler, and may be called the father of the fertile valley.

In the thoughtful remove of the nearly eighty years since the publication of this flowing tribute by his Montana contemporaries, it is apparent that Luther S. Kelly deserves also to be called that simpler, more enduring, less colloquial thing—*a man to be remembered.*